Acknowledged as one of the great Latin American writers of the twentieth century, **Juan Carlos Onetti** was born in Montevideo, Uruguay in 1909. While working as a journalist in Buenos Aires, he was imprisoned under the military dictatorship in 1974 and on release, was exiled to Spain. His novels include *A Brief Life*, and his best known work, *The Shipyard*, also published by Serpent's Tail. He was awarded Uruguay's national literature prize in 1963 and Spain's prestigious Cervantes Prize in 1980. He lived in Madrid until his death in 1994.

D0992890

Praise for Juan Carlos Onetti

'Onetti's novels and stories are the foundation stones of our modernity. To those of us who are his followers, he brings a lesson of narrative intelligence and of immense love for the literary imagination' Carlos Fuentes

'Onetti's vision is bleak but the pictures he conjures up against annihilation are vivid and beautiful' *The Times*

'Latin American literature has few secrets to divulge to the English-speaking world; but one of them is the Uruguayan novelist Juan Carlos Onetti' *Guardian*

'The Graham Greene of Uruguay... foreshadowing the work of Beckett and Camus' *Sunday Telegraph*

'Laconic, elegant, literary' *London Review of Books*

'I consider him one of the giants of the 20th century, certainly doing things in 1937/38 way before Beckett and Camus' Alan Warner

'This literary landmark [*The Shipyard*] is here delivered in a wonderful translation that retains all the bleakness and poetry of the antihero Larsen as he attempts to salvage the unsalvageable' *Independent on Sunday*

'Is *The Shipyard* a one-off masterpiece? I hope that having reconstituted it for English readers, the translator and publisher will decide to take the rust off the rest of Onetti's works' *Spectator*

Juan Carlos Onetti
LET THE WIND SPEAK

Translated by Helen Lane

A complete catalogue record for this book can be obtained from the British Library on request

First published as *Dejemos hablar al viento* in 1979 by Bruguera-Alfaguara, Barcelona

First published in this edition in 2008 by Serpent's Tail

First published in the UK in 1996 by Serpent's Tail,
an imprint of Profile Books Ltd
3A Exmouth House
Pine Street
London EC1R 0JH
website: www.serpentstail.com

ISBN 978 1 85242 979 9

Printed in the UK by Bookmarque, Croydon CR0 4TD

10 9 8 7 6 5 4 3 2 1

CONTENTS

Part Two

Part One

ITE

The old man was already rotten and I found it strange that I was the only one who smelled the bittersweet, persistent odor; that neither the daughter nor the son-in-law commented on it. They were obliged to sniff and wrinkle up their noses because they were his relatives and I was only a male nurse, almost, a fake, a former doctor.

That was the first of the jobs that Frieda had chosen for me when I arrived in Lavanda and discovered her at 1597 Avenida Brasil, as pretty and as tough as in the old days, and tried to get money out of her—she had more than enough—or the help indispensable to every immigrant who is seeking, like a dignified cuckold, another chance.

Jobs and punishments. Caring for the old man in his death throes, the first of the series of her acts of revenge without a corresponding motive. She and I preferred to go to bed with women and one unmemorable night we had a fight in Santa María and I won, not because I deserved it but because the young woman at stake had more fear of my card identifying me as the chief of police than greed for what she, Frieda, was offering her at the restaurant on the river front, with no intention of making good on her promise. It was a game; and in the small

3

hours of the morning Frieda lost, let a stream of saliva fall into her glass, made up her face and was able to smile at me before getting to her feet to leave and go find her car. At the time it was a small, cream Dedion Bouton. The three of us, at the same table, had been very cordial. The woman, young, skinny, dirty, stayed with me. I am unable to discover any other reason and even that one is not at all clear.

The best part of the experience, of the first act of revenge, was the coolness in the mornings, when, overexcited and horny because of the lack of sleep, I would lean on the iron railing of the Argentine Embassy to wait for the number 125 bus. The best mornings of all were the ones in that storm-filled summer, with mud and chestnut leaves on the ground, that restless air that had been made just for me, that waggish happiness of the old trees of the town houses, the big old houses that had had a name and prestige, the irresolute, roiling sky.

Because neither the air nor I altogether believed in what we had done and seen during the night; and we began the day scorning our tasks, jokingly reconstructing men's love, friendship, sympathy, their simulacrum of faith, their brief and fierce beliefs.

Despite the heat that penetrated to one's nerves, the night had been quiet, and the rituals were repeated with the same impassive scrupulousness as ever. The son-in-law, the captain, came with his wife at nine o'clock, almost immediately after the maid had left the bedroom with my food tray, as I was preparing the first injection.

I blew out the flame of the alcohol burner, put the syringe in the black box and sat down in the armchair again with an open book entitled *Vico's Cyclical Conceptions*. I preferred not to give injections without witnesses. A companion for the night, Frieda said, and Quinteros repeated the title. "Two hundred drachmas a night and the work is negligible," he said hurriedly, as he indifferently rested an open hand on Frieda's knee and recited to me apocryphal snippets of the story of the old man doomed to die and hinted at my possible discoveries in the bedroom, in various pieces of furniture, in the mattress, in his gestures and his last stammered syllables.

Quinteros, who had an ancestor who had chosen to call himself Osuna when, in the 1500s, the Catholic Sovereigns did a bit of ethnic cleansing. But apart from business, he forced people to call him Quinteros as an inane and perhaps satisfactory challenge.

I don't know, exactly, when I decided irremediably to accept human stupidity, Santa María, Lavanda, the rest of the world that I would always be unacquainted with. To keep myself from contradicting. I don't know when I learned to savor in silence my total enmity toward males and females. But my meeting up with Quinteros-Osuna, with his powerful mindlessness, with his incredible talent for making money, brought about an inner self-abandonment, forced me to accept with enthusiasm that form of imbecility which he recognized in me, with exaggerated, almost envious paeans of praise. So I said yes to everything and added details, improvements.

For that very reason, when the captain/son-in-law came into the bedroom and found me reading Clausewitz's invented book, I was able to discuss with him, passionately and imprudently, tactical, strategic or logistical points concerning which it made no difference to him whether concessions had entered the picture provided that I listened in a daze to the discourses that left in their wake for military and world history the conviction that he was never mistaken as to what was fundamental, as to what was of supreme value, as to what would distort the final outcome of any war, whether past or future.

But when Susana, the dying man's daughter, arrived first, I was reading one or another of those novels she calls vulgar that were hidden like a purloined letter on the shelf, at eye level, in the library. Sometimes she asked me my opinion as to which one to take away with her and she always gave them back to me with a sigh, a piousness, a "how disgusting," sick with slowness, thick with compassion. And the old man who was dying had hidden them in plain sight, and she looked at me with a pity, a curiosity similar to the one that I went through in the vulnerable wee hours of the morning contemplating the restless old man who was beginning to submerge himself, timidly and torpidly, in the long sleep, colliding with islets of delirium, muttering words alluding, with minute errors of detail, to memories that were never the whole truth, to events or lies unknown to him, to the man that he had been and now, to deceive me and divert me, was attempting to prolong in those ninety minutes that separate the night from yet another day, that time in which death wanders about loose, offering itself, and a person, by tradition or instinct, carries out rituals for forgetting so as not to say yes and give in. And since she had the habit of standing firmly in place with her feet very far apart to talk, I couldn't help thinking of moist places, of an affectionate little cushion above rigid, indestructible bones.

A book or any sort of printed page, the electric coffee pot, the long, feigned wishes to urinate, my nose in the cold of the half-open window, the sudden cry of birds inside my head.

And when Pablo, the orphan soon to be, came in—each one of them announced by their different voices and the different sounds that they extracted from the steps of the stairway as they came upstairs, drawing closer and closer—I was able to grab the book of Adler's that he had left with me since the first night, raise my eyes, with one finger lying forgotten between the pages. For Pablo, twenty years old, was studying medicine, but he had already confessed to me one night, pacing like a raving madman about that bedroom that would be called a mortuary chapel at any unpredictable moment now, chainsmoking so as help along the panting breath and the respite of the thing that was still his father, he had confessed to me that being a general practitioner was to him nothing more than a trampoline to make a repeated childhood dream that he called psychoanalysis come true. He had a decent, placid, intelligent face, and took pleasure in tossing back the rumpled hair that fell over his forehead.

When the farce began I felt that he was the most dangerous one of all of them, aside from the old man, an obstinate dying man. But when after the night of confidences he brought a small bottle of cognac, I knew that the danger did not lie in him.

I had learned many years before that it was necessary to put Catholics, Freudians, Marxists and patriots in the same bag. What I mean to say is: anyone who had faith, in no matter what; anyone who has an opinion, knows, or acts by repeating learned or inherited thoughts. A man who has faith is more dangerous than a famished beast. Faiths make action, injustice, evil obligatory; it is best to nod one's head approvingly as one listens to them, to measure in cautious and courteous silence the intensity of their leprosies and always agree with them. And faith can be placed and stirred up in what is most contemptible and subjective. In the woman who is one's current beloved, in a dog, in a soccer team, in a number on a roulette wheel, in the vocation of an entire lifetime.

The leper is in his glory when he falls into error, exudes phosphoric odors in the face of the slightest opposition or the mere suspicion of it, seeks to stand up for himself—to stand up for his faith—by trampling heads or tender, sacred intimacies underfoot. To conclude—I am thinking of Pablo and of his age—a man contaminated by any sort of faith swiftly reaches the point of confusing it with his own self; it is then vanity that attacks and defends itself. With God's help, it is best not to cross their path; with one's own help, it is best to cross the street to the opposite sidewalk.

And if one night Pablo asked me defiantly and pityingly what would have or might have happened to the world, to mankind, if they hadn't had enough faith to make progress, I nodded my head and silently measured the distance that separates Mau Mau from concentration camps, from genocide and from the greedy animals that rule the world.

All the nights were alike or at the time it was a matter of just one night with hours marked by a storm, a hard and starry sky, a pencil falling, the changes in pulse and temperature. And during this single night I abandoned out of boredom the book best suited to the visitor and looked at the landscape with the multiple curiosities of one recently arrived.

From the motheaten plush armchair, with uneven springs, I contemplated the bedside lamp on the round table, the gleam of the bars of the oversized brass bed, the shapes of the bottles of medicine, the dense shadow of the ceiling and the big standing wardrobe. I looked at the time and awaited the first light of day in the curtain over the window, wine-red in the mornings, black now. I distracted myself by trying to make out, with odious ease, the pieces of furniture and the portraits separated from me by the light, lost in the area where he was resting or tossing his sick head.

But I needed my hundred coins a night. At some far-distant time I would have a run-in with Pablo, a lie for a lie. Every night, or just about, the captain drank coffee downstairs and it was impossible to be contemptuous of his laughter and his jokes.

The memorable time was like this. At a quarter past nine he came into the bedroom with Susana, his wife, Pablo's sister, as much the offspring of the dying man as he was. When they arrived, the deceased was leaving more space between his panting breaths and prolonging what I took to be a pleasurable malevolence, a sudden swift silence between sighs. He was going on living and knew it.

At a quarter past nine on that night in April the captain and

8

Susana. Susana far behind, seeking out the shadow and the stupidity of a fixed, frozen smile, her hands joined over her pubis. Far ahead, military without additional vulgarity, the poor man, the captain, made his way without seeing me, straight to the edge of the bed and halted, standing at attention.

If he could think, the captain that is, he seemed to be thinking with his jaw resting on his hand, looking down at the old man. To make mock of him or out of affection, the half-dead man began to nod his head, and bared the memory of his false teeth, protecting himself, in the face of the vague din that the world forced upon him.

The captain ceased his examination and turned around to greet me.

But she, Susana, my dead man's daughter, the captain's wife, Pablo's sister, was slow-witted and muddle-headed; I regretted having made her, in the beginning when I invented her, stupid and absent-minded.

"At your orders, general," Vélez, the captain, almost shouted, as he knocked one shoe against the other and saluted me. He was as happy and as sure of himself as his grandfather might have been in the year 1904 respectfully saluting in a field tent, next to a cookstove camouflaged with eucalpytus branches. Saluting the imminent approach of dawn as he stood in front of the barbarous, illiterate *caudillo*—his color doesn't matter—expanding his thorax and his movements stiff because he was the bearer of good or bad news, of an arrogant pride.

"Good evening, captain," I replied, barely laying the book aside.

As usual, I felt that the moribund old man was awake and lucid, making fun of Captain Vélez, of all of us; or perhaps the years and illness had placed him in a superadult time, which had nothing to do with old age, and was looking at us from there and found all our words and movements amusing, filling him with disdain and tenderness as though he were distractedly watching the games of children or insects.

Although he had spoken, almost smiling, looking at me, I knew that Captain Vélez's words were not a greeting and were meant only for the wasted thing without any thighs, lying stretched out full length in the bed.

Without bending his knees, trained in gymnastics and logistics, Captain Vélez leaned over till one of his ears touched the sick man's muttering mouth. I could see in profile the joyful gleam of his little black eyes, the black mustache, which his smile elongated.

"Don't worry, general," he said. "We'll send in the cavalry. And don't worry about the artillery park. We have bullets and a gang waiting to wipe out those cowards."

As so often happened, because of a sense of duty and a perverse habit, I was the spectator. And something else, now. I was the medium of transmission that the captain was using to pass the planned message on to Susana: her father was going to live for ten more years or at least he wasn't going to die that night. "If he were in serious condition, if there were any danger, I, who punctiliously honor an officer's stripes, would not be able to behave like this, happy, joking, giving him a friendly punch on his bones."

Furthermore, in speaking of tactics and battles that his grandfather had told him about, in speaking of Mausers, bridges and cavalry as though he had experienced great vicissitudes and were so sad, coming back from it all, he was partially compensating for a long humiliation in the barracks, he was making up somewhat for the frustration of generations which learned how to make war in theory, only to discover that the sort of wars known to them no longer had anything to do with the future. And above all, his discourses were an invitation to forget a vocational courage, which bad luck had doomed to die a virgin, neither fulfilling itself nor failing. That year, in Lavanda, only workers or students could be beaten up. He did his duty and gave vent to his feelings with no real happiness.

At that moment, more or less, Susana came up the stairs and aimed the beginning of a smile between the brass bars of the bed where her father lay dying. Every so often she turned to look at me and I stood there calmly, with one or another of the books resting against my belly, perhaps having been mistaken in my choice between psychology and war. I nodded my head as if to say everything's going all right and he's dying at this very moment.

But the odor grew stronger, the odor fluttered about like a butterfly, black and green, it came and went, as everyone pretended not to smell it.

She was beautiful, Susana, and was born to marry Vélez, because I know that there exists a class, a type of little girls, young ladies, and adult women who are born to marry upright soldiers; perhaps it is possible to recognize them by the resoluteness of their hips and by the distance that separates their smile from their eyes and the gleam of their teeth. They end up knowing more than their spouses about strength of character and submissiveness.

Then, I repeat, the captain grew tired of stroking the old man's yellow forehead and stood erect, ramrod straight. He was dressed in civvies.

"He's an old barbarian, chief," he said to me; I waited incredulously until he said, "He was at Masoller." He came closer so as to squeeze my shoulder, continually shifting about, jovial, so sure of everything.

"Yes. He's a little nervous tonight. But I'd say he's better."

Because Quinteros, dictated to by Frieda, had said of me: "Two years of medical studies. He would have won a gold medal if it hadn't been for that unfortunate occurrence that, at bottom, was nothing but wanting to do good."

The unfortunate incident, invented by Frieda to humiliate me for weeks at the old man's bedside, was sometimes of use to me to retouch a past. It was more real than my deeds, than my own self. With greater ease than the bloody legs, than the twisted jaw of the adolescent girl I had just killed by perforating her uterus, I remembered my solemn slowness as I took off my gown at the midwife's, in the odd consultation room with canaries and begonias. The maniacal persistence with which I had washed my hands seven times, the amazed discovery of my fingers, the silent prayer alongside the stretcher, the refusal to seek help, the insulting hysteria of the fat woman above the empty rubber gloves on the floor. A memory, a falsehood of memory.

"Have we given him the injection yet, chief?" Vélez asked, as though it mattered to him.

I read somewhere or else someone told me that days don't go by in vain; much less nights: poor Vélez didn't know, and never found out, that at one time or another I had demoted him from captain to lieutenant.

"Not yet, I was waiting. The injection is indispensable, but I don't like the idea that he needs it. Do you understand?" I said.

I didn't understand anything, but the lieutenant did.

"Of course," he explained to Susana. "It mustn't become a habit."

We were alone in the house when I gave the old man the injection, remembering—or someone else resting comfortably inside me remembered—the hundreds of injections I'd given to drunkards, hysterical women, and accident victims at the barracks in Santa María, as I awaited the arrival of a nebulous doctor of forensic medicine or Dr. Díaz Grey, still a bachelor, awake at all hours and forever asking, without smiling or pausing:

"Are you certain it's worth the trouble, chief?"

And I repeated to him the exact words of the tired game that never managed to bore us:

"It's our duty, doctor."

And he did the necessary work and on rare occasions forgot to go on or to end up by saying:

"Your paintings are bad. I like the color sometimes, but you never really learned to draw. However, be that as it may, why don't you say to hell with this filth and live on charity and go up and down the river front with an easel and a paint box?"

I straightened the old man's pillows and clothes and opened the window halfway on the cool, windless night. When I sat down on the bed, he moved about until he was almost fully awake, until his eyes met mine; then he began to rock his head back and forth and quickly murmur fragments of words. The thought came to me that millions of condemned men had already done that before him. Almost from the beginning I had lost all hope and desire to understand. So as a result I diverted myself—when Frieda or Quinteros woke me up at six in the evening—by passing on fantastic, sometimes ingenious, always disconcerting versions.

I saw my lies move across Quinteros's face; the suspicion sometimes that he was on the right track, at other times discouragement. It was, between yawns, my little daily act of revenge.

And I added to it a base, sumptuous happiness trying to guess what words Quinteros would have preferred to have the dying man say, and enthusiastically took the risk of exhibiting false, contradictory textual versions which I had written in previous dawns to keep myself from falling asleep or dying of boredom.

I believe that all my literature was a repetition of the old and stupid need to have a friend and confide in him; it also alluded to obligatory mistrust, to secrecy and cunning.

I had only to see the drunken or tired face of Quinteros at the accursed hour of six in the evening; to see his suits and ties; to hear him talk of friendship and selflessness; to remember how much he paid me, always punctually and unstintingly, to tell him about the swaying of the old man's head and the, I suppose,

13

intricate childhood memories burbled by the black, toothless mouth.

It took only that and the presence of Frieda, almost always in the background, playing at indifference and mockery, to understand that it was a question of money; a great deal of money.

Afterwards, I don't know when, one evening as darkness was falling, time to go to work, embedded in the single night of the first punishment, I arrived at the street that is inexplicably called Agraciada—Lucky Street—and from the corner caught sight of the van and realized that something had ended. The first of the brief lives I had in Lavanda. I crossed the street, sat down at a table leaning against a window whose griminess and transparency were acceptable. It was called a café and I ordered coffee, casting furtive glances amid vagrants and curiosity-seekers to spy on what was happening, with professional exactitude, in the house opposite, the house where I had alternately read Clausewitz and Freud, where I had given useless injections, and I sat there thinking of my past without managing to put it in order.

When the van left I turned my attention to calling Quinteros, certain that he was sleeping off a hangover. I thought of the penetrating sounds of the telephone ringing and confused them or mixed them up with the injection needles. Never again.

I let the phone ring until he had to wake up and answer half-wittedly. I said to him:

"It's 6.35 p.m. Medina speaking. You'd best make a note about this. I came to punch in on the time clock and first off I saw a van that made me feel sad and surprised. After that, four guys that I wouldn't want for myself, with dust-coats, gray or sky-blue, the light is bad. They got out and took in a crucifix, a wooden overcoat, six candelabra, an album that would tempt me to write a novel or the diary of my life. They added mysterious things that must be indispensable because death is always a mystery. I think the result would be the same. Did you note anything down? I'm really calling you out of a sense of duty. To congratulate you and to get you to go to the square root of your little sister."

I hung up so as to kill his voice and from that night on our friendship improved, I had less contempt for him. Of course we never spoke of the subject again; and when some time later I was obsessed by the thought of returning nobody was more patient, kind and helpful than Quinteros. But he didn't do it in order to pay me for my involuntary silence.

THE VISIT

Long ago, when we were all twenty years old or a few months more, I yielded to the temptation to be God, knowing it to be an absurd, dangerous one, and respecting my limits. I was in Santa María, during a sultry March with vague threatening signs, the deafening din of storms, as though the weather had accepted the pattern of behavior of the people from the other side, from Lavanda, with the river in between.

This temptation, when it is genuine, prefers to visit the very poor, those in despair, those who haven't fallen into the trap of a tidy fate.

Everything was as easy and as error-ridden as a first-year arithmetical calculation: with what I forgo I can make someone else happy.

The result was a Seoane seventeen or eighteen years old, a legitimate emigrant from Santa María, and his mother. Seoane was the surname of the girl, the woman, and I never knew whether the child, a boy, was my son. She had always played the game of creating doubt, of misunderstanding, of making jokes that weren't funny. They were now in Lavanda and it seemed to me to be the proper thing to do to hold with one decadent finger a paper tray of sweets and visit them each month, when the moon was full.

It meant getting involved willingly and unwillingly in the

16

memory of Seoane as a little boy, in the room, in the roving images of the lad in the dark and ill-smelling apartment, the fat woman with her head covered in coiled wisps, in plastic curlers, in hairpins, the irritated sadness that came pouring out of us, out of the furniture like sweat.

It must be, and it is difficult to begin to say this sort of thing gently: old age, poverty, dead pasts, to go on saying them that way.

But that never happened to me with María Seoane. Despite the cheap presents that I never forgot on any of my visits and that she thanked me for, politely and almost mockingly, only to bury them immediately in the filthy disorder of the room, the one and only possibility was dialogue that referred, sentence after sentence, to the errors of the irrecuperable past. She, the repulsive fat woman, knew better than I did why she proved herself capable of summing it all up by inserting in the conversation, at intervals, sucking on the maté sipper and sighing:

"There's no going back now."

And it was true for us, for all lovers who have met again, for everyone. I could counter her only by my eagerness to understand, half sharing María's intelligent malice, reminding her of the neutral, almost always absent head of Seoane as a young boy, who was perhaps my son, who perhaps had played at being the real half-idiot substituted in the cradle by the inevitable tribe of gypsies that had camped in the right place at the right time.

After one of my shameful peregrinations, I brought sweets for María and a silk tie and a banknote, a blue one. And there I was, after María Seoane's hello, caught in the trapped, motionless heat of the apartment, entangled in the pretentious poverty, in the little red velours carpet, semi-threadbare, with stains of nights and spluttering bottles, of dogs, a distant and impatient dog. Locked in a small, unbreathable, dark world, with gauchos and Dutch peasant girls, porcelain or plaster, framed magazine covers.

María wasn't thinking only of me to have accumulated so

much distastefulness with the aim of annoying me. She and her men friends. María placed her trust in other things, more direct and more certain.

Nor had she deliberately furthered the lower-middle-class odor, of daily failures, of base desires chewed over by unknown people, going back twenty years, before she arrived in Lavanda, desires that had gradually adhered to the walls and that perhaps I could scrape off, today, with a fingernail.

Of course the wallpaper had changed, from one time to another, one hope to another. But the odor of all that had merely grown stronger. The door frames, in particular, very wide, which were successively painted gray, ivory, cream, gray, smelled, spiteful and stubborn, of Italian Sunday dinners, of receptions of mutual medical benefit societies, of necessary steps to be taken in order to retire.

I didn't know whether on that holiday of one sort or another Seoane, seventeen years old, would appear and expose his face to my slow scrutiny; nor did I know if I would manage to see him; nor, I repeat, did I know if he was my son.

María left me by myself so that I could look, smell and invent at will, so as to take off her worn-out decent dress and slowly return, with the useless smile of revenge or brief retaliation. It didn't surprise me for I had been showered with similar smiles of females, whom I thought I had made up, and put them on display over millions of years, as a new model of the season, just born, without antecedents, without risk of being recalled.

It didn't surprise me, I repeat. I have known kindnesses, sacrifices and exceptions. But she came back, as any woman would have done, so as to reiterate, boringly, with her own caliber of subtlety, who María Seoane had been at eighteen, when each time we met I persisted in seeking her averted eyes and was certain I smelled on her the odor of another recent male. The smile was meant to show me what I, an unconscious ally of her congenital imbecility, had turned her into.

She came back now in a dirty, ragged bathrobe; she had managed to age, to put on remoteness.

"Because of the flies," she said in her brand-new hoarse voice, as she closed the windows over the iron jalousie. She slowly lay down on the couch where Seoane, my possible son, slept; with the languid movement of old she bared half of one leg and asked me for some cigarettes. I threw her a package, a box of matches.

Too bad, I thought; an old woman a little younger than I was, repulsive, clumsily handling a twenty-year return. For a moment, overcome with heat and drowsiness, she lashed out at me, calling on stupidity and wickedness for help. It was easy to hurt me; the difficulty lay in finding new ways, in keeping hatred and sluttish courtesy in balance.

She breathed a little, puffing out her big tits, she spoke and it was like again finding oneself without refuge, in the monotonous, steady rain, with no wind. But her voice was not only the spoiled offspring of alcohol and tobacco; it was hoarse and deep, at times almost inaudible from aphonia, at others strident, emerging by force of will from nothingness, from silence. She knew or suspected, dissimulating with hiccups, with deliberate lapses of memory, coughs and aloof smiles. In my ear her voice sounded alien and fraught with mystery.

"If you came, it seems to me, to see the boy, I imagine you're wasting your time. He always bolts from you, it must be instinct, but sometimes, when he's alone, he calls out for you and misses you. I found that out from his sketches. He tries to cover up, of course; but I'm his mother. He went out with friends, the sort of friends he chooses, to go to the movies or a basketball game, to whatever shitty lie that occurs to him. He always lies to me, I can prove it, I don't worry, I don't even listen to him when he answers my questions. Or else he doesn't bother to answer, sometimes he comes home at dawn or early in the morning and he's taken it into his head to get drunk. He doesn't come, it gets to be past twelve, and one of these days they're going to bring him home to me dead; I think over all the bad things that could happen, and that way I prepare myself. You doubtless remember Heyward, who came to the Detachment every Saturday night and said to you . . ." (He said to me that he was dead drunk and I always knew, by his tone of voice, by his smile, that the sentence was one he'd stolen. But it was true that almost every Saturday he came to the Detachment at midnight, filthy dirty and with his tie crooked; or else impeccable, blond, letting a grin slip out that lighted up his suit, the grimy exhaustion he'd dragged all along the river front, from one cheap tavern to another, looking, sometimes successfully, for an adolescent boy who'd say yes after haggling. Heyward. When he met up with me he asked for shelter without affectation, as though he'd arrived at an inopportune hour at a friend's house.)

"I'm at the end of my rope," he'd say, using dirty words or decent ones. "One hour more and it's curtains for me. Not on the streets; inside me, for myself. If that should happen, you and I know that there's only one solution, one ending. A bed with bedbugs, and I'll leave tomorrow."

I always said yes and gave him a cell. Later on, at noon, he would leave on the counter twice the amount of money that he'd have paid to sleep for the night at the Plaza.

She went on: and her hoarse voice surprised everyone except herself: alcohol and tobacco, from breakfast till time for bed.

"But don't be nervous, I'm not thinking of telling you once more that he's your son. What pride, if you take a good look at yourself? How much money does he get out of you? Unfortunately I baptized him Julián, and years later people told me it was a name that brought bad luck. If you can, have a look at him and that's all. Then tell me afterward. Do you remember when you were younger than he was and even painted a portrait of the Pope, whose name at the time I don't remember? I wanted to talk to you but I found out right away that I can send and receive secret messages and I hope they'll tell me when the time has come. It hasn't come yet, but it's no use because you were always evil-minded, a no-good I mean to say, who never believed in anything. It doesn't matter, but if you want a little diversion . . ." She patted her gray hair as she smiled, consoled, at some absent figure. "But I opened the cupboard beforehand and we're going to have a little glass of contraband anisette. Maybe you still remember: I preferred anisette at La Enramada and you those half-liter glasses of Paraguayan rum."

I poured the anisette as I tried to make out what the trap was. They were tiny glasses and I could drink lots of them because it was a good-tasting drink, not too sweet.

The cigarette smoke unhurriedly changed from gray to a sky-blue, almost uniform in the heat of the hermetically sealed room.

"Dead," she said and for minutes afterward her voice refused to speak; she lighted a cigarette to relieve the difficulty and gargled some anisette.

"Dead, some night, some early morning," she went on. "I don't know if I told you that he gets drunk every day now and some night they're going to bring him home dead to me, and when he's not plastered the only thing that matters to him, besides eating, is squandering the little money I have, just about, I can almost say he doesn't bring a single peso home. Julián. He spends the little money we have for food on canvas or pasteboard and paint. And like one of his fathers, I swear to you on this cross and because of calculations that can't be wrong that you were the father, and because of the fact that you painted the portrait of the Pope . . . All he does is paint, get drunk and sometimes bring home money that I have no idea where he gets it from. Every once in a while I go and buy him a bottle, just like that, at least it keeps him painting in his mother's company. You men."

The anisette was good but nauseating. I shook my head, imitating regret, pain, doubt, bitterness and compassion.

"Since he's not going to show up," I said, "you could let me look at the paintings."

She gave a happy smile, as though she'd been waiting for me to ask.

"He'd kill me, he's already told me so, if I let anybody see them. They're in the attic. If you could leave me between fifty and a hundred."

I filled her glass, pushed the bottle certified by the Spanish government over to her and wandered about hesitantly till I found the iron stairway in the patio, only slightly twisted out of shape.

I turned on a dim light and could see, by straining my eyes, that in a turmoil and with no talent Seoane had gone through every school, every style of painting, from the bisons of Altamira, painted by Picasso under contract to the French government, to the kaleidoscopic games that were already going out of fashion.

But, sweating and with my back hurting, I discovered, as always happens, some paintings, a very few, that Julián had painted for Seoane. I brought them over to the light, scoffing and envious. Like me, Seoane didn't know how to draw; but his handling of colors was discerning, assured, dazzling. The paintings were not meant to say anything to anybody; they were silent, oppressive and aloof, done by Seoane for himself and no one else.

When I went back downstairs, the woman said: "I thought you were going to stay up there in the attic forever."

I was a little drunk but still dignified enough to fill the tiny glass without its spilling over.

"I like the paintings," I said. "I want to see him and talk to him."

"He doesn't want to see you. I told him things that were lies and things that were true. I think he hates you. But we don't talk about you anymore. If he paints rubbish like that that nobody can understand, then it must be that he takes after you. Papa. But the funny thing is that none of you can be sure, let me say."

By "you" she meant the two of us, all men, a race that María

22

Seoane had taken great pains to hate for at least fifteen years and that now had as much in common with her as ants or horses.

It got hotter and I didn't accept her invitation to take off my suit coat; I went on defending myself, putting up with the tie around my neck soaked with sweat, behaving like a polite visitor, smiling now and again, looking at her in her drunken state, inventing a purifying suffering for myself.

"Because it's better that you"—the voice, softer now, went on—"you men, make me feel sorry for you. That way I don't let myself be carried away and do something crazy, get my own back. The boy is like you, not physically, I mean. Of course I feel as proud as any mother. But don't get the idea that I've lots of illusions. To begin with he doesn't have any strength of character or if he does it's only a tendency toward evil. Like you. I had him, I brought him up." She raised her plastic-toothed smile toward the ceiling and slowly stretched out one hand to search about for cigarettes; they she stretched her bare legs out and I could predict, almost word for word the monologue:

"Yes, the first time we met and you took me out to eat and sleep, I kept telling you about Josesito. Yes, the first time, a gesture that seemed good to me as long as it lasted, I was just a kid, I couldn't go back home and I lied. I went on lying. Lying is like going to bed with men, because in the beginning it's shameful and then later on you start to enjoy doing it."

"Poverty," I said to cheer her up. "In the beginning it isn't anybody's fault."

"I'm telling you not to talk about the beginning," she shouted in a rage, raising her head off the pillow; another cigarette, a swig from the bottle.

I wanted to break her nose with just one blow, almost without moving, barely stretching out my arm. But I thought and said:

"Don't shout, dear. I've also had my share of suffering." I shouldn't have laughed. Perhaps the phrase had been readied a minute before. But it could be true that in an unlocatable beginning, twenty years before, I had had my share of suffering; the time was right for believing in such things.

In reality María Seoane could cause me suffering only by making Seoane unhappy, whether he was my son or not. It no longer mattered. And by being clever, I had learned to protect myself even from that. She now described the new sufferings that she wanted to inflict on me. Because the others were there already, the always surprising comparison with what I remembered; the decadence, the obesity, like something alien, that turned her into the mother of her own self. There was the hesitant attention of those flat blue eyes, still the same, encircled now by the numerous tiny miseries of skin grown old. There were fatigue, sluggishness, the touching remains of freshness, the thick varicose leg that writhed so as to add to the vehemence of the accusations.

But above all, almost palpable, the accelerated dimness of her brain, the grotesque imitations of her humor in bygone days, the incomprehensible echoes of her character were there and reverberating. The indubitable beginning of María Seoane's old age was there, in the room, fetid and harried by summer. Her teeth that were too new, the sad provocation of her restless thigh.

"It doesn't matter to me anymore," she said, "but everything would be different if you'd behaved like a man twenty years ago."

She hated males because she couldn't live without them. She went on talking above my useless wait for the boy; twenty years back I had stopped being a male because I wouldn't marry her, because I was already too expert at moving about without effort between the dense lies she indulged in anew every day, as furiously and persistently as though it were a vice; twenty years back because I hadn't publicly and legally agreed that the ex-fetus she showed me was my son. Because I had looked at the purple face of the foul-smelling, wailing worm that they showed off to me as though it were a trophy; because I had had my doubts and laughed.

24

In any case, Seoane wouldn't be coming now and she could spend the boy's absence reciting:

"Because I agree with you that in the beginning neither you nor I was to blame. We didn't even know how to blow our own noses, as the saying goes, and they were already teaching us that you boys had a little cock and we girls didn't."

(The justice of the peace and the neighbor women agreed that there was a resemblance; but I had someone bring me a fresh bottle to the courtroom and kept smiling, saying no, suspecting the child of scandalous and fantastic resemblances. When I said that the baby boy's nose and that of His Honor the Justice of the Peace hinted at a future similarity, and no further documentary evidence was forthcoming, from that time on possible resemblances, gossip dragging in names, were inevitable. It ought not to be forgotten that Brausen sent me to Santa María when I was forty years old and already chief of police, already head of the Detachment. There was an antecedent. When I was around ten and had Prince Orloff as my teacher, I disappeared, I was in limbo until I was forty. I am speaking of years as they occur in certain places; here, in Lavanda, for instance.)

"Ah, yes; they have a little cock and we girls don't." She was covered by the bathrobe now, mildly drunk, looking at the grimy, vague wetness of the windows, smiling and rocking back and forth. It seemed like the middle of a literary salon, on a Friday at five. "And we had to believe it because it was true. How many twenty years? No fooling. I had happinesses, real love affairs. As long as they were rare. Men: in front of others they're so nice and so good. With a woman, always superior, bed, silence, vulgarity. And we, the girls, not being able to live freely the way they do, go to camps, invent trips, not having hours or even days to go back to Mama. And if you want to hear it more clearly, we girls can't take advantage of a lantern without a flame to size up how big they are whereas they can fondle our tits, our ass. And we girls who were unimaginably eager for it, and silently reciting the prayer of St. Judas Thaddeus for it, had to say what did you think and who do you take me for. And if, besides, a girl gets married or gets involved with a boy who's a whole lot dumber than she is, and that happens nine times out of ten, in an argument she always has to take a step backwards and say yes, that never occurred to me. You're right. It's true, I grant you, that we cuckold them and then make up some story about a ring, about a lost wallet we found or about somebody who came by selling on credit and keeps forgetting to collect. It's only fair; and for every time we cheat on them we light a candle, in the cathedral, at the feet of the Blessed Virgin. But the cuckold goes on being a poor dolt and the whole business of the presents, the lies and the secrecy is as dumb as the husband is. Then later, we don't have men; only what may be better: the presents we lie about, the hour stolen under false pretenses, the taxi on the corner and the shy moistness that makes us remember the real one. Sometimes, so great that it's boring. After that nothing more except repeated stinginess, and then nothing at all. The enraged husband, the shit in the diapers, cooking. And always, Medina, ever since my tits began to show, you males, whenever you get together, in a hurry to pass judgment. Because a girl, a woman isn't a person, she doesn't get that far, she's only a body or a thing. Until she catches herself a husband and the story I've been telling you begins all over again.

She stopped talking. We fell silent and she took another swig, lighted a cigarette and smiled in self-satisfaction at the window.

I remembered other monotonous visits, other mutual sentences with or without Seoane. Our past might have been sordid, unavoidable perhaps. But the present was worse, as is usual.

The Portraits

Bed, food, or pesos to eat on, the room, the attic of an apartment on the Gran Punta de las Carretas, an expensive residential neighborhood. At least, Frieda asserted that the prices at the supermarket were twice as high, almost, as the ones paid by people who lived in other obscure parts of the city. And furthermore she was annoyed if someone said apartment or flat, or apartment instead of the right word: penthouse.

So I lived in a penthouse on the Gran Punta de las Carreteras and not even today, remembering, thinking, if thinking were possible, can I understand the reason for Frieda's semi-protection. I could only suspect a vague fear of blackmail, of the words drunk and dissolute; but I was, I am, certain that Frieda could believe me capable of any major baseness, but never of that one.

Nor did she need me in bed, although she knew me to be ever obedient, ever curious. As for me, my self-abandonment in those days was almost inexplicable even though, I suppose, easy to understand.

Cut off from Santa María because of a crisis of pride, I wandered about, more or less lived, among the inhabitants of Lavanda with a power of detachment, of criticism, patience and self-surrender that made me happy or not suffering for many months. I looked at them without ceasing to see myself; I spoke the right phrases almost always and very seldom did they take them in the wrong way.

I went about among bodies and voices without wandering off the path that they had imposed upon themselves, tenaciously and involuntarily, forgetting the hour of their death, amen, not knowing that time does not exist, that there is no such thing. But I had known since childhood, and kept my secret to myself like a disease.

I wandered about aimlessly, playing with a bunch of coincidences which—I already suspected as much—could only come about in Santa María, the lost city. I nonetheless persisted; I relied, among so many other things, on the fearful force of recently arisen superstitions that have a greater power than those that are inherited. I had nothing to do with the inhabitants of Lavanda.

I was thereabouts when Frieda von Kliestein invented my second job for me. The name assigned this job went more or less—it was a time of great lack of precise details—like this:

"I wouldn't bet again on Medina the male nurse, paramedic, or bedside physician. I don't know. I said so many things to help you."

"To help me to kill him, to help them kill him."

"That's right, all joking aside. I said so many things that maybe I talked about Harley Street and about Medina the baronet. It must have been comical, but who remembers? The baronet bit is getting to be amusing again. I bet, I lost, and I never have regrets. I told them: this much is certain, Medina was the lord of darkness in Santa María. How macho Medina was with his pistol under his armpit. But I also talked to them about Medina who had been painting little pictures since he was a youngster. So rich and so sweet. Medina, of course, is a man and knows how to punch somebody out when I meow and can punch anybody he likes without asking my permission. But you were a failure, there's no way around it, the corpse died on you when you weren't taking care of him, fulfilling the sacred duty of spurring him on to die a good death. I wept a little; I wept for the great misfortune and for your failure. I remember that I was reasonable. They cried too, although I'm sure that, today, they will have forgiven you. But, in any event, you'll have to use one of your other talents to earn your living. I told you, from the beginning or from another beginning in the filth of Lavanda that all I could give you was a roof over your head, maybe cigarettes, maybe booze. But not food. So that now . . ."

"I understand, you poor whore in reverse. I'm leaving."

"I'm not throwing you out. I'm moving you, that's all."

The new plan was in effect now, and I wished to share it with others out of impure generosity and out of the amusing temptation to have witnesses. I pushed her down on the couch and she was expecting it because she gave up without a struggle, with moans very close to the truth. She laughed only when she again spoke of art and of my paintings.

Frieda for her part stuffed herself full of egg whites, went twice a week for a singing lesson. I teased her about it, mentioning the Colón and La Scala, calling her Maria Callas. But she didn't get annoyed; she didn't intend to sing in operas without having first won fame singing in theaters, clutching microphones, mastering jazz to the point of sending crowds into ecstasy. And then I said to her:

"Bye-bye, Bessie. Don't break the piano."

And we were at peace.

Another time, remote and without the ability to feel pain, the past, adolescence, an imagined Reverend Father Antón Bergner who had looked at the repulsive painting of His Holiness that I had painted, compelled and cajoled by my spinster aunt, devoid of a future. Father Bergner looking at the portrait that occupied a third of the height of the wall; it was a present, it was badly done and unpleasant to look at. He had known me since I was a child, he remembered my face, which changed through the years and clung for no reason to adolescence. And it was my aunt, the headmistress of the school, who brought the picture to the church and offered it with a touching certainty that she was purchasing in exchange a recompense that no one could give her on earth. As though she had executed the painting herself, and perhaps that was true. But I, the nephew, existed; that youngster who had decided to run away with the indispensable clothes, the train ticket, a little stolen money and a few pots of paint. Father Bergner also knew that I had come back to invent for myself a studio in the old market of Santa María. He never found out, because time was against him, that Brausen had made other arrangements, that I had left the studio for the Police Detachment; I could never foresee myself in another old market, in Lavanda.

Perhaps Bergner had learned of the arrival of Orloff, a photographic artist, a connoisseur of all the arts, in the city founded by Brausen.

Orloff, he too a prince or a grand duke, who became furious when he was called a photographer, persuaded my aunt by means of an album of newspaper clippings in various languages, along with his contempt and the serenity of a cynicism that appeared to be legitimate and inherited. I never found out the price; but Orloff managed to become my teacher and twice a week I went up the uneven staircase of his house in order to learn how to paint.

I took my pieces of pasteboard, my box of oils and brushes, my ration of cigarettes home with me; I wasn't able to leave anything in the dirty room, redeemed by a window that overlooked the river, because the grand duke stole anything and everything, drank the pots of paint, shaved the pig bristles, concocted mixtures of turpentine and linseed oil.

I never had another teacher, I said, and no other conceivable one to compare with him. Because Orloff received me with a bow, set up my easel for me next to the window, asked me for cigarettes, didn't address me in the familiar form and never forgot the prologue:

"You have no talent whatsoever. Paint all the rubbish that comes to your mind. I have to put up with you for an hour, but the time goes by quickly if we talk together."

Then he brought out a bottle of brandy from the darkness and filth of his photo labyrinth, which was also a bedroom, and told me the most beautiful lie I've ever heard; from my grandmother with her fairy tales, the wretches I could corral in the Department, Frieda and her inanities, and all the miserable rabble that I have to put up with today.

So, slow of memory, whispering state secrets that would take the Russian Revolution back to zero, Prince Orloff, carried away by a small initial worldwide hecatomb, leaned over to pick up off the stained floor the plot that he went on reciting to me in the afternoons, drunk at times, at other times delirious and cautious. I learned about the Tsarina, Michael, Nicholas the adolescent, Xenia, George, Olga. I learned about Tatiana and Anastasia, about Rasputin and Yusupov, about the immutable loyalty of the Grand Duke or Prince Orloff, anchored today in Santa María, the one and only possessor of the secret of Tsarkoe Selo of Ekaterinburg and that of Admiral Kolchak. That is to say: all of them dead, but, yet, notwithstanding, here Orloff was, laughing shielded by his gray mustache and looking at me with rage and disgust. There was never a useful morning, he never looked at my paintings. But there was no doubt that the secret with a capital S lay in the last words of Admiral Alexander Kolchak, entrusted to Orloff as the sole possible key to the Restoration. And the grand duke or prince, hidden in Santa María like a microbe, like a bedbug in a mattress, kept his mouth shut when he was drunk and awaited drunk the order that couldn't be long in coming.

He laughed only when he talked once again about art and about my paintings.

"A studio in the market they're going to tear down," Frieda said. "My sworn word about the cigarettes and the booze still goes. There's furniture, there's a restaurant downstairs, you have a credit at La Platense to buy canvases and paints and anything you need. I'm going to send you a friend, Olga, who has urgent need of a portrait, the way one needs, I suppose, an abortion or a little bag of heroin. I'm going to send you lots of women friends, the ones I have left over."

A SCENT OF TERESA

Now it was as delicate, sad and remote as a scent that time had aged on a handkerchief. Sometimes it came, nothing announced its arrival beforehand. Generally, in dreams: I saw Teresa's face or her way of walking. The places were capricious and its structures disconcerted me. Never a word, never a direct look that sought out my face. In the dreams, silent ones and ones in color, I saw her pass by, sometimes raising a hand to feel with my fingers the message that Teresa was unable to give me. But when awake I always remembered her in a cruel way, hardly changed or faded, which filled me with furies and blasphemies.

GURISA

So Frieda's magic and the eurodollars that the family, terrified by her threat to return, sent her from Santa María, brought it about that at the end of summer the water beat against the windows of my workshop in the market, came in through the holes clumsily stopped up with odds and ends of cardboard. I had known, for many months, that as a painter I was sick, doomed. I knew that only what I imagined could matter to me. Nonetheless, I spent hours looking at my paintings, my peasants of any race that had risen in rebellion, my fishermen, certain of their appeal, of the affront of their misery. Because they hadn't yet ceased to exist, to live, on the canvases, on easel paintings, on the walls, in the slight shelter that the bed and the floor offered them.

The two ruined rooms of the studio. I worked—if happiness deserves the obscenity of that name—slept, sometimes cooked there. And there also began there, by chance, through God's wishes or Frieda's cleverness, what I am now endeavoring to tell by fits and starts because it was impossible for me to paint it.

Staircases and halls, grease, old age, drafts, bad smells, a brief, ominous silence, cries.

And thus, I remember, there began the curious little hell that there is no need to read but I'm writing it. Through the foggy windows, between eight, ten, and noon, the changeable, damp morning struck me in the face. On the floor, to the right a dead pipe, a live book that an Andalusian had written. I still had a contemptible innocence, Castilian towns, elderly señoritas, foreign dust and respects without a cause floated by.

On a Tuesday, in February, a fifteenth, I stretched out on the bed to recognize myself and hurl silent insults at the knocks on the door and its relative protection of the identity of the knocker. Already awake, feeling nauseated, set down once again in another day. Before me were the hour, affectionate stupidity, the stubborn female on the canvas, standing with her feet apart, the farce of work, the hope of company and wine.

The dog spoke. I put on my trousers and opened the door to let Olga in.

Not very far above the rotting, a sour ferment and the restless odor of rats, amid staircases and hallways, old age, persistent efforts to collapse, shrill voices.

Just that for the time being, so that each one can go on constructing the market that no longer exists and that Frieda gave me as a gift.

I never tried to find out who lent Olga the dented, stuttering Ford that she used in order to arrive implacably and strip naked in the market, studio, workshop or apartment; the car she offered me so many times to take me to somewhere that never existed.

The bad part, the good part was that in those months worth remembering I preferred, to any offer from the outside world, to execute the painting urged on me by Frieda. The portrait of Olga.

Now she was there, more solid by the day, invariably arriving at noon on the dot, a little desperate at times, playing at getting drunk on the half-bottles she brought or found there. I listened to her saying yes, thinking of the nude, keeping her at my side. She was a big-boned peasant woman, with blond hair and broad mannish hands.

Yes, Olga had been married, she no longer had a husband and I managed to know nothing of the details of the story, despite hearing the sound of her sentences amid her fits of weeping. I made a portrait of her face, a timid try and a failure. It got lost among so many other things. A bust in profile, ill-defined; a memory that mattered more than the details of Olga's black blouse, in part invented.

We both knew: it was not the head that we were looking for but the nude. And a special, dedicated nude. In my memory the face of the first portrait takes a step backward and doesn't bare its secrets. It revealed itself only slightly, was mistakable for someone else.

Furthermore we knew. Like two soaking wet puppies, looking each other in the eye; without any other hope of shelter, we knew that Frieda was unnamable, that from some place where there was laughter she was manipulating the tiny story.

And then there came or I dreamed the girl disguised as a Chinese, who smiled, with learned sweetness, so as not to understand our questions and our thanks. I anointed her, of course, with the floating peelings of a sweet fruit whose name we were unable to guess. She, the Chinese girl, was wearing a long black dress, had coiled braids covering her ears and this helped her to smile; to fail to understand, to slowly say no by barely shaking her head.

Either she had been present or she hadn't, and it makes no difference. I didn't talk about her to Olga because that afternoon, or before, I had lost hope and accepted the modesty—any answer that wasn't true—of Olga's vulgar answers.

For two or three weeks of bad weather, in November, of hot and cold, of rain and mist, she came to visit me and to cry, to lean down over the illustrations in art books as though they really mattered to her, looking at a secret. We didn't speak of the nude, I didn't hint at it, it was forgotten. I painted peasants who would never wage revolution, golden with harvests, geometrical hands, black open mouths, upraised hands.

Until one afternoon she kept smiling, inviting me, and spoke my name. I turned around, with the wrong idea in mind, thinking I understood. I abandoned the infuriated woman on the easel amid sheaves of wheat and slowly walked toward the couch.

"What's up?" I said as I cleaned a spatula, looked at the various stains on the rag, thought of framing it: it would no doubt win the top prize at the national salon.

"I thought that now was the time, you idiot. I want the nude. I need it and you always knew that. It's something like that, difficult, like asking you for money or a present. A thing. But the painting is mine and you don't have much time left."

"All right," I said unhappily.

We were looking at the rain on the dirty window and the rainwater wetting the floor, we drank out of the same glass until it began to get dark.

"We had a white stallion that they called a dapple gray, it ate out of our hands without biting us," Olga said. "We never rode it and I don't know what happened afterwards. One of Papa's quirks, something odd, I always thought."

"It was a filly, Olga. We'll begin the painting tomorrow."

I had to think of her naked before seeing her. It didn't interest me to know why I had agreed, what she wanted, needed the portrait for. I went on thinking of her naked till dawn came, and, still undecided, all morning long. I was also undecided when we were together again, at siesta time.

And all of a sudden, on the second day, as I recall, she managed to loosen up and relax the smile aimed at the ceiling, at my face, at troubled memories.

She began to look in a friendly way at the rain and the brief moments of chilly sun. She bent one leg and devoted herself to being more beautiful, more gigantic, white and round. She also became punctual. She arrived at siesta time, described her improbable recent lunch, slowly ate the leftovers she found. I heard her wandering about, telling the air, the studio, gossip about little theater projects that would make the culture of

Lavanda immortal, gossip about actors and authors, of unborn babies doomed to an early death. I smoked my pipe lying in bed only half listening to her and waiting.

I was never really able to discover the cause, the motive that made her fall silent around three o'clock in the afternoon and leap to her feet like a soldier at reveille.

"Excuse me," so as to strip naked.

Many, many times I wanted to change my sensation, to make it perfect, or closer to the truth. But even today I still feel the same way; she stripped naked as though she were taking the slip-cover off a piece of furniture belonging to somebody else, as though she were peeling potatoes or fruit for a dinner that we weren't going to have.

Then she threw herself down on the old coverlet of the couch—overflowing with memories—and lighted a cigarette. Every few minutes she raised her head to look at her body, her torso of a child, her long powerful legs.

She often asked, the poor sweet unfortunate thing:

"Is it all right like this? Is it going to take much longer?"

She wanted, she needed the painting for herself, so as to give it away as a present, like a Trojan pony, in a vain attempt at revenge. But we both had no idea how glorious it is to fight for a failure and we stubbornly went on.

During inhumanly hot afternoons, she preferred to stretch out naked in the studio of the dilapidated market. She talked about her mornings and her beaches—the brief happinesses that bring reconciliation in Lavanda—but I knew how not to listen to her, I had her again. I approached the growing white body, ordered capricious, pointless poses. The heat mingled Olga with the smells of oil of turpentine and the rotting market.

December was beginning when I thought up a common father and two mothers. My mother was unknown and twenty-nine years old. For her all I needed to do was to invent a guileless and gentle female, with a perpetual smile and no precise address. Like

Olga as far as the bones of her body and her hunger to believe were concerned. Mine was more difficult and came to my mind more swiftly.

My young mother whom I'd never seen wouldn't have been able to imagine the lack of importance of all that. A naked woman in front of a man who wasn't her husband, a man who idly fondled her body on the long couch stained with paint and a great many things. Naked in the cellar of the market, chilled to the bone or sweating, placid and docile.

She hadn't promised anything that I had wordlessly forced on her: not to look at the painting without permission. At first the portrait was a glorious white and pink vulgarity that climbed up independently onto the canvas and settled itself comfortably on it, eyes, an unconvincing smile, a striving for hair that would reach to her shoulders. But in ten days I knew that that wasn't it, that I—or the naked body—one of the two of us was wrong. I threw the painting out into the street one drizzling, drunken night, and we began all over again. I at least began.

Olga didn't ask questions. She let time go by and one afternoon she said, in an almost resigned monotone:

"I already know why that portrait can't ever be finished. I already know that Frieda asked you for it and Frieda doesn't lie to me. But you kept putting things between us, all the time. The bad part is that you promised and that I need it right away, before I thought I would."

"Sometimes things come out well and other times they come out all wrong. But unfortunately you need it right now. So now I'm going to do what doesn't matter to me, what I didn't want to do. It's easy and quick that way and the man will have your body on the wedding night. In a different way, naturally. The way children might come from their fathers. As ridiculous, as touching, as useless."

She laughed, gave out the long murmur of a laugh. Sometimes

I compared by unlikely memory of the little girl with the heavy-set woman who was trying to surrender herself on the couch.

She grew ugly for three days and then went back to her solid beauty, to reproducing almost exactly the lines and the color of the portrait, the believable pose.

We also compared—I think—the very brief, almost entirely avowable past, of her childhood with the little world of miserable, illogical squalor—forgetting, lies, and confused shames—that she was now obliged to tolerate and expand.

She laughed again as though she were infinitely older than I was, as though she were revealing that she had discovered my secret. I looked at her for a time, in amazement, feeling grateful that the world still had surprises and innocences in store for me.

"Because if that's the reason," she bargained.

The bad weather had returned and the afternoon light set traps for me. I looked at her in the painting and on the couch. Her left buttock had a green, rosy glow; the other suggested a memory of hair in shadow; her neck suddenly rose up, confidently support-ing itself on misfortune.

I slowly approached as the claps of thunder broke, thinking of the dead years that nobody buries, absorbed in the happy and resigned warmth of the couch, in the fleeting odor of the storm that invaded and exacerbated the putrefaction of the market. And very vaguely, as she opened her legs and her mouth, I also imagined the odor of the girl and everything forced me to throw myself on top of her. Olga moaned before I had even touched her; she stared cross-eyed at me, and a slaver of supplication drooled down one cheek.

I found out that she was the maternal peasant beast that I had supposed. Nor did we talk about ourselves afterward. Nor of the nude in oils that was to arrive at the bride's house on the very day of the wedding.

Dressed now, she asked a question as she stood by the door. I was lying on the couch, having retrieved my pipe, listening to it rain.

"Are you still seeing Frieda?"

"Very little. Much less than you."

She left without banging the door. It went on raining and once again I thought of her affectionately and dreamily. I didn't think I'd made her happy, remembering her tears on my arm, I saw myself using a colored cloth, to dry her cheeks and blow her nose, to protect her from the rain on the roof, from the cries in the market, from the injustice and blindness of life.

The afternoon repeated itself, with fears and preferences, as the nude made progress on the canvas and Olga preceded it, coming to resemble it more and more. I no longer needed to turn my eyes toward her to look at her and copy her.

I am speaking now of Olga's inevitable intelligence. She could well have had it in her cheekbones, in the calm brightness of her eyes. I am speaking of that, by happenstance, because at the time she never spoke to me of love. Naked, enormous and childish, hugging her knees, she spoke only of the idiot who preferred a well-reared and well-off virgin.

But I knew Roa, her ex-lover, and I had sold him two paintings and he almost reached the point of paying me for a third one. In no way was he an idiot; I couldn't confuse him with the man that Olga persistently described to me, repeating herself.

Naked, infuriated, as big as a mother, Olga hurled insults and ate, bread soaked in oil with garlic and thyme in it, barely moved her glass to ask for wine. All she talked about was the painting and—without naming him now—Roa. But I was carefully watching her secret rage, her way of tapping cigarettes before lighting them. Because she was always aware and always kept remembering that I had been with Frieda or had made my unusual escape to the house in the dunes so as to walk all along the beach to look for the crests of waves breaking, to collect shells and to make fun of myself. That, self-mockery, is restful, helpful and purifying.

One afternoon I asked her:

"Would you like to be called Gurisa?"

"That's not a name for a person."

"Of course it is. Would you like me to call you Gurisa?"

"Yes, whatever you please. Anything except something that's an insult."

The nude was ready and packed and arrived at the house of Roa's bride on the wedding day with a card in handwritten capital letters that said: IT'S A GOOD THING TO COMPARE THE PAST WITH THE FUTURE.

A JOURNEY

Quinteros said, or goes around saying, that the idea of employing my five senses in an orderly way could lead me to discover someone from Santa María as much a fugitive as I was, as devoid of documents and condemned to fear and hypocrisy.

Quinteros is lying. That is not a reproach because lying integrates and completes his personality. But I wish to state and leave behind in written form that the idea and the period of madness were exclusively my own. He did nothing except help me and encourage, for his amusement, my various deliriums.

I was looking for a brother, an outcast, a stateless person like myself; someone who had escaped from Santa María without Brausen's permission, out of disgust with Brausen and everything that flowed from him. And I trusted that one of my five senses would serve to discover what I was trying to track down, would help like a confidant, a dog's sense of smell, on my spy mission.

As on any Monday, Wednesday or Friday, between seven and eight in a warm October dusk, I was leaning with my overcoat off against a display window of the Palomino Pharmacy, in the Calle Isla de Flores or Carlos Gardel, waiting for the water with the little syringe in it to boil in the back room. Bored, motionless, watching the crowd of female customers asking for tranquilizers, health, beauty and eternal youth, only to disappear as one and immediately be replaced by others. When in a small empty space, between me and the corner with the telephone and the broken-down scale that invariably showed ten kilos two hundred grams, the girl appeared. I can remember, and can be certain that I am not lying in this regard, the light of her square white teeth, the angle of her head bowed submissively and mockingly as she waited. The attractiveness of her nose of a little kid, her faded blue jeans and her body just beginning to mature cannot belong exclusively to her in my memory. But what surely was hers was the touch of vulgarity that made her upper lip bulge out like a slight swelling, an immutable pregnancy.

I obstinately persisted in being mistaken from the beginning, from the tinkling of the coins with which she tapped, to attract attention, accompanying the song that she was thinking about from her window. She was not, I repeat, without either rage or frustration, what I had been searching for in Lavanda for such a long time, without facts, without aid, without even having convincing plans or real single-mindedness. It happened before I came across Quinteros or the Anglo-Saxon gentleman, it was at a time of uprooting, of the awkwardnesses of a newcomer, of those hours and endlessly long days that for me took the place of the minutes that followed when I woke up in a stranger's bedroom.

It wasn't that, but on the contrary it was the girl, an unborn quality of a small number of years, a quality that none of those chosen to inflict the injuries for which there is no defense, provoked by the presence, the passage, the laughter, the brief suicide and defiance of girls, will ever even attempt to explain. Those who can understand already know this, the others will never understand and, moreover, they don't matter.

"Ah, Medina, over forty years old and showing the ravages of being old and a foreigner. No more rows, Medina, not again, not even this one time."

But a sixth sense told me yes, that it was Santa María again, that the skinny body, bent over and ill-proportioned, had the prestige of a lighthouse, contained within it the trail, the side road, the shortcut able to lead me to the way back.

In the back, amid boxes and packages, in the miserable, dimly lighted, airless room, the water refused to come to a boil for my little syringe, the unknown liquids and powders refused to mix together to fill the prescription. In the precarious solitude, in the sudden silence that fell I recited toward the reflection of the lighted blue cross above the sidewalk:

"Monday, Wednesday, Friday, between seven and eight."

I spoke as if reciting a rosary of troubles so old it could no longer distress me. And I was certain that the sign of recognition was going to be given me, clear and indubitable, through my sense of smell.

In the spring it was inevitable that I should call to mind Santa María and its river, so different from this one that they called a sea, my river with the other shore visible, with its island in the middle, with the regularity of the raft or the ferry, with the precise chromatic distribution of motor launches, barges, yachts, row-boats, heads of swimmers. There in that little cubicle called a pharmacy, motionless, half lying down, waiting for the injection and for hope, so bored at times that the tedium seemed to make persons and things fade away very swiftly, calling to mind the friendly vastness of Barthé's pharmacy, the vegetable coolness of the basement filled nearly full of bags and boxes, his fat, white, evasive face making promises between a blue flask and another that was red, offering consolation in his affectionate eunuch's voice.

Until next Monday, Wednesday or Friday, the man who gave injections said to me, feeling out the terrain with a little smile, as I fastened my belt:

"It seems you took a fancy to that girl the other day."

"Which one?"

"You know which one, the one with the hand cream and the expectorant, the one who was tapping with coins on the counter to accompany the little ditty 'Let's go to bed because we need some rest.' "

"Intelligent," I said to him.

The pharmacist without a degree, who had studied medicine, was fair-haired and short, with a mustache whose long ends drooped, and a squinting or clouded left eye.

"Intelligent," I said to him calmly and gently. "I'll bet you liked her too. You too would prefer to have her here instead of me, to look at her with her panties pulled down, to look at her buttocks and with a little cleverness something else as well and give yourself the pleasure, such an innocent one, of sticking the needle in all of a sudden and feel her hurting just a little bit. But that little beastie can't need injections."

After five minutes of driveling repetitions on the subject of the apostolate in the back rooms of pharmacies and the asexuality of the patients, the weak and the needy, he agreed:

"Of course one doesn't stop being a man even so."

And he gave himself the didactic pleasure of a few little vindictive remarks:

"Don't get the idea that she doesn't need injections sometimes, not of vitamins though, but of hormones. You can't have heard her very well when the two of you were alone the other day for just a few minutes and I was working in the laboratory. Because she was here yesterday and it wasn't even from seven to eight, it must have been in the middle of the afternoon. An imported German product that has never yet failed me as far as I know. Two ampules of one cubic centimeter each given at twenty-four-hour intervals. If she, her friends, or the pimp who takes his cut on that corner is on time with the bribe, you can meet her near the Plazoleta del Gaucho or by the side of the seminary after nightfall, just after seven, as you said, and that was why I was laughing in the lab. The other day was an exception; you had no way of knowing that she made a sign to me and besides the cream and the expectorant she went away with a box of sanitary napkins in the package."

"And I would have sworn . . ." I began to think. But I persisted, I dug about furiously in my presentiment, in the mingled odors of the pharmacy, in the ill humor, a week old now, that had grown worse and worse because of my craving for tobacco. Ever since meeting the girl I had limited myself to fewer than five cigarettes a day so as to strengthen my sense of smell so badly mistreated for years. It was not the wounded vanity of knowing that the girl in jeans hadn't allowed that gaze of hers to fall on my person, a male and a macho, but on just another customer instead. That wasn't why I was in a rage for a time at the pharmacist who gave injections. It was my old repugnance toward, disgust at, and at times hatred of whores, a nice little whore in this case, of anyone able to adulterate the happiness offered by beds. And I remembered signing the little yellow identification books, with photographs that had always been taken long before and fake dates, authorizing the free exercise of prostitution within the limits of decency and the district.

The injectionist must have had a presentiment that this was goodbye, that I would never be back to reveal any sign of gratitude or disappointment, because he added sadly, looking at the corner with the shelves:

"The whoresons froze weekly wages. But maybe for that very reason the measure excepts hustlers. So I can't tell you. A few months ago, she was getting three hundred and the price of the room. They call her Victoria."

I was touched. During our brief relationship I had never made any attempt to be gracious. He was there, blonder and more fragile, pathetic, with the little syringe still between his fingers, stoic, trying to make the farewell easier with an unconvincing smile.

"I understand," I said submissively and fraternally. "A matter of being relatives. Nepotism, the opposition press writes."

It took me two nights of searching in faces immobilized by habit and make-up, in incredible, ill-matched outfits, beneath tall coiffures, constructed by patient master carpenters, of searching without being able to stop, at a steady pace and resisting the temptations to go astray, in the semi-darkness of the gray wall of the seminary or in the blinking light of a neon sign above the horse and the cavalry lancer in the little square. The pendulum of the dark handbags with long handles, a metronome, a come-on, a free sample of what I could do for you. Then, recognizing in the easily mistakable restless little whore, who kept going in and out of the group of her colleagues, who suddenly stood calmly on the corner, alone and disdainful, ready to take flight, to be insulting, to be reluctant, recognizing with an exhausted joy the girl from the pharmacy, Victoria, the promise of Santa María, of the past, of a return, just because, to the mystery of simply being in a specific place on earth.

I smelled her as we talked. Still three hundred and the room, a special price for me, service included.

I smelled her without ostensible anxiety as we went down the street, three or four quick blocks, to the whorehouse. I saw, in the room, that she hadn't changed much; she was still wearing pants, ocher ones now, and a jacket; all I would have to do was wash her face and muss her hairdo to have her again, bending over again, showing me her little kid's nose, her mocking mouth active now, the touch of vulgarity and cynicism, swollen now, growing, overflowing, that had set me to trembling for a second, Monday, Wednesday or Friday, in the Isla de Flores pharmacy.

Frantic and hiding the fact, glimpsed with a deceptively clean body thanks to a professional deformation, traversing in addition the vulgarity of the synthetic perfumes that it was necessary to lift up and peel off like thick transparent crusts, I thought I recognized—by way of breath, armpit, genitals, exhaustion—the words, beings and things which books enumerate and which will come back once more.

("It is easy to draw a map of the location and the layout of Santa María, in addition to giving it a name; but it is necessary to beam a special light on each place of business, on each doorway and on each corner. It is necessary to give form to the low clouds that drift above the bell tower of the church and the roof terraces with pink and cream balustrades; it is necessary to distribute distasteful furnishings about, it is necessary to accept what one hates, it is necessary to transport people, from who knows where, in order that they may inhabit, pollute, be moved to pity, be happy, and squander money.")

Denying my solitude at the cost of some effort, legs spread apart above the slight nausea, the slight fatigue, I persisted in locating barely detectable odors not yet entirely disappeared suitable for doorways, corners, rooftop terraces, furniture, people, innards, faces. Not forgetting—I did not forget—the widely dispersed odor of herds of cattle in the vastness of the countryside, the milky odor of the colony of gringos.

"Everybody must tell you the same thing," I murmured, flattening one hand on the bosom of the girl, Victoria, keeping her from leaping out of bed, washing and dressing. "Please lie quietly. I'll pay three hundred more. But I'll tell you afterwards and not before. I'm not saying that I remember you or that you look the same. I'm saying that you might look like your mother or your older sister, somebody, a woman I knew once, long ago and far away, in Santa María."

"Santa María," she repeated.

"Up there, right there. Have you ever been in Santa María?"

I felt as though instead of renting the woman I had seduced her; I felt, smiling and lying still, so afraid of making a wrong move.

Santa María and the bonfires that make the resin bubble and the dead leaves writhe as night falls in April. Dung and that unexpectedly captured odor, scarcely threatening, of urine in the dunghill. The traffic back and forth of banknotes in furtive business deals, marking them with the unmistakable grime of having been fingered. Tobacco and smoking-hot coffee in my office in the Detachment, the acids in the little laboratory, formaldehyde and death in the morgue, also small but big enough. The odor of the young ladies hidden away that is afraid of giving itself away. A little farther on, like someone who is heading toward the Colony—that scene, if I were to see it, is altogether changed, I've been told—honeysuckle, pastureland at dawn, orange blossoms, the land always propitious, ribs being barbecued amid invisible trees. The great fruit warehouses along the river, the rusted iron of the shipyard, the stiff superstitious trousers of the fishermen motionless on the pier. Those who are optimistic and persevering repainting, with an eye out for the good season, little houses, rowboats and dories on the beach at Villa Petrus, heating tar for caulking. Inside a house near the old main square, abandoned in what we used to call the parlor, the walnut wood of a silent piano, a straw sewing basket with spools of thread, buttons, a length of worn-out elastic, a tortured pincushion, an envelope of lavender with no fragrance left.

And above the barely faded landscape and our hours of happiness, misfortune or lucidity, the conflict, in the exact middle of the sky, of the greens that came from the farmlands and the violent leaden colors of the river, heaps of unwinnowed grain and dead fish.

And, again in my office, the tepid air, unpleasant, unmistakable, so much like phosphorus, that confined the sweat of those being interrogated, the offspring of anxiety and fear, after several hours of traps and questions, violence and affection. I myself, Medina, the man who never tires, taking breaks to wash, shave, revive with cologne on my cheeks and brand-new cautious lies. Or simply night in Santa María with its moon or its drizzle and the commingled, incomprehensible vapor of so many thousands of simultaneous dreams.

I breathed once more the air that we had created and I became a believer once again. A brief faith, precisely the size of its possibilities. Because she had never been in the lost city; neither she, Victoria, nor a possible mother or sister, although, it's true, you're right, a girlfriend who's married and they don't want to have children, she's had abortions, and the husband is a very unusual sort who brings her breakfast in bed on Sundays and does the shopping and makes barbecue sauce and takes her to work and brings her home on a motorcycle, you can't imagine, this friend of mine whose name is Gioconda was in Santa María a few years ago to sign her name on a will that in the end left her only a few funny-money pesos and then, after that, she sent me a couple of postcards from there that I still have, but she never lived in Santa María either and the money from the will came to her unexpectedly from an aunt of her husband's, and as I've already told you he's not like anybody else; they broke the mold after they made that one.

I got dressed slowly and gave her the money she'd earned and the rest as well, half of the fiasco. People were walking about in the patio, knocking on doors and whispering, as all the odors of the room quickly hardened, taking on once again their vulgar and hostile air, they rejected me the way a steel chair rejects the poor wretch who tries to rest in it for a while so as to move people to pity and explain his need of consolation or money.

A CLUE

A while ago I was wandering around the studio in the old market and I suddenly realized that I was seeing it for the first time. There are two cots, chairs with sprawled legs and no seats, newspapers, several months old, turned brown in the sun, nailed over the window in place of windowpanes.

I was wandering about naked to the waist, bored with lying stretched out, since noon, breathing the accursed heat that the roof collects and that now, always, in the afternoons, overflows into the whole room. I was walking around with my hands behind me, hearing my slippers slap on the tiles, alternately smelling each of my armpits. I shook my head from one side to the other, breathing the smell, and this, I could feel it, made a grimace of disgust spread over my face. My unshaved beard brushed against my shoulders.

The brief adventure, the eleventh or twelfth first hope had ended, and not forever, last night, and not forever because memory and forgetfulness would continue, unhurriedly, with no imaginable regularity, biting into, altering my memory, lending, fancifully and surprisingly, to it new purities to the old man and the old woman, the dimly lighted corner where big bunches of herbs baptized by Linnaeus before or afterwards lay head downward, named after a laconic Indian already turned into an iguana or a stone, after a sly gaucho, after a mulatta who smoked—

a washerwoman, a witch, a midwife, one suspects—before or afterward.

For each branch, moreover, the name of an organ, a bone, nervous confusion, inability, or mere bad luck. The series of strokes of bad luck—and their infallible correction—that go to make up life and all possible fates, I thought then or think now and who knows with what indescribable difference, with what new stupefaction I will think about this tomorrow, within precisely one solar year or on the very eve of my death, amen. And amen as well for the toothless old couple, so sweet and still sustaining the mystery of love, looking without apprehension on my ridiculous groping about in error, smiling without understanding and—oh, envy—no need to understand the tricks of my phrases, of my gestures, of my sense of hearing.

And also and above all, now or last night at seven on the dot, coinciding exactly with closing time and postponing it, the little couple of likeable oldsters in the greenish hovel of herbs and possible sicknesses, turned yellowish by the feebleness of the asthmatic streetlight forced on it by the rains in Baigorria or Rincón del Bonete, or the droughts, which we must call, and why not, implacable, endless rains. Or the team of perverse and elusive monsters, made obscene by age and vital obstinacy, determined not to serve me even with a false sign that I might twist so that it would fit into my hope. The bastards, so unaware of my anxiety, diverting toward an interminable darkness and dense forest the narrow path that might lead me either to Brausen on the one hand, or to Santa María on the other.

In any case, in the dingy hovel traversed by different odors, the disorderliness, the timid terror of the broken-down musical instruments lying silent which almost formed a wall behind the counter, my expertise as a snooper who sensed in the darkness of the little drawers of the chest, with gilded pulls and smudged label cards with crude, handwritten characters, strings for guitars, violins, violas, cellos, double basses, harps, banjos, zithers, psalteries, catgut, steel, nylon ones doubled back on themselves trying to be fetuses, forming true circles and not imitations of circles, forever without a beginning or an end.

Because the shop was called not only Herbal Flora but also, in respectful smaller letters, Beethoven House.

And the brief adventure, the failure number ten or nine, had begun, as is almost always the case, in the graphic arts room of the advertising agency, less than a week before, when the little boy or the dwarf who runs errands interrupted my outline for an ad for Trevida fabrics that I was plagiarizing from an old back number of the glossy German magazine *Burda*.

"There's a phone call," he recited twice.

That afternoon, Quinteros had said over the phone:

"It seems there's a clue for you. Nothing certain. I can't even give you the exact address. A married couple, two old people who have a shop somewhere out there in Palermo, near the cemetery. They sell herbs, they tune guitars. The street is called Somebody or Other Petrarch, not just plain Petrarch. Do you know it? Well, it's a street infected with funeral wreaths and cheap bars for consolation. I repeat that I can't guarantee you anything; try it. It may be the two of them, the old man and the old lady. It may be only one of them, or neither. If it's them, or one of them, they escaped from the Swiss Colony. Gringos, no doubt."

"Well, I'm grateful to you," I said. I didn't want to give him any sign of my weary and stubborn enthusiasm. I didn't want to believe or trust, I didn't want to endanger the promise. "And at least . . . Or at most: does anyone know, does anyone suspect which of the five senses?"

"Not even that, pal," Quinteros drawled sadly. "The sixth one, most likely. Of course, the sixth from one beginning or another, from this very moment and for all time, while you try the other five. I've been thinking about this and we must discuss it. Don't forget, when you see me, to talk to me about concentration. That may be a good technique, but it takes a long time to explain. In a word, I'd say the sense of hearing."

Quinteros's voice went away and I picked up the paintbrushes again. The little man in the ad was being crucified wrongly and disgracefully, he was trying to raise up an unconvincing head, summon a playboy smile. I thought of the other times before, when he could believe that one of the five was the probable one, but never anything, anything at all, only the sixth fluttering about hesitantly, nervously, until it lost its strength and found no rest, no point of support.

That night, not yet another one, the night of Quinteros's call, I went back to the agency after dinner, put a bottle, glasses covered with paraffin and a package of cigarettes on the director's desk and looked around for the most expensive paper to send myself a report on errors.

A draftsman of a circle of hell, as in all advertising agencies, art departments. Frieda and Quinteros had managed to get this life for me too.

EXACTLY THE THIRTY-FIRST

When the whole city knew that midnight had finally arrived, I was in Frieda's apartment, on the Gran Punta de las Carretas, alone and almost in the dark, looking at the river and the light of the beacon from the coolness of the window as I smoked and went on stubbornly searching for a memory that moved me, a reason for pitying myself and reproving the world, contemplating with an exciting hatred the lights of the city that were moving toward me on my left.

I had soon finished the sketch of the two children in pajamas who were amazed every morning at the invasion of horses, dolls, cars and scooters on top of their shoes and the mantelpiece. In accordance with what had been agreed, I had copied the figures from an advertisement published in *Companion*. The hardest part was the drooling expression of the parents peeking out from behind a curtain and keeping myself from using crimson to X out the sketch with a "Hurrah for happiness," in hairy letters drawn with a sable brush.

But instead I was able to devote the forty minutes that separated me from the New Year, from my birthday and from Frieda's promised return by painting a new little placard in green letters for the bathroom. The old one was faded, spattered with soap and toothpaste stains. Moreover, it had been done in dreadful cursive letters, in that calligraphy used on the little placards that cretins hang on the walls: a little house, a big heart, welcome; young boat, old captain.

I had bought a present for Frieda that was awaiting her, wrapped in sky-blue paper, next to her glass, the bottle of rum, the little plate with shiny polished fruit, nougat and nuts, in the place at the table that she usually occupied. I had also bought her a cigar and a package of razor blades for her to cut her hair with. Although we had been living together for only a few months, these presents were traditional for the anniversaries that we observed or invented. She thanked me for them with insults of an astonishing obscenity, sometimes convincing, she promised to take her revenge, she always ended up accepting my good will, my esteem and my neglected understanding. Her gifts, on the other hand, were jobs, ways of earning a miserable salary, contrivances so that I would forget that I was living on her money.

On Saturday nights, when there were lots of people, when she started getting drunk, Frieda went to sit on the toilet and for minutes or quarters of an hour at a time, as nobody went to look for her, she sat there almost motionless, with her balloon pants pulled down to her knees, cutting with a razor blade, with avarice, the hair that covered her forehead, her eyes fixed, as alert as a bird, on the little placard pinned up between the medicine cabinet and the sink, the same placard that I was doing over for her so as to surprise her, with Baudelaire's verses that say: "Thank you, my Lord, for not having made me a woman, or a black or a Jew or a dog or a shorty." Nobody who used the toilet could leave it without having recited them in prayer.

But on that New Year's Eve we had wanted—or we had enveloped ourselves in lies until we had promised each other—to be alone and try to feel happy. She had sworn to turn down everything, dancing pupils, customers in her dress shop, unexpected proposals, so as to be alone with me before midnight. I didn't have many things to give up in order to promise her the same thing.

It was not happiness but it was less trouble. Frieda would arrive, but not before the New Year did. We would eat something and devote ourselves, as experts, delaying things so as not to spoil them, to getting drunk; I would ask questions with pretended interest so as to get her to repeat the monologue about her childhood and adolescence in Santa María, the story of her expulsion, the fanciful, variable reminiscences of the lost paradise.

Perhaps, when the night was over, we would make love on the big bed, on the rug of the master bedroom or out on the balcony. It wouldn't matter to me whether we made love or not; but I had never known a woman as competent at offering continual surprises, as ready to confess. When it occurred to her to go to bed with me and being drunk forced her to talk, it was like possessing dozens of women and finding out everything about them. She might, moreover, agree to celebrate the New Year by lying on her back on the floor or on the bedspread.

I was smoking and downing rum with lots of water in it, in the window, when horns began tooting and shots rang out. It was impossible for me to devote my thoughts to myself, so I thought about María and Seoane, my son, I forced myself to suffer and to accuse myself, I remembered anecdotes that ended up meaning nothing.

Everything, simply, had been or was how it was, in such and such a way, although perhaps it was in another, even though every imaginable person could have offered a different version. And I, unquestionably, not only was unable to be pitied but didn't even manage to be believable. Other people existed and I watched them living, and the love I devoted to them was merely the application of my love of life.

Midnight had already been forgotten in Lavanda. The lights on the Ramírez side grew fewer and fewer and the couples attending the ball at the Parque Hotel would now be going to and from the beach, when the New Year really began. A black man's timbrel sounded again, deep-toned, lonely, untamed, in the vicinity of the barracks, and made the words spoken hard to distinguish.

But I recognized Frieda's voice, uncertain, giving in, losing its energy. She shouted "Himmel" and I walked through the apartment, went down, in the dark, without making a sound, a few steps of the stairway leading to the garden and the entrance.

The only light there was down there came, dimly, from the Proa. But I could see her, firmly planted between two parched flower beds, looking athletic, shifting her vigor from side to side, as a monstrosity born of tubercular parents, blackish and wearing skirts, its head fantastically enlarged after a day's work by a cheap barber, said to her: "Because as far as I'm concerned, you filthy bitch, because if you thought you were going to make a fool of me, because if you go with me you aren't going with anybody else." It slapped her face with its hand and Frieda let it; then it began to hit her with its handbag, methodically and tirelessly.

I sat down on a step and lighted a cigarette. "Frieda can flatten you just by moving one arm," I thought. "Frieda can send you flying into the river with one kick."

But Frieda had chosen to begin the year that way; with her hands on her buttocks, exaggerating the width of the shoulders of her tailored suit, letting herself be manhandled and enjoying it, answering the blows with the handbag with her hoarse "Himmels" that sounded as though she were asking to be hit some more.

When that obscene creature tied of hitting her, the two females wept and made their way out of the garden to the street. I saw them stop, panting, and walk away embracing each other. Then I went back upstairs to turn the lights on and offer Frieda a nice welcoming of the New Year.

I had her beneath the luxury of the floor lamp, or else only she was there, in the armchair, with her blond hair hiding her forehead, her mouth contorted by vice and bitterness, her right eyebrow raised as always and curving now above a black eye. With her bleeding parted lips, to which she refused to apply any remedy, she forced me to see the New Year in by talking about Santa María. From the age of fourteen she had devoted herself to getting drunk, causing scandal and making love with all the sexes foreseen by divine wisdom.

I say this in homage to her, she who proved herself to be more Catholic each Sunday and who in the small hours of each Saturday night filled my apartment—paid for by her—with women who each time were older, more astonishing, more abject. She spoke of her provincial childhood and of her family of Junkers, absolutely to blame for the fact that now, in Lavanda, she had no way open to her other than getting drunk and repeatedly causing scandal and making crapulous love. She talked until dawn on that first of January, of unfortunate encounters and other people's faults, plastered since before she arrived, stroking her almost completely closed eye, enjoying the pain of her swollen, parted lips.

"It seemed to me," she said, smiling, "you aren't going to believe me, but it seemed to me that Seoane was on the corner."

"At this hour? And besides, he would have come upstairs to see me."

"He might not have come to see you."

"Yes, dearie," I said.

"Not to visit you. Maybe to spy on the apartment, to see if you went out or came in."

"That could be," I agreed, because I didn't like to talk about Seoane with Frieda, and perhaps not with anybody at all.

She spoke, like all women, of an ideal Frieda, she was amazed at the unending triumph of injustice and the lack of understanding, she searched about, she volunteered the names of the guilty parties, without hating them.

She didn't say anything about the inexplicable repugnance she had felt for anyone hitting somebody on the face with a handbag. I was already accustomed to her need to bring home women lovers who each time were filthier and cheaper. Since time lacks importance, since simultaneity is a detail that depends on the whims of memory, it was easy for me to call to mind nights in which the apartment where Frieda allowed me to live was peopled by countless women whom she had brought there from off the street, from bars down by the port, from Victoria Plaza. There were pretty and well-dressed ones, with a few pieces of jewelry, with bangles, with dark suits set off by pearl necklaces.

But recently there had been an abundance of insolent and filthy *mestizas*, foul-mouthed, a lighted cigarette dangling from their lower lip. Frequently the heated dialogues kept me from sleeping and I would leap out of bed and wander about the apartment chewing on a cigarette like a little olive branch, moving about with difficulty among the women crouched down on their haunches, sitting on the table, lying with their legs apart on the couch, kneeling in the kitchen, changing their clothes in the bathroom, taking the sun or the moon on the red tiles of the balcony.

"Roa paid," Frieda said. "He did the right thing, that makes for a better beginning of the year and maybe it'll bring him luck."

The banknotes had fallen from my chest onto the table. I picked them up without loosening the rubber band around them; they were hundred-peso ones.

"Did he pay for everything?" I asked.

"Give me a drink and a ciggie. That poor tramp. But it's so nice to let them do it to you over and over, do whatever they like with you, and not even suspect who you are. To let yourself be had till suddenly it occurs to somebody that it's all over and done with and then one stops putting up with it and taking pleasure in giving in and with all the eagerness and happiness in the world the worst possible thing imaginable. Out of revenge; and not out of pride, or out of eagerness to even the score, otherwise why does the pleasure all of a sudden lie in hitting out and not letting oneself be hit. Right?"

I understand," I said. I listened to her making the roll of bills dance above my hand.

"Are you going to help me? When the time comes, I mean, if it ever does."

"Of course." I put the money away in my trousers pocket, filled a glass with rum and gave it to her, put a cigarette in her mouth and gave her a light.

"Whenever you like. Did he pay or not? What I mean to say is, did he pay for everything, and for good and all?"

Frieda stood up, overcome by a fit of laughter and toppled over on her side onto the floor, spattering it with spittle.

"He deserved it, for being such an imbecile. On the day of the hasty wedding in the room where the presents were on display he saw the indecent portrait, the painting of Olga in the nude. He might have let people see a perplexed look cross his face, one that said I don't know and I don't care. That's what he should have done. But at the end of the honeymoon he writes to Olga. The usual thing, poor dummy. 'The only love of my life and everything will go on the same as always.' Give me a drink. And he adds reminiscences and details. Olga comes to see me, hesitating between disbelief and happiness. Since she was born stupid, I had no trouble stealing the letter from her and got busy making photocopies of it and blackmailing him. Poor Roa."

She hugged her sides and then assumed a childish expression to listen to what still remained of the night. "I think that dirty bitch kneed me in the belly. That's nothing. Yes, he paid for everything. I told him it was the final installment. I don't know whether that's true, I don't know whether within a week, when he's playing with the kids and the presents for Epiphany I won't appear to ask him for more money. Roa's money doesn't matter to me any more. As you see, I kept it for you. What matters to me is to fuck him up, that's my relationship to him and it'll have to go on being that way."

"Frieda," I said in a very loud voice. She stirred in the armchair and finally raised her head. She was drunk, her smile was that of a little girl, tears were beginning to fall down her cheeks. I put the money on the table, making sure it didn't fall off. "This is a bad state of affairs. You must put an end to this business with Roa."

She shrugged and sat there looking at me as though she loved me, with such a sad and surprised smile, as she languidly moved her tongue to reach her tears.

"As you like," she said. "Give me another drink, we're going to celebrate the New Year."

JUANINA

Dead from insomnia, scorning exhaustion, I sometimes left the first hustle and bustle of the market at daybreak, took a bus and went to Frieda's house in the dunes, all by itself, almost lapped by the water. I was always ridding myself of a prophetic dream or was impelled by it.

Sometimes, out of cleverness, cheating as though I were walking sideways, I had myself blessed before the journey, before the attempt to overcome my having been stained by water, receding, sweet and foul-smelling, swollen and rotting amid the infinite flock of wholesome, useful waves.

I went inside the cathedral, cool, too vast, nearly deserted. I prayed on my knees, avoiding with difficulty that distraction of the virile flames, almost motionless on the altar. To one side, to my shame, there would be the portrait of the Pope I had painted, with childish false pride; worn out by time: a XII, a XXIII, a VI. Painful draftsmanship and color, emetic reds and blacks, eyes that endeavored to show faith, acceptance of fate, unsought sacrifices. Now the eyes grew more lifeless, like prunes, with each visit.

They were always there, the old man, his farce and mine, a little more tired than the youngster I had painted; than the memory of my fanatical aunt, naïve and tight-fisted. The hard-hearted old lady who found out how to get to heaven.

I wish to recall now the times that I escaped from the city by fulfilling my oath not to take a pen or paper with me. They had promised me: for a second I would see the height and the color of the perfect, unrepeatable wave. Such a vision can compensate for all the rest of a person's life.

At seven or eight in the morning I would arrive at Frieda's wedge-shaped house in the dunes, look at her sleeping, accept the miserable breakfast she offered me, stale ham, hard rice. On mornings when luck was with me, a raw egg. But Frieda is not greedy, she becomes neither fatter nor thinner; perhaps hunger doesn't exist for her, perhaps her food consists of calming her asthma with a shot of adrenaline.

On certain mornings, always unpredictable ones, she kept me company on my stubborn search up and down the riverside. Neither winter nor good weather made any difference. It was enough for her to glimpse my profile, to hear words from me that were far removed from us and from the truth, to contemplate distractedly my footsteps so as to learn, without its mattering to her, of my desire to walk along by myself or with her.

Here, in those long-ago months that I feel like calling to mind now, another woman, Juanina, appears, on a cold and cloudy morning when Frieda chose to go on sleeping and I again went wandering along the shore looking to the right and hoping to make my discovery. I breakfasted at Cristiani's on two gins that made my bad humor brought on by hunger even worse. In the doorway of the tavern, Cristiani assured me that the weather would continue to be dreary though it wouldn't rain. I looked at him growing older in the gray light: dressed in balloon pants, with his childish gaze smiling at the sky, barefoot as usual so as to absorb the earth's radiations.

For a second I sensed the danger, but I didn't have the strength to escape. And Cristiani said:

"You who are a painter, sir. Why don't you make paintings to show humankind the danger of atomic bombs . . .? What I mean to say is that people talk a lot about it, but they can't even imagine it. Instead of bullets, hydrogen."

I felt like offending him, but I answered slowly, gently:

"You're right, Cristiani, it would be a good thing, it would be better. But humankind isn't going to look at my paintings. You can be sure of that. And it's possible that after the bombs paradise will begin. Nonetheless, you and I share the same view of things. I'll have to think about it. Right now, what I want is a wave, to paint a wave. To come upon it by surprise. It has to be the first one and the last one. A white wave, dirty, polluted, made of snow and pus and milk that reaches the shore and swallows up the world. That's why I walk up and down the beach."

He nodded, intimidated, as though I were repeating with perfect accuracy a scene acted out many times, with his damp bright blue eyes trying to make me stay a while longer. He crossed his arms over his chest as he rubbed one foot against the other.

"I read in a book a while ago . . ." he began. "It was a problem of purity, the danger that delicate things, clean things, would fall into dirty hands."

I couldn't tell if he was saying that in reference to me, or to those who had control over the bombs. I was certain, at least, that Cristiani—a vegetarian, abstemious, chaste—didn't believe in my purity.

"Give me another gin," I said to him, going back to the counter. "I have a long way to go and this is the best time of day. I have to discover a wave that looks like the very last one. I'm not asking too much. Just that it looks like it in more or less the same way a fetus two months old may resemble the woman one loves. I have to discover it. Certain things belong to the realm of mystery, Cristiani, you'll agree."

He served me my gin, brought me the change, stood there staring at me in silence. The counter was between us.

"I too discovered something. A few months ago."

I didn't want to listen to him. I picked up the coins in a friendly and affectionate way, smiled at him as if the same secret separated us and raised one hand as a promise. I went out into the dull light, into the cold of the morning that was almost gone and walked amid rocks and tamarisks till I set foot on the wet beach. I looked at the roiled water, lighted my pipe and started off again on my useless stroll. I walked along for a kilometer, I saw a rotted boat, the breaking of the flat sea foam on the beach, protected my pipe from the wind that was rising. Then I saw the dog lying near the waves, not moving at all.

I sat down on the sand some twenty meters away from the motionless, enormous yellow animal. The wind made the cold even more penetrating and all of a sudden I understood, forever, ill at ease, clear-sighted. I could paint whatever I pleased and do it well. Peasants, portraits, the painting of the Pope that would continue to hang in the church in Santa María. But never the wave promised to Cristiani, the crest of dirty whiteness that would say it all. Never life and its reverse side, the fringe it shows us in order to deceive us.

I was washed up, peaceful, frozen in the morning cold, still not quite forty years old.

The night before we had been present at a third version of the Santa Rosa storm at the end of August—nobody can argue about other people's superstitions—but spring alone had appeared in the rachitic shoots of the trees, the pleadings of the tomcats, the personal longings.

It might well have been, I remember, ten o'clock in the morning: the beach was now sunny, cold, and an aggressive wind was stirring up the sand. I rose to my feet, walked along slowly, keeping my eyes on the little curled-up figure.

I walked on until the big yellow dog turned into a person and a woman, yet another one in the story that even though it's true won't be useful to anyone. So, I repeat, as I was searching for an impossible wave, or pretending to search for it, Juanina appeared, embedded herself in the world.

I saw her sitting on the damp shore, atop the shallow pool that the waves kept forming over and over again. She was wearing an old dark-brown coat and hugging her knees; every so often she shook her head and raised it, her hair as short as a boy's, black, sketched with Chinese ink and a brush.

She was sitting there on the shore, getting soaked to the bone: dampness, sea foam, and seaweed were creeping up her clothes, taking possession of, dangling from, her stubby thick shoes.

I also know that she was doomed to slip and fall and that this way could be as good, as unfortunate and dangerous as any other. I walked closer and looked; perhaps her slow eyes hadn't taken in my face, my beard at first.

But I could see, from the very first moment, the desperation turned into a callus, proud and cynical, permanent and impersonal hatred. Less then twenty, her neck too long and sad, her bony, sad face, her curved nose, tiny and having difficulty breathing. I saw the portraits that could be forthcoming from that head; I did not foresee the future.

Motionless, my legs spread apart, almost touching her, I tried to light my pipe, I wanted to greet her, find the magic phrase able to change her back into a dog again, an error, nothing at all. Because I needed to paint that profile, I moved about hesitantly among old prologues, I wanted never to have seen her.

"Bitch," I said with a smile. She barely moved to look at me again, growling, inexpressive. She appeared to be or was very thin. I couldn't calculate her age now.

"Little yellow dog," I corrected.

She remained still, the skin of her face and hands purple from the cold; every so often, regularly, a grimace contracted her smile. I sucked on my pipe for a while, I slowly bent down till I was squatting on my haunches, alongside her, I too above the ever-shifting puddle. We remained silent, looking at the whirlwind of seagulls on the rocks and for a time it was as though each of us was acquainted with the life of the other. But this sensation came easily and, as always, it was wrong.

Another pause, then I asked uncertainly, rudely:

"What's the trouble? Because everything can be straightened out although with no guarantee of happiness. Or even that the way the matter is settled will be better than what was wrong originally."

She was sitting with her head resting on her knees and finally raised it and smiled listlessly at the water, without interest, as though she had heard my pronouncement many times. Maybe she was drunk or high on some drug, or maybe both, or perhaps everything had begun in her early childhood. Her scrawny little head gave no indication of her age. Other things flowed from it: controlled distress, time-worn antagonism, refusal to surrender. I needed to sketch that profile.

"What is it?" I calmly persisted.

"Everything?" she said mockingly, not smiling, not looking at me.

"That's not possible, but it might be best."

"It's not possible, it's long. There are lots of stories. This story begins with an aunt."

She went on looking at the water. With every minute that went by, she seemed to me to be skinnier, a deeper violet color, sicker.

"Talk to me about today then; if you care to. You on the beach and your ass in the water. What happened last night? We'll talk about your aunt later."

"Last night?" She seemed not to understand, she hesitated.

"Or at dawn today, this morning."

"There's nothing in it for you. I saw that right away. There's just the aunt. A present. Her name is Mercedes."

She was feeling her buttocks with a child's fear, not trying to hide it.

"Why did you come and what does it matter to you? Just one thing: killing her. Would you help me?"

"Of course, it's possible, if you say so. To kill Aunt Mercedes. But you have to tell me why. Or else we'll invent the reason between the two of us. But talk to me about right now. I know it's around noon and I find you sad, drunk, rocking your ass back and forth in a puddle of water."

Then, standing up, she was a newborn camel on two feet, cynical, mocking. The foggy landscape stretched out motionless and the greens and blues of the water went calmly on. Scrawny trees on the beach were turning green to the right and to the left. Above all, farther on, the water, once again, impassive. She and the recently arrived heat presaged a torrid storm, the slow rain of the summer season. As always a motionless white yacht, a quartet of boats playing at winning, with different colors, with a fat man on the poop making his siren wail in vain.

Now she finally moved her head to look at me and try to find out who I was. The endless story of Juanina begins more or less here. I stroked her wet forehead and repeated:

"Beginning with this very moment, with last night or this morning. And you must take those clothes off. Come with me."

Looking sad, she appeared to think for a minute. I spoke to her as to a child; I had to sketch that nose, the eyebrows that gave signs of joining together. I saw her tremble as she laughed.

"Are there flowers?" she asked.

"No, there aren't."

"I don't mean here, of course. Near the road, in the privet."

"There aren't any there either."

"It doesn't matter," she said to reassure me. "I already knew that, it was a joke, I know this place, I may even know it all too well. My name is Juanina but that's a lie too. Do you really want me to tell you everything? Everything, what a dumb word. And then you'll take me to your place to dry my clothes out. Because I can't go to the hotel."

I put a wide-open hand on her little boy's head.

"Get moving," I said to her. "Do your lying later on, when you're dry and cozy."

She threw her head backwards, with a look of hatred and disgust on her face.

"No," she said, "I prefer to pay beforehand. In the end it always turns out to be cheaper."

Then she lay down on the sand again and leaning on her hands and feet crawled backwards till she was out of the water; she lay on the sand, rigid, mouth open, eyes closed. She was neither short nor tall, she bared her teeth without smiling.

"If you'd like me to tell you, and they all like it, bend down. For years, ever since I was a little girl, I've kept coming across people who want to help me. There are so many kindhearted people running around loose. It's odd, isn't it? But I always pay the price. That's the way it goes. Last night I went out with the fishermen again. I like being with them, at night, early in the morning and on the river. There were four of them. I paid and I'm not complaining. Men are so ridiculous. You're better off not knowing the details."

She smiled scornfully with her thin lips, her nose quivering, looked at me for a moment, blinking for an instant in the sun.

"But there's nothing to talk over. There were four of them, and me, and a little black who did the cooking. Is that enough for you? It was enough for me. I can add fishermen and little blacks."

She lay there laughing for a while about things that were far away and shook off her lethargy.

"Let's go," I said to her and touched her thin ribs with one foot. The brown coat was old; but the wet shoes, the perfume that came to life again with the sun, the length of her white fingers and her fingernails, made Juanina's first story unconvincing.

She leaned on one elbow and was able to sit up. With her dark

71

glasses on her forehead she looked at me, still laughing, perhaps at me now.

"My aunt," she said. "I like that better. Up until yesterday I was staying at the hotel, the one where they rent horses, and I ran out of money. I paid the bill and come out here to live on the beach. I made up a story and left my suitcases behind. But when we came back, with the four fishermen and the little black, we made a fire, grilled sea-bass and a demijohn of wine appeared from somewhere."

The sun was stronger now; I lay down on the sand, apart from her, afraid I'd scare her and lose her.

"What else?" I said.

"Still about today?"

"About you. Yesterday or last year."

"Okay, listen. If you've come to protect me . . . I can get along without help. You know what you can do with your pity. Keep walking along the beach. As soon as I can get up I'm going. To visit my aunt, of course."

"We're going," I said in a low voice, without looking at her. I had already thought of a dangerous plan. "Tell me as we walk along, if you like."

Now she was the one who was on her feet and she was skinnier and smaller than when she lay stretched out sleeping; a sudden distress bolted out her cynicism for a moment and made her bend over double. Before starting out for the hotel—worn out and finding it difficult, but nonetheless standing implacably erect—she spoke to me as though she were spitting on my horizontal face.

"And thanks for everything, for your curiosity. I can't bear well-mannered gentlemen. I've had diarrhea for more than a week. There's also an abortion that can't wait. Maybe I'll give the fetus to my aunt as a present. It was some consolation at least, last night in the boat, to think that it had already happened, that I was pregnant again. There wasn't any danger, not that particular one at least. Now you can go to the . . ." Tears were beginning to fall, as she stood there, so skinny and lonely, on the beach, with her back to the river; I could half-open my eyelids so as to see the tears that were trickling down to her lips, down to her chin. But it wasn't weeping. I never saw or heard her have a real crying spell.

She didn't say where. I listened to her farewell with my eyes closed, I let a certain length of time pass and then I turned around and saw her rocking back and forth on the sand.

I had Frieda, I had almost two thousand eurodollars in some corner of the Market; an abortion and the beginning of consolation cost a great deal less if one lives in Santa María. But we were in Lavanda, the name of an African tribe.

"Yes," I thought, "I read somewhere that for curing diarrhea and pregnancy there's nothing better than a good hip-bath in a cold puddle."

THE INVITED GUEST

I came across Juanina at the hotel and we had lunch together. I came across her is a manner of speaking and everyone chooses the one he pleases. I had told Frieda the story, indifferently and without pressing her, keeping close watch on my affection and my purposes.

"She's young and pretty. But she looks like a boy."

"You probably liked that. It's not every day that a person comes across pregnant boys."

It's likely that I was more incredulous than Frieda; I couldn't be entirely confident of the nonexistent Juanina I'd invented. Perhaps other misfortunes were born of that, some of them bothersome, another of them decisive.

Juanina had looked at me on the beach and in the hotel, face to face, honest and hypocritical. One of the last communiqués of the government of Lavanda had forbidden, with plausible whereases and wherefores, anyone to write "eyes in the shape of hazelnuts" or "hazel-colored." Just as it was forbidden to surround, to highlight, a form with an outline in white or black. Clever painters use cobalt blue or greenish smears that bring diapers to mind.

But the reader deserves the truth and, furthermore, we all know that the truth is always revolutionary. Juanina sat there looking at me with hazel eyes, without blinking, without her entirely believing in me either.

Frieda and I listened, in the pauses, to music on the radio. It was, I believe, a German before Bach and the man, his music, were always right. They told me that the only thing that mattered was to paint. That it was necessary, even for the hygiene of the soul, to do without women, friends and money, to lose all interest in landscapes and oceans, never to accept, never to take seriously the meaninglessness of a world, of a life that I didn't make myself, that were forced on me, that are there, outside and inside, implacable each time upon awakening, without anyone's having had the courtesy to consult me, to ask my opinion, at least, about some petty, and, apparently, unimportant detail.

I forgot my answers, my objections almost immediately. The man playing music on the radio proceeded from one phrase to another, from one tempo to another, invariably being right and saying so in a miraculous way.

Frieda asked me for a glass of water so as to take a pill. I was smoking, with an air of boredom and drowsiness, lying stretched out on the curved chaise longue. She knitted for a while; then she asked me with a smile, her eyelids lowered:

"Does it have to be here? Wouldn't she rather go back to her aunt to kill her or recount her memories or tell a new story? Doesn't the aunt have a lot of money for her and the grand-nephew on the way?"

"Fear not. She'll go to her aunt or to the devil sooner or later. I see it as a problem of patience, of pity."

"How many days?"

"I don't know. It depends on your patience, on your pity."

"But she already told you what you could do with your pity. I suppose she'd give me the same advice."

"A week? Two weeks? Though maybe she's already gone."

The German went on tirelessly playing on the radio.

"Let her come," Frieda said. "The worst part is that you'll

have to sleep with me and not be alone with her and not exaggerate this sudden kindheartedness. So touching, I swear. I never suspected. We can take a nap, can't we? Then afterwards you can rush off to save her."

I began to take my clothes off as I thought about the girl or woman, about Juanina, in the regiment of fishermen, about life and about the cowardice that keeps so many millions of those condemned to death from living it.

And after the almost invariable ceremonies that kept me from tiring my back, I lighted a cigarette; I listened to Frieda sleep, I felt at peace and humble. It was no longer a question of cowardice but of the chance to live. It's not always a question of going to bed, I thought, even though it is for women, despite their feeling love and talking about it, suffering from it and chatting about it. It was a question, I think I remember, of escaping from cities, from comfort; of respecting oneself, of being hard, selfish and cynical, of fulfilling a destiny or satisfying a caprice. And if there is no such thing as destiny or caprice, there is no inevitable reason for mercilessness, protests have a meaning and complaints are assuaged in a haggling voice, the voice of a lady amid the din of a marketplace.

Let everything that happens to the poor devils be welcome. Let them accept it as a substitution they deserve, if they reach the point of understanding it, if they learn to enjoy it with the help of their congenital stupidity, of their innocence, of their impotence, and of the grace of Brausen. He is my last card, and instinct advises me to keep it unmarked.

I slowly got dressed and discovered that the weather had turned hot again; I found the necessary money in Frieda's handbag and began walking on the hard dampness of the shore to the enormous glassed-in porch of the hotel.

Without having said so, Frieda and I were right. There she was, in the hotel bar, with her suitcase on the table, having a soft drink, calmly digesting, as if it were habitual, her night long past, her four fishermen. Her coat, still wet, was hanging from a chair.

I went over toward her—she recognized, expressionless, my sparse beard—and proceeded to the counter to ask for a plate of sandwiches. I took it to the table and in a while the waiter brought me the soda, the double rum, the cigarettes I smoke when I'm all keyed up. I sat there, not moving and not saying a word as she repeated, looking at me, the dirtiest of the laughs that she had come out with that morning in the sand. Then she began to eat as though she were famished; I then took a big swallow of rum and sighed, almost at peace.

She had eaten half the sandwiches when she turned her head toward the tin container of enormous ferns in one corner of the dining room, of a very light green, protected for years from the cold and the winds blowing from offshore. The girl seemed more healthy, more solid and authentic, more dangerous than on the first encounter.

"*Merde*. That brings good luck," she said. "Why did you have to come back?"

I stroked my beard so that she wouldn't sense the meaning of my smile.

"My name is Medina, I don't know if I told it to you before."

"Thank you. My name is Juanina and I tell it to everybody."

"I don't know. I was certain I'd run into you."

"It happens that way sometimes. I was able to settle up with the hotel. I have a bus to catch in half an hour."

I looked at her, looked at her again as I raised the glass and accepted the fact that I would prefer to kill her rather than allow her to escape without copying her profile. "Even if it's only once and she's moving, even if it were only a line biting its tail." A profile with eyes that any police clerk would have described, bored stiff, incredulous or certain and not afraid of being mistaken, as being a light chestnut color. Now they were green. Nor were the eyes dominant in her face, which had grown slimmer, but they revealed more about her than her words and her movements; they threatened to narrow to an almond-shaped slit and didn't do so, as they looked they were calm and wide open. Friendship, pity, desire were not provoked by her youth or the unsuccessful simulacrum of sincerity with which she was now looking at me.

Everything came from the strange shape of her eyes, of their arbitrary emplacement in their sockets, of a harmony with her cheekbones. They had seen a great deal without their betraying themselves by lines around them, without resignations on the part of her skin. For now, at least, she could look at me like that, with eyes that I considered so easy to paint twenty times, and come closer to the truth after useless words. Serene and fresh, reddened by insomnia or the wind on the beach. Whereas the remainder of her face had been shaped and trained to lie, her flat eyes expressed nothing. They simply were; looking without apprehension or hope. And so Juanina appeared, for the first time.

I interrupted her gently, almost unwillingly.

"There isn't a bus, I can tell you why right now. I'm a little drunk, just groping along the edge of happiness. But in my case it's not important and I can order another glass. You already know I'm a gentleman."

"An old man," she said. "You must be over forty. And it's easy to manipulate old gaffers and it's so great to make them think that they're the ones doing the manipulating."

"Yes," I said, "over forty." It's sad but I don't have anything to do with it and for Juanina it's going to be much sadder.

"Shit," she translated as she ate the last sandwich on the plate. "You aren't forty yet, not even with that beard and other ways of lying."

"And the fishermen, were they, are they, younger?"

"Some of them. But that's a different matter. They're there but so is the sea and the night."

"I understand."

"No, You can't."

"Who knows? I could tell you a story. When I was teaching design in a high school. There was a special day, without classes and without a strike. An inspector of secondary school education had died. Much older than I was, of course. A day of mourning was declared, and classes were suspended. Then amid the squeals of joy I heard two girls, fourteen years old, chatting together as they put on make-up in the patio. I remember that they were under some scaffolding that had been erected because masons were working to shore up a wall in ruins. One of the girls said: 'What luck. Do you realize? We can make *chiquichiqui* all after-noon and earn piles of money' ."

"*Chiquichiqui?*" she asked without feigned innocence. "I didn't know that word, but it's enough just hearing it to know what it means. And you were shocked, you refused to teach any more classes and now we have a well-dressed beachcomber."

"That's not how it is," I said, looking around for my pipe. "It was a surprise, I grant you. They were fourteen years old, we had classified them as well-off middle-class girls. No real need to be prostitutes."

"Come off it. Maybe they wanted to be."

"Maybe. But I retract the story and refuse to argue." What mattered to me was not to let her disappear. "At any rate, this bus has already left."

"Thanks. I've been watching the clock the whole time. Is this pity again?"

"No, it never was a question of pity. Maybe it's a question of a sleeping sickness that you were fated to arouse."

When she stopped laughing, I looked at her scrawny bones, her sharply profiled, quivering nose. For lack of talent and a raging white wave that would stand still for me, it was that, that bold, vulgar head that I needed to paint.

"No," I repeated distractedly, "it's not a question of pity. You interest me because my collection of odd creatures is very limited at present."

"Thanks. Use *tú* with me."

"All right. It's the same as with books. One puts them on display, lends them, and the library ends up empty or toothless. Moreover, there's still a moreover that I confess to you and others that I don't, I want to paint your head. Bring it back to life, but not overdo it, and paint it. God tells me that there's going to be a storm, rough water, a big haul for fishermen. It's best if you come to my place."

She smiled looking at the revolting blue plastic tablecloth, with roses in relief. I had only to touch her to feel a shiver.

"Do you know you're a good bastard . . . do you know that?"

"Yes," I said to her, "but not always. That's why we're brothers and sisters. That's what we're here for."

"And afterwards at your house. Where there'll be a fat lady, who may or may not take me in, who'll help me watch you puff on a pipe. Tonight?"

"She's not fat. She's different from you but you'll understand each other. I'm certain. I don't know how or why, but you'll understand each other. This afternoon, now, in a little while. I can't guess how it'll end. It's best that you come and see. She must be awake now."

"It's all the same to me. I'll go and look at her yellow fangs, I'll put up with her patience. Is it many blocks away?"

I took a little of Frieda's money and called the waiter over.

"I'm going to have one last drink," I said to her. "Go to the toilet or the latrine. It depends on habit, need. Stay as long as you have to, it'll be a good thing if you're as pretty as possible when I introduce you."

She looked at me for a while, as though she were the one condemned to paint a profile; then she swung her handbag back and forth and left the bar of the hotel.

She stayed locked up in the lavatory for so long that I couldn't keep from imagining her sitting down in there and I immediately remembered something sad and beautiful that a woman had said to me when I confessed to her that an angel or Juan María Brausen himself, in person, had whispered the order to me to do a painting of a back street that ran through a gray area of an abandoned city until it reached an ambiguous silhouette on the horizon.

I don't know anything except how to paint, to put oneself in a painting and bear the suffering must be like feeling and thinking in a total way, with one's entire body and oblivious of one's body. I remember, at the beginning of adolescence, when I was hardly more than a little girl, sitting in the isolated latrine of a big broken-down country house, certain that I was all alone, reading pieces of an old, torn, dirty, yellow newspaper on a rainy afternoon as it was getting dark. It was like that, nothing and I, everything and I. And if a candle end was flickering, threatening to go out, so much the better.

FRIEDA SAYS YES

The first afternoon, the first night, were not hard. Frieda waited for her dressed in a neatly tailored women's suit, collapsed on a chaise longue in the sun, on the north side of the house, which always seemed to be pushing forward into the water, knitting, her gaze hidden by her dark glasses. I couldn't guess what it was she was knitting and it's likely that she didn't know either. She had just bathed and had a new, severe coiffure. She smiled at her without animosity, calculating.

"Hi," Juanina shouted, standing erect in front of the porch, with her fists clenched in the dampness of the yellow coat. "I'm the little whore that your husband's brought home from the beach."

"He's not my husband," Frieda said mildly. "We're a little bit crazy, sometimes more than a little, but never that crazy. We're prudent loonies."

"I beg your pardon," the girl said and for the first time she seemed to me to be disconcerted. Frieda went on calmly knitting; she didn't have yellow teeth; she accepted the girl's presence as a natural event that went a long way back. She spoke of the thatching of pine needles and branches that covered the roof of the house and kept the rain water out. She said, vaguely, that someone would have to climb up and clean it.

After having tea we went to the beach. There weren't any

fishermen getting ready to go out to sea; the enormous black boats rocked back and forth at anchor. We talked about the weather and the obligatory places that the three of us had visited by ourselves, at different periods. When I saw that Juanina was turning green, I looked at Frieda and we went back to the house.

Frieda knitted in silence, I put logs on the fire even though it was only slightly chilly. Both of us listened to the rumbles of thunder from a storm that was moving off and the sounds of the girl vomiting in the bathroom.

"Is she going to sleep with you?" Frieda asked indifferently. She went on knitting. I knew her.

"I thought I'd bring the horsehair mattress downstairs and make a bed for her near the fire. But it may be a lot of work. I can sleep with her or with you or in the doghouse, if only you had a dog. As you please. The house is yours, the kid is yours, I'm yours."

"If you're going to sleep with her even though she vomits on the wedding night, then it's true love. I remember that you always hightailed it away from me when I was sick, when I was coming down with a cold."

"No, unfortunately. It's not love. I only want to make a portrait of her, a sketch at least. The rest is yours, if you're interested."

"You always took off like a shot to get away from sickness. Not out of fear of contagion of course. Merely out of disgust. But what would you prefer to do? Bring the mattress downstairs, fix her up a little virgin's bedroom or lie smelling her all night long"—and she went on tirelessly knitting the green yarn.

"It wouldn't bother me to smell her. Everything can turn out to be useful. But if you want the *droit de seigneur* for your nose . . ."

"You can go to hell with your whore"—and she went on knitting.

"I told you that all I wanted was to paint that head. The girl has a bus before one o'clock and I need to sleep."

I rummaged in my pockets and took out the rest of the money I had stolen from her. I laid it on the table.

"Whenever you like, give her the money and send her off."

"Aren't you going to bring the mattress downstairs?"

"No, I'm tired. I want to sleep for a whole month."

"I'm sure of that," Frieda said and went to knock on the bathroom door, to talk in a whisper with Juanina. Then she came back to the armchair and sat there for a while looking at me in silence. "The dumbest one or the best," she said with her old half-smile.

We heard the last uncertain thunderclaps of the storm, the intermittent pounding of water against the walls.

"Or both," she added. "There wouldn't be any point in asking you if you remember a time when you wanted to paint my profile. Ah, it was mine and nobody else's. But don't be annoyed, I'm sure you really wanted to paint it."

"I did, more than six times, I'm sure."

"More than ten. I can swear to it." She put her knitting down and sat leafing through a book. "I don't know whether they were good or bad. They say yes, they say no and I don't understand. But listen to me calmly; as I hardened myself to pose with the face of a stupid female, the only thing that mattered to me was something else."

"Yes, that's no news to me."

"But it wasn't what you think it was. All you ever really think of is that and painting."

She rose to her feet and carefully put her knitting on the back of the chair, picked up the book in one hand, with one finger buried between the pages. She appeared to be happy and at peace, watching the fire now, younger-looking.

"I'm going to sleep upstairs, by myself. Even though you're tired and sleepy, I'm sure you're going to take care of everything.

The kid's taking a bath now and there are deodorants and antiseptics on the little table in the dressing room. After all, I owe you many things, though whether I repay you for them or not doesn't worry me. Many more things than the ones you may suppose or guess. Don't worry about the money or the smell. I'll wake her up early tomorrow."

She went to the cupboard and brought me a bottle of rum and a siphon of soda water. Surrounded by the rain I listened to the sound of her slippers going upstairs and that of water running in the bathtub.

CARVE BLANCO

But at twelve o'clock the following day, without a watch, certain of the time because of the heat and the patch of sunlight on the floor, Juanina was lying alongside me, sleeping in the nude and face downward, in the bed that I'd improvised. The curve that your waist makes and the short line of fuzz between your buttocks that you don't see. I slipped out of bed so as not to awaken her, shook off my drowsiness and the rum under the shower turned on all the way.

Frieda was knitting in the deck chair, in shorts now, although disguised in a baroque woman's blouse, with her dark glasses, but having moved to the south side of the house, facing the river they call a sea. I had a glass of milk in my hand, embedded precisely in the middle of the whiteness of the day. She greeted me with a smile and we didn't move, neither looking at each other nor speaking.

A folded newspaper was thrown over the wall. I read the headline: it looked as though not one student, not one policeman, had been murdered, no one had been raped yesterday. I handed her the paper.

"Were you happy last night?" she asked.

"Yes, not very, she doesn't know how, she fell asleep right afterward. I think she's really ill."

"Maybe you're getting old, Medina. But I listened and I swear that you saw God's face."

"I'm not entirely certain. There are so many minor gods. Must you knit? I don't know what or who it's for; but it's necessary that you knit. I understand; it completes the picture. I also understand why the girl is still sleeping, why you didn't wake her up early, why you didn't give her money to get her out of your life. Forever, naturally."

She sat up straight and let her knitting slide down onto the wind-scorched grass. She wasn't angry.

"Medina," she said, "you can think whatever you like. You can even think that when all is said and done the rest of the money you stole from me is still mine. I thought I pitied her, that it was impossible for me to let her go away sick."

She slowly assumed her sad and forgiving expression.

"But there's another alternative. There's no point in your hearing it, it's part of the truth."

"Let's hear it," I said as I rolled the newspaper devoid of violence into a ball; the heat and my hunger were bearable.

"Go on. I hope you've bathed. As your foul-smelling baby doll begins to stir in the bed and doesn't even know where she is. But she must be used to that. The truth, the part I'm going to tell you now, is very short."

"Thanks."

"I woke up at six and went down to the beach. I don't know when I decided to let her sleep till she dies, to throw you out, to hide the money and go on knitting a coat for a three-legged baby. To knit until something unpredicted, unpredictable by me, happens."

She rose to her feet laughing and in a little while I heard the screen door of the kitchen slam. I stretched out on the grass looking at the white curve of the waves approaching. So that I was dripping with happiness in the sunlight and wouldn't have a single blessed eurodollar for twenty or thirty days yet, and the pregnant youngster had only the faint hope of getting money out of a hypothetical aunt to give it to a fat midwife, soaked with blood and understanding enough to get in turn the calcium-consuming fetus out of her.

I was almost naked on the grass, drowsy from weakness, doubting the existence of the aunt or imagining her by turn as skinny, fat, dressed in mourning, aloof, enveloped in fabrics with inharmonious, furiously clashing colors, wide sleeves with lace trimming, dry and shriveled up again, her stubby hands paralytic from the weight of her rings and a big solid gold cross halfway buried between her breasts.

And if we were left without an aunt, it was not impossible to get the necessary money by painting the portrait of the girl (if she agreed to get bored stiff not moving, if I was able to do it). On the same beach, a couple of kilometers to the east, Carve Blanco lived, all alone, drunk, with his collection of records of Gregorian chants—as far as he was concerned music had stopped and died there, a thousand three hundred years before the sunny morning on which I was idly thinking about a way of introducing a little air into Juanina's uterus, about the odd night just past, when she said, as though I were paying her a price, "Do whatever you like to me, but do it quick because I'm dying to get some sleep," and I did so.

Meditating on Frieda's three or four probable reactions and on my counterattacks, which had to be swift and resolute.

Carve Blanco, I was certain, would pay, robbing me, enough money. It wasn't the first time he'd signed checks for paintings, sketches or what he persisted in calling gouaches. He was rolling in money, but the only thing he got drunk on was a harsh wine that Cristiani sold and that he himself toted home on foot, in the middle of the afternoon on Saturdays, in ten-liter demijohns, from the dreary tavern to his glass-walled house, bent over crooked, plodding on indifferently and wearing sandals. Winter or summer, his scorn barely showing, making certain of his solitary nights and early mornings of wine that hadn't been aged, of Gregorian chants, of useless and hopelessly entangled memories, of delirious futures.

He really didn't like anybody and this gave him a respectable impartiality. Apart from the recorded chants and an occasional stray dog, what interested him was painting, the details of a picture that would resemble what he would have liked to do, so many years back, and that only now were forming, in his moments of lucidity, a thick paste of failure that very seldom ached.

He didn't like women or men who were past adolescence. But he could recognize a good painting by merely looking at it, contemptuously, out of the corners of his crossed eyes. And if they coincided with the foggy nostalgia of what he had tried to do it was possible that he'd be critical, it was possible that he'd haggle cruelly and cynically only to end up buying, signing the check. He never kept cash in the house.

In order to bless it, to give it warmth and skill, I hid my right hand, the one that was to paint Juanina's head, between my shorts and the skin of my belly. House flies and a horse fly awakened me. The hand was competent and pliant.

But this other beginning was difficult. I found the two of them in the cement cube that Frieda and we friends of hers call the living room. They had eaten lunch without inviting me; they were sprawled out, Frieda in an easy chair, Juanina on top of three orange cushions. They were waiting for the coffee in the fat round glass jug to be ready and meanwhile they were lying to each other with sympathetic smiles, with little pats of their hands; capable of smuggling their contraband across any frontier, affectionate friends of a whole lifetime, permanently united, with no need to say as much, against the world's ingratitudes, against the evil race of men.

I accepted the cup that Frieda pushed across the table, lighted my pipe to quell of my hunger and stayed for a while leaning against the wall, effortlessly enduring the jumble of signals, the feminine cryptology with which the two of them pretended and perhaps managed to be by themselves. I felt wide awake and amused, full of peace and disquiet and the bad humor and happiness that are needed to paint well. I waited for a pause between two hoary falsehoods.

"I've just discovered that the three of us need money. Frieda's money order has been held up longer than usual and I can't go on stealing money she doesn't have from her."

The word "money" caused them to notice my presence; but they looked at me without the least interest.

"Carve Blanco, our private anchorite, must be fed up with seeing Frieda's face, her little round tits, one or another of the holes up her ass. So surprising because of the size of them. What's more, as we know, they can't inspire the anchorite very much. He'll sell them for a profit some day and that's the reason why he bought them. Not products of genius in any way, but they show craftsmanship and he knows it. I almost always failed to get him to buy landscapes and still lifes. They're probably my best work, but they don't interest him. The walls of his house can't hold any more Friedas, full face, in profile, in three-quarter profile. The house is very beautiful but as silly as they come. We need money, we need a novelty so the guy will buy."

"I can see it now." Frieda said. "A portrait of a girl in the nude would be refreshing."

"Money," I repeated. "No less than a thousand eurodollars, no less than five hundred. You must know what an indispensable item abortions are in a family budget. No. No nudes. A knitted sailor's pullover, an oilskin fisherman's hat. That's best."

"And what if I don't want to?" Juanina said. "What if I don't let you paint my portrait?"

So I got down to work that very same night. Juanina with the very wide-brimmed straw hat that Cristiani had lent me and a sweater of Frieda's. The girl tolerated the oblique light of a floor lamp that was almost close enough to touch her; Frieda knitted the poncho for the St. Bernard, without saying a word, barely murmuring the numbers of stitches in the pattern, and humming in a soft voice one of her favorite songs, "Stormy Weather"; I, slowly and surely, the inventor and master of chiaroscuro. But the girl held her head in an impassive, defiant pose, looking straight ahead, her black eyebrows meeting; her motionless head completely apart from us, isolated on the lofty heights of an independent solitude, hers alone, as if just born, just dead.

And it surprised me—I note it down so as not to forget it, since I never saw it again—that minutes after I began to paint her portrait, Juanina's face began to be veiled by a vapor over her forehead that disappeared if I gave her an order, a piece of advice, in a loud voice. Her face and her soul, pliant and elusive, so close and buried in the mist, soothed and almost absent, tenaciously keeping up her silent dialogue with the invisible enemy, with angels that persisted in not appearing, in not being.

THE WAY

And they went onward, unaware, going through the wine of the first Mass, the struggle for their daily bread, ignorance and stupidity.

They went onward, happy, distracted, very seldom doubting; so innocent, relaxed or tense, to the final hole in the ground and the last word. So certain, ordinary, silent, reciters, imbeciles.

The hole had been awaiting them without real hope or interest. They went on their way good-humoredly; some of them leaned on others; some of them followed along alone and smiling, talking softly to themselves. In general, they discussed plans and spoke of the future and of the future of their offspring and of revolutions great and small recorded in books clutched beneath their armpits. Certain of them waved their arms about as they rambled on about memories of lovers and faded flowers that bore the same name.

THE RENDEZVOUS

Frieda was not interested in the progress of the picture. It was enough for her to learn that the ocher and blue with which I put the finishing touches on the canvas came from old paint pots that belonged to me, that it was not necessary to contribute money of hers.

Perhaps she made a remark only once, yawning, on a freezing-cold early morning after a night of drinking a great deal of cheap wine.

"Are you sure that Carve is going to buy that from you? It looks like a Modigliani from the days when the Italian was learning to clean his paintbrushes. Or from the times when he was already dead and practically rotted away. I always suspected that that was how it would all turn out, ever since I saw her, ever since you brought her to me to give her something to eat and cure her insides with Talipectin. It resembles her a little, I admit. It looks like something odd and nasty that happened to you all of a sudden. But the world is saturated with Modiglianis. Why add one more to it?"

"Maybe. I couldn't portray her any other way."

In all truth, we were in no hurry. A pregnancy twenty or thirty days old is very young. Frieda gave us everything, shelter and food, coffee and bad wine by the demijohn, organized brief strolls along the beach. Despite all the signs of spring in the sky above, warm weather hadn't yet come or came only to go away again. But I was working furiously in the afternoons on the three sketches of nudes—there had to be three—and on the portrait, the head with the neck out of joint, the hair lying flat with the broad yellowish parting in it that divided it.

Frieda furtively spied on them. I thought that, despite everything, she liked them and began to fear fire and the knife. We both knew that it wasn't wise to speak of the paintings before they were finished and, perhaps, sold. Before I grew sick and tired of seeing and painting Juanina, I'd get the money from Carve, I'd cheat Frieda and Juanina to a limited extent and invent some trip or other so as to leave the beach. I came to think that they'd find a way to live together without bothering each other.

And so, when the first part of my work was finished—the head and the paint spots meant to form three nude women—I asked Frieda if she wanted to visit Carve and deduce how interested he might be in a rendezvous by night. She agreed, obedient and happy, anticipating failure.

When she returned, Frieda announced enthusiastically:

"He said yes, because it's not good to let grass grow along the path of friendship, the 'narrow path,' he called it. But there were lots of demijohns about and it was barely five o'clock in the afternoon and nobody can imagine what sort of mood he'll be in tomorrow at nine, which is the appointed hour, which presupposes that he's not planning to offer us a meal, because he's always been stingy with other people. And there was something else. Putting illustrations in order, tolerating the Gregorian chants without signs of fatigue, or pretending that he was putting them in order and tolerating the chants, Heriberto was there, leaning over the big table. And Heriberto has always liked you, and I think there won't be any purchase agreement if you don't show any signs of how likable you find him. It's necessary to make sacrifices when it's for a noble cause. I for my part don't intend to waste the death of a hundred cows that I foresee as the night's grand finale. The sad part is that this poor innocent, your little spring model, will be obliged to witness such horrors, that will seem to her like the little secret kisses that schoolmates give each other compared to her aunt's teas at five o'clock on the dot. And I remember now that we don't know if that relative is a spinster, a widow, a married woman or a bawd.

THE ESCAPES

Juanina's sittings almost always ended up in bed. On a mattress, a new one at least, practically a soft one, that Frieda had laid on the downstairs floor. Both in the lies and in the bellowings and the silences a strange, multiple past could be perceived. In any event, it seemed as if nobody had taken advantage of the time spent with her to educate her. Or in any case she didn't take advantage of the time she spent with me.

Once a week I climbed upstairs in the dark to Frieda's room. The old habits were taken up again, the round shapes of love were recovered and I dropped off to sleep in peace.

I remember having calculated that it would take two weeks' work and discipline to finish the three proposed canvases. The head had to have as close a resemblance as possible to Juanina. The two nudes, paint spots on a pure white background, obsessive to the point of illusion, had to be ambiguous.

I looked at her emaciated body, forcing her to close herself or open herself. She obeyed with her childish, distracted smile, so unconcerned about me, about the probable existence of the world. The next day it was necessary to ask her to hide her revenge, her scorn, her smile again. I found her weaker and weaker by the day, more and more vulnerable. Sometimes she straightened up to light a cigarette, without warning.

"You're a good pair of motherfuckers. What brought the two of you together?"

What she gave, offered, lent was only the touching thinness of her body; and that body could be dressed, separated from me for all time.

Then, as she sat smoking on an uncomfortable kitchen bench, she preferred them, she dragged them about, hooking one foot around them, she spoke of her aunt with so many variations, so many hatreds and signs of tenderness, so many contradictory descriptions that I reached the point where I was practically certain that she didn't have an aunt and that she found this absence sad.

It was likely that, of the trio, the least unhappy one was Frieda. I didn't know anything about the girl that could be believed and for me life was not a matter of good luck or bad; it was an everyday occurrence, regardless of what happened or didn't happen. But it seems inevitable that the word "happiness" has a meaning and that any number of idiots, without premonitions or terrifying pauses, fling themselves on top of it belly first, surrendering body and soul to it.

Frieda, for example, while not surrendering, seemed to be certain of her life and her victory. A question of years. Every night, when I was in bed with Juanina, she brought us hot-water bottles, as the heat slithered away she arrived shortly after dawn—she never knocked on the door, was never bothered by what she might come upon—and talked to us about the weather, about a brief future, about fishing incidents. I used to catch a glimpse of her smile and always saw that she attributed no importance to what she was saying and that with every maternal movement she was patiently diverting herself. I would look up at the ceiling, Juanina would pester her in silence, with hatred and respect.

Frieda once asked:

"Did you two work much on the little paintings today?"

We didn't answer her. But one time too, perhaps the last time, Juanina struck the right note in her most childish and drowsiest voice to answer:

"He made me walk around naked, coldly, with neither of us in the right mood. Smoking his stinking pipe. He's a pig, if you'll pardon the word. Then he painted for a while out of hatred and with every brush stroke he berated himself. Then we made *chiquichiqui* till morning, ma'am. If you'll pardon the word."

THE LUNCH

The head, the profile, the line of the nose, began coming in as great numbers as when one sits down on a bench in a public square and surrounds oneself with seed to attract pigeons.

As far as the ambivalent nudes—two of them—were concerned the story was different. With the head I could recover and celebrate my old, eternal, newly arrived wisdom. With the hints of nudes I experienced yet again an oft-repeated illusion: that I was someone else, that I was painting in a different and better way. But we aren't dealing with paintings here; just with a book, a story. The self-surrender involved and the explanation aren't worth going into.

I contemplated the first nude for many hours, I knew that it was made for me, by a miracle, by a lack of understanding, and that I would sell it to no one. Or almost no one.

I slept till noon, wrapped up the painting, the sketches and the nudes that could be exposed without major danger, without its mattering, to men's stupidity. In the afternoon I lay in the sun with a bottle of wine and slept. I didn't want to talk to the women. Then I walked along the shore, like a superstitious roulette player, playing the game called "at any moment the ideal wave may appear and perhaps I'll understand it." It was indispensable to look at the water indifferently, to walk along with my mind elsewhere.

I began being hungry for lunch when I came back from my failed attempt and found Carve sitting in front of his house in one of those stretches of sand that Cristiani called a terrace. He was drinking wine and in his case it was difficult to be certain whether or not he was drunk; or if he was managing to waver between lucidity and dull-wittedness. I asked him for a glass of wine as he said to me:

"Nobody ever sees you anymore."

"I walk along the beach all day long. You can see me whenever you like from the ten windows of your house."

"They're always closed. Records and I. Nothing else. I don't need anything else."

I thought of the liters of wine and of whichever Heriberto was on duty. I forbore to mention them.

"I think Frieda organized a get-together here tomorrow night."

He put a package of cigarettes on the table.

"That's true; I didn't know you were anywhere around," he said after giving me a light. "Though one can never guess your whereabouts. Or even intuit them;"—he took another swig—"it happens to me with other people. You can have lunch with me, you can stay here to live, for as long as you like. But as for what you have under your arm, it's no go; I don't have any money, I'm not thinking of buying nor do I have the means to."

I lighted my pipe and sat watching the rhythm of the pairs of dolphins.

"I don't have any money," he repeated.

"In all truth, you never did have any money," I said. "A few thousand pesos once in a while. I only brought this so you could see it, before one of the two of us dies. It'd be a shame. Moreover the only thing I paint is waves and I don't sell them."

Sitting on the steps I could smell him frying ham and eggs. I looked at the sea, awaiting the impossible wave, with my portfolio at my feet. Every so often, Carve came in a sweat to get another drink from the demijohn and offer me another.

"No," I said in an indifferent voice, looking at the dolphins. "I never drink before nightfall."

"At some juncture, however," he said. "Or is that a new procedure for selling paintings?"

"It's possible; on occasion. But, I remember, there were women; that world was different. I didn't come to sell anything; I came to show you. After lunch; there's time." I raised the demi-john to wet my lips, out of politeness, so as to keep him from being a poor solitary midday drunk on that beach; I pressed the cork in and murmured sadly: "I sell only waves and the wave that I would be pleased, or not, to sell you, hasn't been painted yet. You can't even see it, a fake wave that would represent it, pass on gossip to me, tell me the truth in advance, hasn't even broken on the shore yet."

"So early and already drunk," he said happily; he went back inside the house. But there was no such thing as a wave like that and I hadn't reached the point of believing in its absence so firmly as to begin to paint it. It wasn't a wave of the Pacific, it wasn't a Japanese wave; let me make that clear. Perhaps it didn't deserve my signature at the bottom. It was a turbid wave, with a dirty white crest (add, out of modesty, as someone said) the color of an opal: a filthy mixture of urine, eyes that had burst. Elements: bandages stained with blood and pus, but already faded; corks with blurred brand names; gobs of phlegm that could be mistaken for clams; saliva from an epileptic, bits of plaster without sharp edges, remains of vomit, bits of old and bothersome furniture, semi-decayed sanitary napkins—but, any beach of ours: everything absorbed by the wave and forming its foam, its height, its respectable dubious whiteness.

I watched, already very far in the distance, the dolphins leaping up and diving down. I had many things to complete my ideal wave; but I would die without seeing it. I wet my tongue again from the demijohn and left the jug in the sun.

We ate ham and eggs as we talked about many things and people.

"You're afraid of Gregorian plainsong," Carve said, "Yet it's the beginning and the end. Maybe that's why you're afraid of it. As the Goncourt brothers say, people become subtle, intelligent when shit begins to compact itself in their intestines. That's why I mention Gregorian plainsong."

"That may be true," I said. "I've often thought the same thing. But so what? My mania is painting, though. Let all of music explode, be dammed up in Gregorian plainsong. I paint."

"I make war," he said, laughing, as he lighted a cigarette. "Well, you've walked for blocks to show me the portfolio."

"Yes, but the food hasn't had the same effect on me yet. I don't feel spiritual. Please pass me the demijohn."

It must have been around five when I pretended to be drunk, took the portfolio out from under the table and sent it flying onto the couch.

"You can turn up your nose as long as you like. Nothing begins or ends here. It's not Gregorian plainsong."

I went outside, to the stairs, to the beach; I didn't want many things, but I confined myself to thinking that an abortion cost five hundred piasters.

Half an hour later he came out to sit alongside me, on the stairs, looking at the water as I was doing. Everything was green and silver fish leaped in the air and dived back into the water. Almost in desperation I thought of the remains of a shipwreck for my wave. Maybe we went out into the sun, into the air that was beginning to grow cooler, close to an hour in silence. When it began to get dark, he stroked his mustache and said, unenthusiastically:

"How much?"

"Everything?"

"I'd except certain things."

I began to laugh covetously, not making a sound.

"Except certain things? No, no; everything or nothing. All of it for a thousand maravedís."

"You're mad," he remarked sadly.

"For some time now. If I weren't mad, I wouldn't offer it to you, I wouldn't make you a gift of the portfolio for a thousand. I need the money. Did you look at the heads and the nose on the heads?"

"They're very good. I looked at that and other things."

"I didn't paint other things. Neither for you nor for myself. There are only bristol boards and pasteboard."

He let a certain time pass, a whole cigarette's-worth.

"Are you living at Frieda's place?" he asked.

"Yes, just for a while."

Then I discovered the pairs of dolphins, diving down and leaping up, rhythmically, without interfering with their movement forward.

Fishing

I came in without paying any attention to them and knelt in front of the stove. Frieda went on knitting an endless greenish brown pullover, for a giant not yet born; Juanina was biting her fingernails and didn't look at all happy or hopeful. I didn't break the silence and then after a while I said to them:

"We have the money. Or we're going to have it."

"You two have," Frieda answered; she picked up a stitch she'd dropped before asking in a soft voice, her eyes lowered:

"When are you leaving? Did you get as much as you wanted?"

"Not one peseta more." I was sure that they'd been talking about me till they heard me come in. "I think I'll have it tomorrow. We're leaving. Juanina to live with her aunt, and I to the studio. I have to invent something useless."

Frieda didn't say anything and went on knitting the monstrous pullover that wasn't for me.

Juanina said:

"I was on the beach this afternoon, I couldn't help staying on there. The fishermen were there. We're going out tomorrow at five."

Frieda sipped at her glass of raw rum and gave the mysterious smile again as she knitted, the endless pullover, the warm garment that no man could wear. Juanina drank half a glassful in one swallow; I hoped that her cough, the burning in her chest, would go away.

"What?" she asked aloud then.

We didn't answer her. Frieda went on knitting with her gentle, knowing smile; I looked at what remained of a piece of wood taken out of the fire. Juanina swallowed the half-glassful still left, leaned back and burst out laughing. We didn't pay any attention to her. She finally said: "I'm cold. Who's going to bring me a hot-water bottle in bed?"

We didn't fetch her one. The first light of day was beginning to dawn, and I had gotten everything I'd wanted from her and knew that she was used to that and let herself be had out of hope, out of indifference.

"Does it bother you that I'm going out with the fishermen?" she asked. "All you have to do is say no, to shake your head."

"It's just that I don't believe you really want to do it." I lighted a cigarette and thought that I was awake now for the rest of the morning.

"If there's no aunt I'll kill you. You can do whatever you like today because it's a desperate love, even though you haven't realized it. But last night we were happy, or I was."

She suddenly got to her feet and kissed me on the forehead. She went about looking for warm clothes in the murky light. She left without making any noise. I lighted another cigarette and in a little while I fell asleep again.

(She had been laughing without meaning to make fun of me; she didn't believe it, that was all. But since I was madly in love with her and moreover she didn't matter to me, I could dream her in the gray morning, going down to the water's edge, little, all hunched over, cold-blooded, seeking to wound the world and, in passing, me too perhaps as I lay sleeping, absent, all bundled up, incapable of loving her in the way that she had imagined love.)

THE SALE

At nine p. m. the moon lengthened our three wavering shadows, stumbling up and down on the treacherous dunes. Toward the east the obdurate pulsing of the stars. I was carrying rolled up the epicene nude of Juanina and Frieda had the drawings, the more or less successful rough sketches tucked in her neckline. The girl was running, rolling about in the sand, preceding us or allowing us to go ahead of her. We entered the light from Carve's veranda: an oil lamp hanging from a long iron bar, an antique octagonal lamp.

The first to come out and greet us was Heriberto; he appeared to be making fun of us in a mild way, to know and to be telling us in advance what the remainder of the night would be like.

"We were waiting for you."

"It's nine on the dot," I said, as the women shook hands with him; I went inside, shoving them ahead of me, and led them off to one side toward the large armchair where Carve was pushing a pencil across large sheets of wrinkled paper. The demijohn alongside him, on the floor. Five glasses on the table, two of them reddened all the way up to the rim.

"Punctuality is the politeness of idiots," Carve said. "Those who have nothing in their head other than the memory of the rendezvous. That's impossible for me, I always arrive late. They can wait for me."

He wasn't drunk yet; just the high-pitched, plaintive voice, the very slow movements of his hands, sketching in the air now, the pencil touching his lips like a cigarette.

"Heriberto," Carve said, "fill the glasses."

The boy lifted up the demijohn, almost full, with one arm and poured the wine, for Carve first, then for the women. As he handed me my glass, he winked at me.

"Ah," he said. "You drink it with water."

I followed him to the kitchen, full of empty bottles. He leaned down into the refrigerator and came up with a bottle of Haig, half empty.

"Have a quick one. That wine is for the poor and for drunkards."

I took a long, slow swallow and handed him back the bottle, which disappeared immediately, clinking noisily against other glass bottles.

The women had spread the nude and the sketches out on the table; I saw Carve hastily put his eyeglasses on and raise his head to look at the ceiling. Then he said:

"The painting. Hang it up vertically."

This was done; one corner for each of the two women's hands; he stepped back and put his glasses on again.

"The same merchandise as always," he said, smiling.

"Almost," I said. "But keep looking. I've never done anything like this. It may not be good or you may not like it. But it's different from everything I've done before and I couldn't tell you why."

"Music," Carve said, still looking at the painting, and Heriberto crossed the room to put ten records of Gregorian chants on the player. "It'll do." He took off his glasses.

The two women took a rest and the painting lay rolled up on the table again.

Then I drank a glassful of the repellent wine, which immediately mixed with the whisky.

"You had time to look at them as long as you liked yesterday," I said. "So nothing is beginning or ending. It's not Gregorian plainsong."

I went out to the veranda, I went down the stairs till my feet hit the sand, I took my espadrilles off and paced back and forth. I had to see the painting and sketches, I had to think of five hundred florins for an aseptic abortion. The sea was phosphorescent and flotsam and jetsam from a shipwreck came to my mind for my wave. With my espadrilles in my hand I went back inside the house.

The cast of characters was the same, but the scene had changed. Heriberto was sitting facing a kitchen knife stuck in the table. He was drinking whisky straight out of the bottle. Carve, pale and nervous, turned his head to look at me, as though he were seeing me for the first time, and said:

"Ah, it's you."

Frieda and Juanina were on a long unpolished bench, locked in an embrace, cheek to cheek. The four glasses full of wine on the table were a bright translucent red.

Carve looked at the table again and I saw a drop of blood on his ear; Frieda said, in a monotonous, bored voice:

"That's enough of this. I'm leaving."

The scene immediately became calm once again and for a few seconds it seemed to me that I was looking at figures in a waxworks museum.

"Give him the money," Heriberto ordered.

Without turning around, Carve stretched his hand out to me with the check for a thousand leis that he had already written.

"This is for everything," he declared.

Heriberto gave a drawn-out drunkard's laugh. I took the check as Frieda and Juanina got up from the bench. Then I went over to look for one last time at the portrait of the nude girl.

Outside the moon had climbed higher and our shadows were small and shaky as we walked in silence over the dunes.

SUMMER DIES

As we were coming from the beach a windy, sandy afternoon set in; we had our heads lowered and my breathing was a little heavier, more anxious than Juanina's. We reached the house and saw that it was closed, silent and blind; we saw our suitcases at the top of the stairway at the entrance; we saw, nailed to the door the sign that said: SUMMER IS OVER, written in all the colors of my paint pots, we saw, for the first time, a ginger cat sitting mewing its abandonment.

We opened the suitcases so as to get dressed on the porch, behind the house, by ourselves, invisible from the river front. Juanina said a dirty word for each garment she put on. I was keeping close watch on a black cloud when the first drops fell.

"I'm certain that that big whore knew it was going to rain," Juanina almost shouted as she resigned herself to looking for her yellow dog uniform and putting it on. "And what happens now?"

"Now we're going to the corner where the buses stop. But your money. They aren't going to cash the check for me here. Did Frieda give you the address of the apartment?"

Juanina contrived a smile in the rain.

"Of course. The address and an offer to put me up."

"There are only two beds. She must be thinking of throwing me out."

"I don't know. Or else thinking up combinations," she said.

"She might be in love. It's possible."

"Women make me sick. Really sick. Just the smell of women is enough to make me feel nauseated." I knew very well that she was lying.

"Did she tell you so?"

"She didn't have to."

We were now on the corner where the buses stop, isolated from the world and its memories by a furious and crafty rain. Water fell in my eyes, in my mouth. The yellow dog protected her head with a shower cap.

"She offered to put me up so that I could rest after the abortion. If my aunt didn't agree to let me stay with her. Give me a peso.'

I rummaged in the dampness of my pockets and peeled off a bill. She hid it in the waterway running down her neckline, her breasts hard and almost new-born, and laughed again.

"You've already paid"—she too spat out water—"I sold you my aunt."

"No thanks. I don't need her, I'm not in the market."

"The fact is that there isn't, there never has been, an aunt. This is a dirty trick, it's a deluge."

"That's how it began," I said as I withdrew, motionless, to another zone of cold and disillusionment.

She realized it and asked:

"Does that lie annoy you? Well. I was already an outright lie when you met me on the beach. And now you're going to give me two pesos. One for the bus."

I searched and gave her a five-peso bill.

"Will that get you where you're going? Is it enough?"

"It's too much," she said and now she was no doubt laughing at me.

There were claps of thunder, flashes and zigzag rays of lightning; the rain, arrogant now, grew stronger, more furious still. It hit my head in an imitation of a soft sprinkle, it penetrated my nose.

I said: "It doesn't matter. It's moving off already. A summer storm," and she corrected: "Summer is over." Without bitterness or mockery.

She pushed the suitcases with one foot and tried to embed herself in the wall of a house where they were turning lights on. From her no man's land—we were alone on the corner—she said to me:

"I already sold and you already bought, paying too high a price. You bought another lie, another truth. Calm and patience. There's no abortion, I wasn't ever pregnant. Or in the family way, as poor people say. The work as a washer woman I had to do so Frieda wouldn't tumble to the truth. Now, a favor, maybe the last one. The first bus is mine. You take the next one. I want to be by myself and think about a whole lot of things."

The first bus, hers, arrived, with its red and yellow lights on in the rain.

I let her go and stood there waiting, feeling swindled by love and dying of it.

THE SUPPER

I can lie, but I don't wish to do so here, because it is a matter of a memory and any imbecile can twist the wires of a memory, give it nice shapes, the right colors, place them above a piece of furniture or a chat.

I say that I foresaw the scene from the elevator, between the fourth and the sixth floors, with my jacket over one shoulder, loosening my tie, returning to the apartment, which would be warmer than the street. Frieda would be there, was there, half naked on the couch in the living room, with a pile of German magazines thrown on the floor and a bottle of gin, a glass, a bowl with pebbles of ice on the little low circular table. I had guessed correctly and it was as if Frieda were making a clean copy of the phrases, the pose that I had vaguely thought of in the elevator, it was as if that special form of the woman's bad humor could extend itself not only so as to surround her but also to slip through chambers in doors, dig victoriously into the holes made by the nails holding up paintings on the wood-paneled walls.

I unbuttoned my shirt and let it fall to the floor; I filled the glass and dropped another misshapen cube of ice in it. As I drank, she started in, her voice slow and guttural, not knowing that that night, at least, was doomed to be a fiasco. From the big open window the heat of dusk, still luminous, entered gently, becoming more intense; opposite, the derelict garage of the vanished

112

streetcars, the yellow glass of the soccer field, the calm river traversed by an enormous patch of silver, a rhomboidal boatful of paralytic fish. At times, fortuitously, the patch foretold more heat for the following morning; at others, a storm at dawn.

"A Sunday," she began. "And I haven't seen you since Friday. What suffering since Friday. There are certain characters who have bizarre ideas as to how to spend a Sunday afternoon. Today, for example, since lunch, shut up with that old lady full of sheep shit who wants to convince you that that cretin of a kid is your son. Or has she already convinced you? They say it's possible to find out by having blood tests made. But the worst part of this sob story is that nobody even knows if he's her son or if some woman forgot to sweep him out with the trash or if she borrowed him so as to get money for his support out of you and birthday and Christmas presents. What's more, she lives with the boy in one room. Do you send him to the movies so the two of you can go to bed together or do you wallow about in front of him? The facts of life. It's your duty as a father, when it comes right down to it; some day he's going to have to know how those things that he sees when he looks at himself in the mirror are done."

She took a little time out to drink out of the bottle, nibbled a piece of ice.

"But maybe not. Maybe you trotted down the sidewalks on the shady side of the street, your tongue hanging out, looking like a dog for a gap in a wall, a door left ajar, any sort of crack so as to take the big leap and go back to that Santa Maria that you invented for yourself with the aid of the other tramps. Why don't you tell me the truth? Were you with that filthy female or looking for the city?"

She repeated herself, she was a little drunk now; perhaps, when it got dark, she would find herself obliged to go out and look for women. I finished the glass and went to the kitchen to get myself another drink, a little more ice. Then I sat down in an armchair near the big window; gin and hatred circled about in the heat on the balcony, making it even hotter.

"Not at all," I said to her. "At times I'm afraid I'll reach the point of loving you. Not tonight, of course. They're moments, like a shudder, like a pang of remorse; they're over immediately. But it's sheer terror, I swear to you. Loving you either a little more or in a different way, I don't know which, and mixing that love with pity, believing that you're the guilty party responsible for my misfortune. Terror because I'm sure I'm capable of killing you."

She made a noise with her nose and picked up a magazine to hide her face. She went on drinking, smoking; the sweat poured out of me drop by drop, slow and insolent. I heard the silence of the fat neighbor women who were listening on the balcony next door.

"If you thought that I'm one of those women who . . ." Frieda finally said. "Did you cash the check at the agency?"

"It's Sunday."

"Yesterday or the day before, stupid. Because there's nothing in the house to eat and I don't have a single peso."

Since Friday night I had been stumbling, as always, blinded and well-behaved in the world of twin sisters. But it wasn't one of those things that can be told to people, it was something that required living with a dog and smoking and thinking and turning round and round watched by the unquestioning friendship of a dog's eyes. And perhaps not even then. And immediately, the heat persisted and it was, I forgot Frieda and the thirty-second version of this her litany and imagined myself telling a man a little more brazen, cynical and stupid than I was, that my childhood had been the classic and decisively frustrating childhood of the solitary little boy, deprived of dogs. And if the cretin persisted behind my back I would tell, I would have told the truth. I would have described the impossible dog—and said that in the dusk of gin, twin sisters and Frieda they seemed to me as necessary and as capable of bringing me closer to perfect bliss—I would have conversed in detail and with conviction of a beast like myself, condemned to being classified by the profane as a police dog. Belgian or German, the differences being of no importance, with a slight admixture of sheepdog blood and just a trace, for those who were most intelligent or disparaging, of Doberman, an unpleasant animal that enjoyed a solitary, exclusive bliss.

But I didn't have, we don't have a dog, and Frieda added:

"Did you cash it or didn't you, you orphan and procreator of orphans? The immortal little drawings for toilets."

As I was remembering, back there in the Detachment, a confrontation at high noon between a gigantic scoundrel and his feeble colleagues who twice advised the other:

"And if you're afraid, why don't you buy yourself a dog?"

"Younger by the day"—I looked at her in envy. "The toilets were work done a week ago. I was paid for them and the money ended up at the Morini, because you were sentimental and wanted to visit the ruins of the Market, get a feel for the window of the room, for the studio where it can be said that I lived before you decided to support me, more or less, before we founded that society, that association for criminal purposes on a small scale. What I had to cash on Friday and didn't"—I lied—"was the drawing for the white bread made with milk, opus 513. But I have some money. It's enough to eat on, but not enough for you to get drunk on, I regret to say. Nor is it enough for you to send a telegram to Santa María to demand that the postal money order be forwarded to you."

"More annoying by the day," she murmured, almost pacified, pensive, mustering a smile for me.

I dried my chest again with my shirt and stood there smelling it before tossing it gently in her face. I lingered under the scanty, lukewarm shower, went looking for clean clothes in Frieda's bedroom and discovered on the rug, almost hidden underneath the bed, a watch, the Gérard-Pérrigaux that I had given Seoane as a present a year before, for one or another of his birthdays when I decided to accept forever that he was my son or wasn't my son and that neither of the two possibilities was of any importance.

Dressed now and feeling cooler, I went back in the living room and sat there smoking and looking at her, having resolved not to speak to her of the watch, thinking of lovers' meetings with a definite time limit, when one resorts to stealing frequent glimpses of one's watch so as to make time slow down, so as to measure the minutes that have gone by during the plunge into a caress and knowing that one can still try for another. Perhaps Seoane was my son and had inherited from me that superstitious idea, an idea that was perhaps universal, a rite practiced by all lovers whom time traps.

Now Frieda was naked, her face invisible because of the magazine, her legs spread slightly apart. So, I thought, she knows, or believes much more firmly than I do, that Seoane is my son; hence it would please her to try to get me to make love to her after the boy had, perhaps almost immediately afterward. Why, then, didn't she begin the temptation the moment I arrived, why did she give me time, with her stupid argument and guileful reproaches, to bathe and get dressed again? I thought that her aim now, after the attack that had been no more than a form of defense, was to get me not to bed her in the position forced on her from the beginning, so as to be able to move about, smiling with her eyes closed, so as to compare by remembering, so as to increase her pleasure.

Then—I ceased to look at the minuscule trembling that began in her thighs—it was also possible that they had deliberately left the watch underneath the bed, that she was the one who had suggested it, that the fake carelessness of leaving it there had been invented by Seoane so that I would catch on, so as to leave his defiant mark, his emblem of rancor and revenge. The watch was now in my pocket and I felt with my fingertips the short, black, sweaty viper with the gold head in the middle of the backbone, as I fished out cigarettes and the telephone rang.

"Are we home for whoever is calling?" I asked.

"Find out who it is," she said, without lowering the magazine. "Maybe he has some dollars, maybe he'll bring a plateful of food with him."

It was Quinteros's voice.

"I'm with Mr. Wright. Oh, gloomy Sunday. We're hungry, we don't have a peso and the English gentleman has a bottle with him. Since, on looking at the expression on his face, I see, as though the child were the fruit of sin and his parents the presumed parents of the boy, they might well have thrown them out of the house and there's every indication that there will be a storm, rain and cold. A matter of minutes and poor Wright, here at my elbow, with his sexually hurt look and his breasts full to overflowing with milk . . ."

"Pathetic. Very good news. Frieda will be madly happy and start knitting. There's no need to thank me for that. That's just how she is, she weaves and unweaves. One moment, please, I don't know whether she's in."

Frieda had let the magazine fall to the floor and picked up her glass.

"Don't tell me anything," she said. "That pair of comedians, the exiles from Santa María. Another night of memories and boredom, and I haven't come home yet, even at this late hour, and who knows where I might be."

"As you please. But I've just bathed and I'm hungry. It's true: Quinteros and the Englishman. They've just made it big at the racetrack and are inviting us to eat down at Buceo in some dockside restaurant that you like a lot, the name of which I don't remember."

Frieda walked over and sat down on the couch, one hand raised so as to drink, the other to ask me to wait. She calculated the possibilities of the night, measured the heat and the fatigue that Seoane had left her with; postponing the vengeance and the complicated pleasure involved did not mean a real postponement. She realized that, smiling sweetly at me, so powerful and sure of herself, almost maternal, my beloved.

"If you all swear to me not to talk about the lost city . . ."

"Quinteros? Still there? Yes, I found Frieda and she doesn't know how to thank you enough. So, as we were saying, at the Yate in Buceo, in half an hour."

"In Buceo," Quinteros said with a laugh; he wasn't drunk, he never had been. "No. The young lady can't travel by bus and you know what it's like trying to get a taxi in Lavanda on a Sunday night. As hard as getting the money to pay for the trip."

Frieda had already gone into the bathroom and then it crossed my mind, the thought came to me, I was certain.

"Where are you?"

"Alhambra. But that's not really where we are. We're just using the telephone. And you'd better tell us right away where you're inviting us to eat because there are people who are anxious or have a physical urge to talk over this very same telephone. They haven't queued up yet, perhaps out of respect for the moving social and emotional situation in which circumstances have placed Lady Wright. As I told you, it's enough to see her facial expression and the bottle discreetly wrapped in paper clutched to her breast. Her way of not moving, of leaning against things and standing still. There's just a little something that gives her away. I apologize. She says yes. With no need for questions, she says yes to everything. Well, it's the end result of her having said yes before, nine months and one week ago. Now, with the little baby girl in her arms. I apologize for the second time: she spent half an hour looking at a new display of Colt revolvers in the Ferrando shop windows. But it doesn't worry me, and I beg you to not to let it concern you either. She looked only out of envy and sheer artistic admiration. Gray-blue steel and ascetic functional shapes. Then I explain to her, as you may know, you were born a painter. One last apology: I seem to remember that on a very different night Frieda was happy at a restaurant near this telephone—no, there's no line forming yet, but the look in their eyes—a restaurant called the Gruta Azul or some similar unfortunate name."

"Yes, Quinteros," I answered slowly. "I naturally pray you to go to the devil, on account of the memory. But never mind. The Gruta Azul and the nostalgia for a number of native lands. In half an hour. The same thing will happen again, I prophesy and you already knew."

"It's of no importance, believe me, see you shortly," Quinteros asserted, almost syllable by syllable; I imagined him shrugging as he hung up.

Frieda had come out of the shower and I could hear her high heels tapping in the bedroom, hangers sliding in the clothes closet, her scent of cleanliness and perfume preceding her into the living room. I sat down again facing the balcony and the storm, the first silent flashes of lightning. I sat there drinking the cold gin and tonic, buried in the tender happiness of waiting for her, of guessing at the dress, the necklace, the bracelets she'd be wearing. And once again, with amusement, I thought, it occurred to me that I was certain that Frieda had hesitated to accept the false invitation so as not to destroy with soap and water the physical traces left by her reunion with Seoane which she had resolved to offer me and force upon me. The idea was not mine but Frieda's; it was almost incredible, almost grotesque, almost unpleasant. I calmed down only when I was able to find a word that was the equivalent of those three almosts: the word "moistening".

NECKTIE

On Lavanda or Santa María anyone can know Quinteros, at any
time and it doesn't matter to me because it doesn't go beyond
finding him congenial and won't change anything. But Mr.
Wright's case is different, it matters to me and a vague loyalty
forces me to say what he was like to me, years before the Sunday
night and the storm, in a ubiquitous restaurant. I don't want him
to be fat, a humorless drunk, clever and full of egotistical mysteries. I learned to obey for so long a time that now, without my
having realized it, I can take command of the details.

Two or three years back, including and accepting the time
lived in Lavanda, can be said to be nothing, a today without a
yesterday or a tomorrow, but the passage of which I must accept
out of an obscure politeness toward others. I imagine Mr. Wright
in a dark little street, meandering between villas, a street miraculously respected or faithfully grateful for the superintendent on
duty, a narrow lane winding through the wealthy neighborhoods
of Santa María; small of stature and straight-backed, dressed in
linen and wearing a Panama hat, holding in the same hand his
cane and the thin nickel chain that restrained the restlessness of
his dog, Dick. Mr. Wright in his Indian attire, the odor of strong
alcohol on his breath. Telling me incoherently about a succession
of mysterious robberies that had occurred in that same dusty

street where we were standing, dripping with sweat, I wearing my khaki uniform, my boots and my kepi with a visor.

"Mysterious," I say to him, "because they never steal anything. Nothing that's worth anything. They enter the houses at night. I come out with my dog and search about, Dick searches for trails they've left behind. So far, he hasn't found any."

Perhaps my friendship with and trust in Quinteros were greater than those I felt for Mr. Wright, perhaps I had more contempt for him or liked him less. But between the well-dressed, almost elegant Quinteros, with his flat chestnut-brown hair and the perfect transparency of his eyeglasses and the other man, fat, dressed in dirty white clothes that had shrunk, sweaty and not at all disgusted at the drops that trickled from between his eyebrows down his short violet-colored nose, I chose the Englishman. So that once we'd sat down and ordered the first course and, with the waiter's help, ended our discussion of brands of wines, I chose to invite Mr. Wright to the counter to have a whisky on me, knowing that he was going to tell me:

"You know. No. My sense of smell. Cane brandy."

"They don't have the one labeled Ombú."

"I know. We aren't back there. In any event, begging your pardon, cane brandy."

I lifted my glass to my lips. Why precisely the words "sense of smell" from this gringo? Quinteros is an artist who creates situations, a little sadistic, properly discreet and depraved, incapable of risking his power. How could the Englishman have known about the story of the sense of smell?

"Speaking of whisky, speaking of cane brandy, what does the sense of smell have to do with them?"

His round face, drenched with sweat and innocent; the damp blue eyes weren't lying. A hesitant nostalgia, confusion, almost nothing else.

"What the devil does a sense of smell have to do with the

difference between whisky and cane brandy? Even if it isn't Ombú," I persisted gently, giving him a friendly look.

"A cold, flu," he said slowly, only slightly annoyed. "A bad story, about a stable burned down. Whisky no longer has any smell or taste to me. A story about Montreal, very old, Mounties, redcoats. Oh, he can be called chief. In another story, later on, sahib. At peace now and so grateful. Because I had always imagined a splendid title such as *Colonel Wright's Red Coat* for his mythical or merely false saga."

I chose him so as to obey what an invincible superstition forbade me to do directly, personally, forcing a messenger on me, a separation between myself and the minor infamy.

"Later on we can take a bottle of cane brandy to the table, if you like. Or wrap it up so you can take it with you, or go bar-hopping in the night, a vice that pleases you so much, one of Frieda's manias. Pablito's stays open all night. Two blocks from here, in back of the Teatro Solis. I told Frieda that you two were inviting us, that you'd won a lot of money at the racetrack. It's a favor, I can't go to Pablito's because of a story involving a tiepin. What was the name of the horse?"

I put my old watch in his baggy suit coat pocket, open as though he were waiting for it.

"Tie." He ordered another cane brandy and rolled his teary eyes. "That's its name. I've had many, a great many dogs in my life, and they were all the same dog and there was one whose name was Tie."

"Don't sell it, Mr. Wright; just pawn it. When you see what makes it is you'll realize that you can ask for several thousand. Pablito will understand too."

The mister left without staggering.

Then, while the Englishman and Frieda were having dessert, Quinteros coffee, and I went on slowly drinking the wine, my chair with two legs leaning against the wall, I felt cheerful and sad, full of something that didn't go by the name of remorse, but very close to a feeling of complicity for having agreed to play the game and the move I'd made in it.

"Then"—Quinteros lied, having now caught on—"we decided to bet the little money we had left on Tie. We knew it wouldn't win, it was impossible, an old nag, stiff-legged, an also-ran. But if luck . . . You understand, Frieda, you must understand us because we gamble the way women do."

"Always idiotically, time and time again," Frieda patiently agreed. The restaurant was beginning to fill up, the theater or the movies were letting out, couples or quartets, several giant-sized family horrors piloted by fat women, one step behind the bald men, with offspring in front and behind.

"Exactly, Frieda; you understand us," Quinteros went on. He took nourishment in the form of a glass of wine; implacable, I thought with amusement. "Everything was lost when the chance to recoup our losses came along, everything except the dirty bills that John Bull and I dug out of our pockets. To tell you in words that only a woman can really understand, everything lost except for hope. Better still: the much-fingered will to hope against all hope. Tie couldn't win, you know, and then we decided to bet on Tie anyway, right on the nose. And just look, darling, how things turn out. Lancaster's pupil came through, a fine show against all odds. Imagine a 1400-to-1 handicap."

"Right, a thousand or thereabouts," Mr. Gleason broke in, sitting far away from the edge of the table, between Quinteros and Frieda, almost outside our party.

"One thousand four hundred and no going back on it," Quinteros insisted. "Once the starting gates went up the jockey, Lein, took the lead together with the son of Splendor and it was no use for Negrito to put the spurs to his mount to get his revenge. The horse from the Alequi stud went on running at a steady pace and in the straight managed to spurt past black Pansy. From behind, because it was impossible from the front, the favorite, Distante, appeared again and looked to be about to steal the lead. But,

Frieda, luck wasn't on the side of Marino's pupil because Tie toughened up and kept the lead down to the wire, only by a nose but the lead just the same."

"Why don't the two of you go to hell," Frieda pleaded, looking for her cigarettes. "How much did you win? We could go somewhere else, this place is filling up with kikes." I sought her eyes, all aglow, that refused to look at me; but the sudden voice, which came close to asthma, couldn't fool me. I searched for faces and bodies at nearby tables without discovering any reasons for her remark.

They went on talking, not about races now but of just anything, and the sentences drifted off and fell, intertwining like distracted and ephemeral fingers. My back in the corner, one shoulder almost exactly touching each wall. I looked at my melancholy, still healthy and friendly. The first touches of sadness, the new failure and the different loneliness had reached me, had kept coming to me with the sound of a moth, of a bonfire in a drizzle, of a puppy scratching at a door. I presume. Because when I realized that the holiday celebration was over, those things were already inside me and were building up a secret sickness that was mine, and my mistress, causing no pain but sensitive, prefactory, patiently training my bones. Not a trace: invisible dust particles.

The adolescent absurdity of the said animal and its rebellion had ended, who knows at what precise unlocatable moment. The no to Santa María, to Brausen, to the masochism of imposed responsibilities.

I was the one scratching now, useless and grown old from an age impossible to make out, or returned without warning to my real age, here, in Lavanda, the hostile limits of the city that I had left and lost; my cheeks were caressed, almost every night, at the variable hour of clear-sightedness and cynicism, by the wetness of the saliva that I had spat out so many months before and that was not returned to me, without trickery or haggling.

Leaning on two legs of the chair and on the corner of the wall,

I contemplated the gestures, heard the intermingled designs of the words above the table that eluded, because of their origin, any respectable meaning.

I sat smoking with a smile on my face, slowly drank the rosé wine, said yes to them out of habit, stood up for the reason of the neediest. I was on the outside, sad and scornful, at peace, but I had to come back inside because Frieda looked at her wrist and said:

"Not a word out of you, Medi? As always, as on occasion, above stupidities and the world."

"Above the stupidities that shape the world," Quinteros corrected.

White and wrinkled, Mr. Wright brought his body up close to the table and leaned his elbows on it. His face rounder and more infantile, resignedly sweating its oily sweat.

"There was cane brandy, a bottle promised. Here or in a place with heat that's just a little more civilized. I'm paying, naturally," he said.

"It's midnight," Frieda went on. "It's the hour when tomfoolery enters the picture. Let's go somewhere else."

"Let's go; choose the place, all of you," I agreed. But the voice hadn't fooled me and the opaque, asthmatic tone now sounded like a hardened patch of plaster.

And now it was beyond all doubt because the new symptom knocked against the edge of the table with persistent little leaps; Frieda's broad hand, always as white as it was dead, protected from all inclemencies and from the mere passage of time, dancing its Cossack dance with its red fingernails, an apparently tireless hand, untamed and free.

I began searching again and made a discovery. He was on my left, two tables away, enormous, fat, young, in profile, drinking his wine between brief bursts of laughter that broke off with an unpredictable hysterical violence. He was in his shirt sleeves, without a tie, to the joy of his double chin, his pot belly almost asleep on his thighs, hearing stories and incapable of speaking, adding with his anxious breathing to the insolence and the ordinariness of life.

That was normal, it had already occurred to us more than twice. I resolutely awaited Frieda's eyes, which kept inventing reasons for not looking at me: the blue tablecloth, the bottles of Chianti strung up by the neck far in the background, the bright glints from the paper mâché that lined the walls of the blue grotto, the strained agility of the waiters, the women's stiff hairdos. I waited without moving, as though I were waiting with my hand upraised for the return of a fly until Frieda's eyes were obliged to turn and look at me telling me yes in anguish, exaggerating her desperation and intelligence.

"I agree, everything is perfect and inevitable," I nodded. "Now, as Fräulein goes to the powder room, we'll play up and discuss a probable rest of the night for her to consider."

Frieda picked up her handbag and walked unhurriedly to the little door decorated with a white A, immutably crossing the zone of vulgarity surrounding the back of the fattened young beast, the laughter and the unbearable odor of the minor debasement.

"The cane brandy," Mr. Wright said.

"The best thing, I suggest, it occurs to me, would be to go to the yacht club in Buceo and wait for dawn on the pier," Quinteros proposed.

"Anything you like, whatever she chooses and says, until she herself comes loose from us like a piece of wrapping paper with no need to throw her out."

"If only there were some cane brandy," Mr. Wright began, correcting himself: "When there is some I'll tell you the story."

"Afghanistan or the strange case of the barren village," Quinteros agreed, making his chestnut-brown hair, his eyeglasses gleam. "But you, Medina, are a gentleman. You're right, we can offer Buceo to Frieda. And if she doesn't care for that, something else."

"Thanks," I said to them. "The money."

"Yes, of course." Still smiling, Mr. Wright searched methodically through his trousers and put the money for the watch on the table. I covered it with one hand and asked for the check.

I was thinking, hastily, losing the pleasure of slow and detailed remembrances, of Frieda involved in the mystery that protects the letter A in bars, restaurants, hospitals, railway stations and schools attended by both boys and girls. I was thinking about Frieda, immediately after Seoane. I was thinking feebly of meetings that led to misunderstandings and of postponements, I was thinking enviously of a supposed Medina, in love with Frieda and of a Frieda in love with Medina. I was thinking that for them Frieda's caresses in the ladies' powder room, either seated or standing, given in homage to the sexuality that the unusual lewdness of the fat young manhood awakened, might have been for them, the hypothetical lovers, an act of union, a secret, inexplicable, powerful enrichment of love.

When Frieda returned, swinging her handbag to and fro, the brief appeasement showed on her face; the bill was paid along with an excessive tip and the warm night, with the characteristic persistence of girls, was growing younger.

Anyone, in Lavanda, on a summer night, can lose a woman merely by being distracted. It's enough to drive a car with an eye out for dangers, looking straight ahead, looking to either side of street intersections with feigned rages and close attention.

I don't know where it was that we lost her. Lavanda occupies an area of only a few kilometers on its surface and above it, but not everywhere do there softly glow, until early morning, a few places that sell alcohol and corners that deceptively extend an invitation to customers to come in and stay dill dawn, till the implacable brightness of daylight.

Quinteros drove the Impala so imprudently and joyfully that

the car seemed to belong to him or was, definitely, someone else's, in transit, smuggled in from Brazil or Paraguay with a questionable destination. Alongside him, Mr. Wright sucked on his sputtering pipe, nearly empty, suggesting morgues and mausoleums.

In the back seat Frieda and I were embracing as in the taxi that had taken us, for the first time, to a brothel that in Lavanda goes by the name of a house with furnished rooms. Slowly and deliberately, accepting the failures with touching surprise, Mr. Wright said in an impassive tone of voice, his accent now heavier:

"Nice night. I mean a nice night for us to look about a little."

When it became necessary to accept Frieda's loss we got out of the car and indifferently reproached each other, soiling the low notes until they turned into gentle soprano diminuendos. Wearying of the farce, we mourned Frieda's disappearance; we agreed that no one was to blame and entered a hopeless cheap bar, down near La Mondiola, our faces and hands illuminated by green neon, greeted by the friendly lie of a placard: "Three Trees—Day and Night."

We sat down and asked for the already reheated tripe soup, left over from long before, with every hint of putrefaction disguised with vinegar the highly spiced special sauce of the house. One of us was drunker than the others, but that was hardly likely, and furthermore, it is of no importance. Mr. Wright finally had half a bottle of cane brandy to savor as he drank it down and then burst. Quinteros, his bright yellow hair plastered down, had ordered wine, which he insisted be certified as a 1952 vintage and it was hard for me to accept the fact that he was that stupid, to believe that he believed in the wines of Lavanda. Equaling the stupidity of tourists by insisting that there be a date on the label of the poison that he drank with caution. I ordered mineral water and was readily taken in by the bubbles, because the two of them were fools or else con men, clever enough to easily sell me an impossible, nonexistent territory.

Then, at some time, I looked at the violet light in a high little window and for no particular reason detested Quinteros's flat yellow head and thrust one elbow forward so as to annoy the Englishman.

"I speak to him, Quinteros, but it's the gringo who really listens. Don't interrupt me, I beg you. He knows and keeps his mouth shut; you think you know and confine yourself to hinting. I may be wrong and everything is the other way around. It doesn't matter to me for now, for this dead night that's being taken away into nothingness, clarity, the shit of daytime. You called me on the phone, from telephonic prehistory you give me a call and gave me an approximate address, you suggested to me, unequivocally, that the voice could be the clue."

"I didn't promise anything, I supposed and wanted to help. Without verifiable evidence, of course, certainly, naturally."

"The sense of hearing and the sixth sense," I slowly said twice, thinking that I was the drunkest one of the three, convincing myself so that they would be obliged to believe it. The Englishman's face lit up even more and his exaggerated, colonial off-white suit fitted him even more tightly, as he joyfully and resignedly drank the cane brandy that was not labeled Ombú. The nearly immobile beast, sweaty and self-absorbed, knew. Quinteros, all good manners and public relations, knew, the same thing, or something else. They weren't going to say what it was or give it away, not that night anyway. Then, pushing impossible chips toward a roulette board with thirty-seven zeros all set to swindle suckers, I went on, carefully gauging the lie and the importance of the failure:

"Hearing and the sixth sense. Every detail was faithful, it was just as you'd told me: an elderly couple, herbs, guitars that will never play, other things, impossible objects hanging in the semi-darkness. Summing the whole thing up is easy: I went, I listened to them, I failed. They were innocent or more cunning than you were. And there I was, believing out of superstition, because of the proximity of the cemetery. It would be very hard for me to explain, we'll talk or I'll talk later. At present I am, by your leave, the little inquisitor and it seems to me that the way for us to come out clean, in a sense that you understand, is for us to discuss things for a while so as to arrive at a final solution."

"I'm listening," Quinteros promised.

"Talking," the Englishman said. "You're talking and I don't know why. I mean the mysteries. Sometimes I like them, and at other times I don't, depending on how my liver is doing, I think."

I didn't even look at their faces; their bodies, so different, had the same immobility and a long-standing, invulnerable reticence. I filled my glass with soda water and wine and smiled at the ceiling as I moved an unlit cigarette on top of the table.

"Perfect," still looking at the roof and without hope. "There exists a place, a thing, a thought called Santa María for all of us.'

"I beg your pardon," Quinteros said; he looked at his polished fingernails, the white silver lighter between his fingers. "I'm in no hurry till eight a.m. But the prologue seems long, repetitive and perhaps unnecessary. You went, you listened and you're sure you've failed."

"That's not it, you know perfectly, diabolically well that the little inquisitor doesn't wish, for the moment, to speak of trivial things. I've been stumbling into pitfalls or wandering off on detours. I think there's a trap, but I don't know where it is or who set it."

"I tried to help you," Quinteros said; the Englishman helped out with the sound of his pipe.

"It's possible. It's true that I asked you to help me. But perhaps neither of you can say what sort of help was involved."

"You wanted to search. I didn't."

"Cards face up on the table. Frieda is missing, but we all are keeping a place for her. Me first of all. Escaped from Santa María in Manfredo's boat, a fugitive without a passport or a permit. Kid

Manfredo, the very man I had to arrest or kill. Orders from above; crime, smuggling. Me, Medina. And just as I meet him at the farmhouse whose access was hidden by trees or bushes that have never grown along the edge of that river, at the very moment that I'm a hero, I walk in alone and put my hand with the pistol on the table before he can grab his revolver (zealous guardian of law and order arrests a dangerous smuggler), just then. It makes a person think; but no explanation understandable by imbeciles, the two of you and I, the much-missed Frieda, the people I know or can imagine never approached me that afternoon as dusk was falling, or at any time after that. I've been turning the memory over in my mind till I've worn it out, but I'm still fond of it. Just then, just at the very moment when. You two know the river front, you who aren't in a hurry till eight a.m. The part of the river front at the bend, there where the sandbank descends abruptly and the water is fifteen meters deep within three steps and on summer nights it's full of couples, of naked youngsters and machos playing at being about to commit suicide so that the girls will plead with them and get all hot and bothered. But it wasn't a summer night, it was a fall afternoon and Kid Manfredo was waiting for the sun to go down, with his revolver and one of the bottles stolen from the contraband on top of the table. I recognized him: thin, brown eyes, around forty, white skin with a tan, a markedly receding hairline at the temples. An egotistical, calm look in his eyes, a black knitted sailor's pullover, a cap with an admiral's anchor.

" 'You fucked me, chief,' he said to me, not using the familiar *tú*, neither asking nor accepting.

"It was then, just as I was able to get my hands on him after months, false trails, early mornings as cold as they were wasted. I sat down opposite him, on the lookout for one of his sly tricks every minute and covered his revolver with my hat. Just think: he had three at my back and I had ten with long-range rifles up on the hill with instructions to wait for whistles or the first shot. If they can, Quinteros or Mr. Wright, they help me or try their luck with any sort of nonsense. Maybe they're better off than I am; I still don't understand."

"Naturally," Quinteros put in patiently, "there weren't any shots. Or whistles, even."

"No, there wasn't anything. No facts, Mr. Wright," I repeated, knowing that it was useless, a routine as old as more months than fit in a year, the brief laughter, the glass of wine, another cigarette, the slow stroking of matted hair. The pause that I effortlessly defended.

"Nothing, you asinine brothers. Kid Manfredo raised one finger and from behind came a clean glass. He put one hand to his mouth and filled the two glasses now on the table with the contraband, maybe fake Martell. When a person comes up against a mystery, begging your pardon, an act that he committed without understanding and time passes and that he still doesn't understand, he looks for consolation or support to great events that have befallen others. I reached the point, some time later, of repeating from memory. Paul's words on the road. He filled the glasses without discourtesy and we raised them without a sound or so much as my lightly clinking them, with the three thugs at my back and the black Colt in my paralyzed right hand, Kid Manfredo with his body lolling in the chair with a sudden languor, his eyes half open, pretending to be at ease and bored. We downed our drinks and then it was just the right moment, it was when. If there was anyone in the world I could swear by to guarantee my sincerity, I'd swear, since you and everybody else and maybe even I myself are people who need to have a person swear to the truth. Not the Kid. He didn't need to speak words or listen to them; he was waiting—and perhaps not even that— for movements and things to happen."

"It was then when," Quinteros remembered, without hurrying me, taking a cigarette.

"It was then when," I agreed. "The only thing I can swear to is that I wasn't afraid, that I knew that a wink from the Kid could make the nape of my neck go flying off; but that this wasn't—the autumn sun was already going down—the most important thing."

"Yes," Quinteros said, with a smile that so closely resembled friendship. "I don't want to interrupt, you understand. I for my part would make him blind and a traveling country singer, I would listen to him going about the shacks of the day laborers on the cattle ranches or country estates of Lavanda telling about happenings and accompanying himself on a guitar without a bass string. But Kid Manfredo was a millionaire and his fortune is still growing. Kid Manfredo works for the patriots who are in command in Santa María and in Lavanda. If you came, begging your pardon, to capture him on that late afternoon in the fall as dusk was falling, it must have been because he was betrayed."

"But the launch took off."

"But there weren't any shots or whistles. And don't get the idea that I'm forgetting your sandbank sloping steeply down, the division camouflaged in the woods, the influence of an autumn dusk with no wind. We'll add soft lights on the water and, if I'm not annoying you, a presentiment that you'd go somewhere else. Betting, I'd say, without taking it back, that the old man was betrayed by you. All that is yours, generously granted you, and with no objections. You can use it however you like. Mr. Wright, I suppose, agrees."

"Oh, it's all yours," the Englishman said, and sucked his resuscitated pipe until his laughter was cut off by a fit of coughing.

"Whatever you like. But you two don't understand Chief of Police Medina, nor do I understand the dead. There were no other millions but the bottle of cognac and a couple of packages or so of cigarettes. Accepting money from him would have been the same as staying in Santa Maria or continuing to be me. And let me add, if it's any concern of yours, and it's all the same to me if you know it or not, if it matters to your or not, if you collect a salary in one or in both intelligence services, the fact is that Kid Manfredo is still sailing. If we happen to run into each other, all we do is greet each other with a wave of the hand, a smile, and an averting of our eyes. As you'll understand, that afternoon we discovered we were friends; not very intimate ones but forever."

"And you here, Frieda, all the rest. And he has cattle ranches here and there and he bought, or almost bought, Latorre Island so as to be able to do his work more easily."

"So I heard. And on his travels, aside from small planes, all he brings in is gringo cigarettes or gringo whisky or gringo spare parts for just about anything. He also brings in men and the men bring in submachine-guns and grenades and go and come. You can tell everybody; the Kid and I will go on smiling, counting the dead and the millions that the military announce, sometimes reducing the number, and at other times exaggerating how many. I know, there are lonely people and people who have starved to death. But none of the four of us. I'm including Frieda. All of us with money to earn, all of us with an ambition that, if we were in the same position, would smell bad; all of us with a love or its repellent caricature, all of us with a future headed for the worm farm. All of us with a motive, in a word, and if you follow me. And it was just then when, dear dumb animals, with no possibility of ever knowing the cause, I put away my idiotic pistol, took my hat off his revolver because I was beginning to feel the cold and wanted to protect my head from it. I suddenly felt, without relief or sadness, that I had ceased to have any motive. I poured myself another glass and asked Kid Manfredo: 'What time do we go across?'"

ANOTHER JOURNEY

Because of a tacit promise and on my word of honor as a man, that had never been put into words but had suddenly come over me, I was obliged to tell the now nonexistent Quinteros—who now was called Osuna or some sort of Jew threatened by the Catholic Sovereigns and a convert—I was obliged to tell him of my second attempt to escape.

Apart from the sixth one, the possibility came from, might come from, ears, voices, words, little truths and great lies that everyone ignored.

I never acted like a gentleman with the defunct Quinteros, Osuna, great-grandson of a friar, a draftsman who wandered about the city of Santiago de Chile. I never told him the story that begins and ends in the shop in Lavanda, next to the Central Cemetery, where a pink and ash-colored couple, an elderly couple, kept me waiting with a controlled and smiling hostility. Nothing. It was true, a big old house, marble staircases, he or she in a so-called writing room with windows overlooking the river and one orders violin, viola, cello, guitar strings, and out of caprice, if one so desires, bass violin strings. The two of them and the enormous, disconcerting photographs on the walls: in oval frames, sepia-colored, three or four generations and a careless slip, fresher, grayish, with two minuscule figures to the left of the unmistakable cathedral of Santa María.

And the two of them: the same white hair, mare's haunches for the old woman, almost a dwarf secreting honey when her hand touches yours. He, tall, heavy-set, round and good, positioned in the background at his own request, with just at touch of irony, talking to you with his voice of a chosen low C on the viola. It is obvious that he is trustful and she is not. That they began to play at sex when they were fourteen and still love each other today, and I almost speak of adoration, this being the only acceptable way of loving at the age of eighty, sixty-five or sixty of those years lived together, thanks to irony, jokes, ridicule, unavoidable tenderness.

Yes, Quinteros Osuna; they had been in Santa María, they had not left the Colony since the day that their tiny, impossible, and respectable *Mayflower* brought them from Europe. They did not leave the Colony (if such a thing means leaving) except for Sundays when the two-wheeled carriage hired at first and later on their own took them to Mass in the city. Which was a matter of concern to me for the first time: why, being Catholics, had they left their Protestant German Switzerland?

But, in any case, there they were, surrounded by dead and fresh branches, there they were, there they had been, looking down on me with mild gaiety, waggishly, agreeing that they had lived in the Colony and refusing any explanation that went beyond covetousness of the mystery of their second emigration. They had nothing to do with me, with the supposed group of us, those accursed, rebels, yearning to return.

"It was no longer possible to live."

With no need to touch each other, happy in the certainty that it was not necessary, not any longer, to unite their bodies so as to defend the sacred from any attempt at intromission, sure that time, faith and the God to whom they prayed had erected—and not for nothing—a barricade that separated what is secret from what is filthy. Almost motionless, inscrutable, and to all appearances forever.

Together and smiling, poor deceitful Osuna, leaning on each other unintentionally—or else it was a matter of an intention as old as forgetfulness—so as to make it impossible for one of them, she or he, to slip, to fall, into the always suicidal trap of death. She or he who had loved each other since they were fourteen above and below all known words and all the words that a genius or a stammering imbecile might make up to express the inexpressible, to belittle and besmirch that sixty-five-year-old purity.

THE TEMPTATION

In the prologue of an unbelievable time, I almost utter the ineffable name—Gurisa—in front of Frieda, who was painting her twenty nails. One of her manias.

"What's become of Olga?" I asked in a distracted voice. "What's become of Juanina?"

Frieda looked at me, almost smiling, blew on her fingers.

"Juanina sometimes drops by. Still as rude and mysterious as ever. I don't know a thing about Olga. She phoned once or twice and you weren't in. Or she phoned and I wasn't in either."

I was grateful for Juanina's mystery because I had cashed Carve's check. Nobody knew it, nobody asked. I remembered that they had begun to tear down the old market and I made up my mind to go have a look at the state of my studio, to see what things deserved to be and were able to be rescued.

First I saw the letter on the floor and I was immediately stunned, buried in the din of the demolition. Pickaxes chipping away over my head, pickaxes farther away—in the southern section of the Market—the blows of the enormous steel and lead ball persistently knocking down façades, cornices, partitions. But the cloud of dust had not reached my room and the letter said:

I don't know how long it's been that I've been looking for you calling the lesbian's house and getting nowhere. I

don't know if you're here or if you're alive. Who knows
whether she's hiding you from me, she's quite capable
though she used to be different. Before everything comes
tumbling down call me at the office after five and say
you're my brother because they've taken it into their heads
to control everything. I have lots of brothers. Ciao,
handsome. Olgurisa.

For half a month or twenty days we lived in bed and the sky
turned to dust kept falling into the room; we went out to eat and
while Gurisa tried to sleep I tried to paint, with less faith by the
day, indifferent to the sounds of the demolition of the Market,
but attentive to my inner apathy, to the disobedience of my
hands, to the errors of my eyes. There was no more electric light,
we bought a smelly kerosene lamp and the fearful blows of the
enormous metal ball landed closer and closer each day.

Until one morning the three of us went into the studio/one-
room apartment and the intruder said:

"So you haven't caught on. This is all coming down and we'd
have to pay for things as though they were new. If the two of you
agree I'm calling the firemen."

Luckily, we were asleep, separate but naked. Behind the aforementioned ill-mannered individual was the bright daylight
framed by the complicated geometry of the caved-in wall. The
great murderous ball of the Almighty was slowly revolving
against a blue background already tinged with autumn.

Indifferent to the grimy presence of the man and his sneering
and domineering phrases, I unhurriedly dressed, waved in the air
the shoulder holster with the pistol stolen from Brausen, took
out a large-denomination bill and held it out to him by one
corner.

"Shut up and clear out of here. Or I swear to you that tomorrow you won't be working here anymore."

He hesitated and stopped smiling; he said no more, sought my

139

eyes. I had known lots of riffraff of that sort in the detachment in Santa María. My new clothes or the pistol or my bluff made him calmly grab the money and he went off by walking into the incomprehensible design on the smashed-in wall.

Gurisa was completely hidden by the sheet and blanket lying higgledy-piggledy on top of her. I told her to get dressed to go to the restaurant. I rummaged about in the rags with paint stains and turpentine on them till I found the money wadded up into a ball.

"But I tell you, she's as mean as they come," Gurisa went on insistently in the dilapidated taxi. "It doesn't matter to me that she likes women. But she shouldn't be envious and think she owns you. You pamper her, though. Whenever I looked for you, in the apartment, on the beach, in the market, she put me off the scent every time, she told me she didn't know a thing about you. That she hadn't seen you for months. And now you tell me it was all a lie."

We'd entered the silence of a dark street. The taxi driver saw, as I did, that a diagonal wooden barrier was indicating to us that we couldn't go any farther. But with a faith shared with no one else he honked his horn three times, waited for a moment in vain and said to us again:

"We're going to Nostra's place or we're getting out of here."

"To Nostra's," I answered him. As though I'd said Kuwait or the Falkland Islands.

The failures had made Gurisa angry, filled me with rancor. I said to her:

"I have a good-luck charm and it's the only hope. If you'd put it on a thin finger." It was a little lead ring.

She'd already said no. But that was to be in limbo, with paradise suspended in the sky and the inferno of closed-circuit coitus. And time and shelters were going by. Finally, at some vague moment, after refusing in disgust, with a profile of mortal and unpardonable offense, intermittently outlined by the dreary light of the street lamps, she accepted the ring and said:

"Shit. Another whore."

The magic talisman that I'd offered her, bearing a Judas Thaddeus and a St. Pancras, with a red thread joining the medals, was a present from Juanina.

"It's never failed me," I said to her.

And as, anxiously and resignedly, she rubbed the ring against her visible cheek, we passed by three houses with no vacancies, three houses of assignation, three places of fornication and brief bliss.

Until she, her mouth wide open and feeling ill, confessed:

"Tell the driver we're going to Carreño's. Tell him you're a friend of Carreño's. Larsen,' she added, practically weeping.

I hesitated and was afraid. I thought she was just a touch crazy, but that was quite enough.

"Tell him," she persisted in a hoarse, trembling voice, as though we were already in bed.

I did so and the man grumbled:

"You should have spoken up sooner."

The car hung a wicked U-turn in the dark and we went back the way we'd come, entered a different darkness, in a plausible tree-lined avenue.

"Carreño," the taxi driver said happily, remembering him well, almost a friend.

But Gurisa, with the silver or lead ring on her fingertip, was all absorbed in the steam on the windowpane. And the only thing that matters, I thought, is her naked body, her odor and knowingness.

Carreño's taxi-driver friend had a word with a waiter and said to me: "Room fourteen." I paid and went searching along the monotonous row of metallic curtains. Gurisa had already gone downstairs and spoke with another waiter who had the voice of an invert; after that I lost her in the darkness.

Carreño was generous and had the heat turned on in October in room fourteen, with an anteroom and everything else necessary. But Gurisa wasn't there.

I stretched out on the bed, face up, lighted a cigarette; my hands underneath the nape of my neck, the cigarette ash barely burning my chin. Gurisa lost forever or else there'd never been a Gurisa. Until I picked up the telephone and explained how lonely I was.

Somebody said:

"In a minute. Sorry. A mix-up. It'll all be straightened out."

"Yes, everything always gets straightened out. But too late sometimes. Send me up a bottle of whisky. The least poisonous kind you've got."

It's true that my curiosity, my nostalgia, were getting all mixed up with a confused ranco. Carreño, whoever he was, was innocent of the fact that his employess had confused fourteen and sixteen. But I had said "a friend of Carreño's." And since childhood. So I had to fill up the time that we'd been friends. So I distracted myself by investigating an old and feeble reason for hating him, the memory of a dirty trick he'd played on me in a believable and remote past, when we cautiously lost our way in the dark of the farms that surrounded a city so as to steal green fruit from them.

I also remembered that the manservant, with a foreign accent and almost certainly an invert, had told Gurisa, unmistakably, room sixteen. There's no way out except to tell about it and sometimes details please me, as does the device of the unexpected.

Minutes went by, the bottle came and the servile smile, and it occurred to me—when I had to get up to throw the cigarette into the toilet because there weren't any ashtrays, since the clients take them away with them because they're kleptomaniacs or out of fidelity to what they call an unforgettable night—that my slight hatred of Carreño, the one real friend, a stranger to me, that life had brought me, might be based on what a certain Marx brother had tried to explain to me in Santa María. He was a gigolo with the beard of a ship's captain, and used to say that everything's a question of money.

Then, if the aforementioned brother was right instead of another one more economically bearded, also from Santa María, who was looking for support though not repose in the tribulations inherent in the relationships that one had with one's grandmother, my mild hatred of Carreñito stemmed not from the errors of his men or computers, but from a simple envy that I had never felt before, a poor man's healthy and amibitious envy of a rich one—and now an errant and humble one—with no friends among the satrapy of Lavanda, a poor man without a grandmother.

I sat down in the subdued light of the bed and accepted the fact that my revulsion for Carreñito, never manifested in childhood, was born of the mere fact that he had managed to get his hands on five million so as to pay the bribe that permitted him to turn a tidy profit on the generous house on the Calle Iglesias. I, on the other hand, did not have, among other things I lacked, even one woman in the suite with a living room, bedroom and bathroom.

I forgave, I believed that I had forgotten Carreño forever, when the woman who had made the mistake came into the room, badly dressed and wriggling, more stupid than ugly.

Getting to my feet I showed her the palm of my hand, like a greeting of the Nganska tribe, and put one finger to my lips.

"If you'll just stay quiet, if you don't say a word . . ." I said. "Don't worry, it can all be straightened out."

She agreed to stay in the living room and await her private destiny, separated from me by the transparent curtains. But I was forced to endure hearing, amid her tears, a little handkerchief for her watery snot, the story of her life.

None of you can even feel your way along or lean for support on the edge of the fury, the bliss or the bittersweet disgrace of the little woman—wearing a hat—lost forever in apartment fourteen or sixteen of my buddy Carreño's place.

The little beast wept with her back to me; she respected the curtain separating the little antechamber and the bed. Growing bored, certain of a happy ending, I smoked, barely nibbled at the whisky, relaxed in an easy chair in the shadow:

"The best husband a woman ever had, the kindest, the most macho. And we've got three kids, all of them so blond that they don't look like they're either his or mine. Two, four, five and a half. May God forgive me and you too and everybody who wants to throw stones at me. I don't know what to call it, a rash impulse or having the hots, because all four are mistaken and I don't know if some day, which I hope never comes, I'll meet up with that one again. With you who have seen my face and never in a lifetime can my face ever be forgotten. I don't care whether he's got a pot belly or is a skinny blond who's losing his hair. But the other guy who let himself get lost like an idiot and is entirely to blame and here I am being kept waiting, knowing that I can't go back home after ten, no lie of mine is going to stay fresh till ten o'clock at night. And the whole thing, the three kids, my husband, all because that idiot who maybe made me get lost just for the fun of it tonight, just look at the calendar, this night that was going to be the first time, and a woman imagines things beforehand and can't be sure if it'll happen or not. You understand so much seeing him come from the office next door, all smiles and little thoughtfulnesses, roses, a brief encounter in a tea shop, but already wetting myself to say yes to him, more curiosity than a case of the hots for him, though you may not believe me. Married for seven years and never once, there comes a moment and a woman closes her eyes and that moment came for me, and it's the last one and it's all a big laugh."

She went on crying or making those noises; when I stubbed the second cigarette out against the wall, the telephone rang.

They explained to me once again the equation fourteen-sixteen, please excuse us, we'll fix things right away. But when I went to give the good news to the married woman who'd made a mistake, there was no adulteress to speak to. Not even the odor or the perfume of a woman in search of yet another unpredictable room number.

I went back to bed, had another cigarette. My duty, I realized, was to be worried, to be upset as to Gurisa's whereabouts, to ask the photo on the calendar for the month of March—imported hanging vines, shadowy sheep above a vague whiteness, of snow or sand—where she might be, in what room of the brothel, among what sort of people, keeping what words to herself.

Gurisa, God giveth and God taketh away. It was possible that she would make her way through the labyrinth of rooms, stupidities and telephone cables and come back to me. She might cover me with syphilitic sores from the soles of my feet to the crown of my head or it might suffice if she merely stretched out on the hard coolness of the sheets.

But Gurisa didn't come and when I was certain, when I forgot her variable faces and the curves of her fingers, I stripped naked so as to rub against the sheets, go on smoking and waiting in the peace where there floated other thoughts more important than she was, older than I was. Why, I thought, do they allow someone who is born tired and already on the way back to be born; why is someone born with a lukewarm will, someone waiting for death and Gurisa doesn't come?

Perhaps there was an answer and it was on its way to me, I thought; but a second before that the telephone rang and out came the voice of the exotic young pederastic manservant.

I told him yes, of course, I understand, it's quite all right, thanks, thinking of his buttocks squeezed into black bullfighter's pants too small for him; his fancy shirt, his virile determination not to waggle his behind even though he couldn't help moving like that.

"Everything's all right, Manolete," I said, thanking him again for calling.

"El Cordobés, if you don't mind," he said angrily and affectionately and hung up.

I didn't have all that much money in my pockets, but the bills were already flattened out between the sheet and the mattress; I had cigarettes, a member that swelled up and then turned violet, I had hopes that a woman whose name might be Gurisa was on her way.

Perhaps we were separated forever; I would never again hear her moans atop the sheet or be entangled in the snare of her naïve lies. I was alone and sad, the bottle half empty. Without knowing why I decided to write a letter from a shipwreck victim which, now, she'd never read. In the desk, an imitation antique secretaire, I found wrinkled paper with an elegant letterhead discreetly placed in the upper left-hand corner: Carreño House.

I took a swallow and got to work:

"No, Gurisa, there was no need for anything but bed and oblivion. The fear born in childhood or adolescence of never being in debt to a woman. But you were out of your head and your madness found its support in me, in my own madness, which you gradually gave rise to and used in order to increase your own, little by little, until you and I accepted, mistakenly, the fact that being mad was the equivalent of normal people's being in love. Without thinking, Gurisa, that all the sufferings and happinessses of true lovers barely scratched the surface of our anguish, the desperate and novel desire to know each other's soul and innermost vitals, to construct a hermaphroditic unity that would naturally and joyfully support four arms, four legs, a single brain, a single sex organ doggedly searching for ecstasy and communion.

"If I swear, if we swear, if we promise, Gurisa, to tell the truth about them, the story lasted seventy-two hours, enough time for the protests of the poor and hunger strikes. But being a man and woman who were unemployed because of impossible ambitions, because of their illusory belief that it is possible to commit the sin of lust to its utmost degree—the sole path to the absolute, the eternal and the minor belief in genuine communication—Gurisa and I were never within time. We came and went without anyone suspecting."

I was about to sign the letter when there was another knock on the door. It wasn't Gurisa, but a man wearing a hat, with a pleasant earthy odor of damp soil, or remote spaces, a stranger. But I said:

"Hello there, chief," and he came into the room slowly, swaying back and forth, skinny, short, easily mistakable, and apparently tamed.

I began to recognize him when he walked over to the mirror to pull gently on the wings of the black butterfly he was wearing as a necktie.

I was a little drunk and that man had died years before. He went over and sat down in the chair that I had used to write my letter; he turned it around so as to show himself to me in profile.

"Larsen . . .? Larsen," I murmured, in a funereal voice.

"Why don't you call me Corpse-collector? Collector. Carreño. Coming from you it doesn't offend me." He spoke these words with a subtle, aloof sneer. He barely stirred the silence with a snort.

I saw him grab distractedly and resignedly, the worms that were crawling from his nose to his mouth. When there were several of them snaking across the floor he thrust his shoe forward and crushed them to death with the sound of a brief, repeated sigh.

"Sorry," he said, "it's my illness." He spoke without moving his milky face. "I didn't want to bother you. I contributed a little to the confusion of rooms and the rest was just bad luck. When all is said and done I'm indebted to you and it pleases me to pay up by telling you so."

"In debt to me? So many years have gone by . . . I don't understand."

"If you don't remember it's because you didn't even realize. And so the debt is greater and I have to pay more. Just think: you were the chief of police and I a poor pimp who'd gone broke, which is the worst failure that a man can experience in this world. Santa María. And in all the many times we met, you never even called me *tú*."

"That's no doubt true, I wasn't in the habit."

"Yes, you were different. We treated each other almost as equals. As we're doing now."

The night was wearing on and Gurisa was still lost. And what could this man come back to life want of me . . .? He was now using a handkerchief to gather up the worms and nodded his head as though saying yes to a memory. Then he looked straight at me and said in a voice that was very different, almost soundless:

"Don't worry, the girl will be here right away. As soon as I phone. I found out that you were here another night. With another woman. I didn't want to bother you then because at the time I didn't have what I'm going to show you now. Why did you bolt from Santa María?"

"Because I was fed up, because I was smothering to death, because I hated Brausen."

"And now you're wandering around Lavanda, I'm told, dying to go back."

"Yes, I miss it now. I was born there."

"And Brausen threw me out in a very nasty way. That's what they say. But I'm the same anywhere on the planet. This is where I live and have my house. And with fake mirrors in every room. And they're all bugged too. But I've gotten bored. Because they all do the same thing, mind you, even though they think they're inventing something new. And they say the same inane things or tell the same lies. It's disgusting, but they pay. Well, I didn't come here to talk about myself. But wait just a minute."

He rose to his feet and went over and picked up the phone. He muttered something vulgar and I heard him say:

"Send her up."

He went back to his chair; I was sitting on the bed with the glass of whisky in my hand. The sound of car doors slamming came from below. He smiled, forgiving me for living.

"You can go to Santa María whenever you like. And without its costing you a thing, without even making a trip. Listen: I've never wasted ammunition on vultures, so I've never bought a single one of those books that those who are dying of the cold over there called sacred books, nor have I read any of them. I can't do it, but you can. What I mean is, go through the test I'm proposing to you. Because I got my degree from the university of the streets and you're a man who reads. Listen: a friend told me abut those books in the Residents' Center. And, as we were talking, he showed me a piece of one. Wait."

He leaned down and put one hand into the back pocket of his trousers and took out a black billfold with a metal monogram or decoration. He rummaged about among the bills till he found a worn piece of folded paper.

"Read it," he said to me.

In addition to the doctor, Díaz Grey, and the woman, I had the city where both of them lived. I now had the provincial city where the two windows of Díaz Grey's consulting room overlooked the main square. I was smiling, surprised and grateful because it was so easy to make out a new Santa María in the spring night. The city with its steep drop and its river, the brand-new hotel and, in the streets, the men with tanned faces mechanically exchanging jokes and smiles.

I held the paper out to Larsen, but he raised one hand.

"No," he said, "it's for you."

Another knock on the door, timid, almost secret. I left the bed and opened the door, stepping aside so Gurisa could come in. She had a new smile, which I had seen on another woman's face, who knows where or when. She came in, standing tall and straight and walked past the owner without looking at him. The latter barely tipped his hat, but I had time to catch a glimpse of his sparse gray hair combed forward, like a thin silver skullcap meant to minimize his baldness.

I sat down again, Gurisa stretched out on the bed, at my back, and I heard her open her handbag and light a cigarette. From then on it was as though she neither saw nor heard Larsen, as though he felt that he was alone with me.

"Brausen." He stretched out as though to take his afternoon nap and lay there inventing Santa María and all the stories. It was obvious.

"But I was there. So were you."

"It's set down in writing, that's all. There's no evidence. So I say to you again: do the same thing. Stretch out on the bed, and invent too. Make up the Santa María that you like best, lie, dream up people and things, events."

"You haven't asked me so far what the devil happened to me," Gurisa said to my back.

Larsen rose to his feet and squashed to death against his nose, with his index finger and his thumb, the last worm.

"Think about it," he said. "It's easy for you. You can stay here as long as you like. At no charge. There's room service, for meals I mean."

I got up to go with him to the door and despite the worms I didn't find it repellent to shake the cold of his hand.

I went back to the bed; Gurisa had made an ashtray out of an envelope and was holding it between her breasts.

"This is going to be an honeymoon," I said to her. "We're going to stay here for a few days till boredom sets in."

Gurisa smiled happily.

"Really? The whole time together?"

I nodded and she added:

"Then I'm going to find some way of changing those curtains. They're horrible."

PART TWO

ALMOST TRAMPLING UNDERFOOT

Almost trampling underfoot the hands of beggars and thieves, Medina entered the shadow of the arcades of the old market of Santa María and stopped to take off his hat and wipe his forehead with his handkerchief. Faded, pale, the large cloth sign read: WRITTEN BY BRAUSEN. He might or might not have left the key on the dashboard of the car, but it didn't matter. He breathed hard, looking over his shoulder at the ragged riffraff, silenced and treacherous.

As on every Saturday afternoon, the men were seated in a horseshoe, barefoot or in espadrilles, wearing sombreros, scratching their armpits or poking their fingers inside greasy paper containers or oil cans with scraps of food. A few naked and swollen-bellied children snaked their way along, avoiding the idle bodies and dodging swift slaps. A few old women were knitting yarn dyed rabid colors. "Till nightfall," Medina thought; "and the gangs of adolescent boys and girls and motorcycles and papa's cars who discovered the filth of the market this year."

(To get plastered and dance half smothered to death at Barrientos's place or the German's, the boys with reddish checkered shirts and the long locks of a filthy woman; the girls, the ones who are going to shine brightly for two or three summers and then explode and go out, the girls with their tight-fitting cowboy pants and unbuttoned blouses. And when it begins to get light and trucks arrive loaded with fruit and vegetables from the Colony, they'll take off like a flash for the sandpits of Villa Petrus to play at switching partners, a game with surprises. Then, when the invaders' bursts of irrational laughter begin, the supine flock of bums and scroungers will stand up and stretch as one and begin moving off and separating so as to take their places in the hovels that the city offers them, each one on his own, with no need to make plans together and negotiate. Maybe the women will disappear with the kids or just take them and put them to sleep in the shack and come back with powdered faces, to maraud, to wait for the Colonists to come out drunk and haggard from staying up all night. And tomorrow, Sunday, or when the painful brightness of the moon comes along, the formal accusations will begin to rain down in the Department, where the cell is a moth-eaten room that at one time was a bedroom, the accusations against persons unknown.)

He put his handkerchief away, put on his old-fashioned hat and stared straight at the broken-down and submissive smiles that they had kept turned toward him. He was standing in front of the market, beneath the furious white sun, so as to perform a fake act, pious and pointless. He put one hand in the pocket of the jacket he'd taken off and rained coins down on the shifting area where snot-nosed kids were running around.

Leaning on his counter, Barrientos had seen him as the dusty Ford came to a stop, smoking in the light from the street. Worried and resigned, he watched him get out of the car, cross the beginning of the siesta, slowly and casually make his way through the sinuous line of drowsy bodies. Motionless, wavering between an atavistic hatred and an obscure unavowable sympathy, remembering his transgressions and translating them into fines, stubbornly resisting removing from a table the bottle of contraband cane brandy he'd brought over to a customer, he saw him halt in the shade, wipe his face with his handkerchief, throw a little pile of coins at the swirl of ragged kids. He remembered his most grievous sin, hidden in the basement.

"The son of a bitch," he thought dispassionately, professionally. "Two or three pesos. The amount it costs him to bribe them. And he must feel like God, right now, or at least free of all sin listening to the retired whores who give him a 'Thanks señor chief,' wagging their snouts and needlessly covering up their empty sagging tits and looking at his goodness reflected in the grateful faces of the young roughnecks who would gladly, and he knows it, plunge a knife into his ribs.

Barrientos saw him come ahead in the shadow, white, tall, thin, ridiculous, meticulously dressed in white, with nothing dark about him except for his tie, loosened a little, handing outside his jacket, and his hard impassive face tanned by the sun. He saw him stop again, hanging back a little, his legs slightly apart, already in the damp, fresh, fragrant interior of the market, and look from one side to the other, with the swift, alert and ambitious glances of the occupation that he had chosen or that he had to thank someone for and accept.

He saw him, young and old, cordial and no one's friend, measure with an overbearing nod of his head the dark vastness of the empty market, and then come ahead to the counter where he, Barrientos, was waiting, readying answers without moving, cleverly apathetic, framed by the multicolored posters advertising various liquors.

Medina took his hat off again, without greeting him or before doing so, and his bony face turned toward the table, the only one occupied, where a little old man, freshly shaven, was holding a pipe clenched in his teeth and twiddling his thumbs facing a bottle of cane brandy on which no customs duties had been paid at the border.

Barrientos straightened up slightly and said with a smile: "Hello there, chief."

He saw him run his hand through his stiff, short, black hair.

Then, as always—every Saturday night for months at the beginning, when Medina had just come back to Santa María and had perhaps dropped in at the cheap bars in the market just for a little diversion—as each time he saw Medina smooth down with unconscious rage his anachronistically young, stubborn hair and joylessly bare his sharp-pointed white teeth, Barrientos calculated without hope what and how much there was about the chief that was different from Santa María and from all the men he had ever known.

"What'll it be, chief? With soda, as usual?"

"No. I want some of that cane brandy, with soda." He pointed with his chin toward the man with the extinguished pipe.

Barrientos went over to the table and fetched the bottle. After pouring himself some, Medina leaned down to look at the table and stroked it with his fingernail.

"For me, it's on the house. But is it worth the risk?"

"Yeah," Barrientos said offhandedly, punching the cork in with the palm of his hand. "There are lots of customers and they pay for it."

"Sure . . . Queers and little whores?"

"Them too. But they're not the only ones."

"Do you think Santa María's a disgusting city? The thought crosses my mind sometimes."

"I couldn't say, chief. I don't have much to compare it with. It seems to me it must be like all the rest of them. Can I take the bottle back to the table? It's the only one there is."

Medina looked at his face for a moment and said yes. He stood at the counter by himself and it was as though he were alone in the empty market and, through his own choice, alone in the world.

He tilted his head to one side to look toward the street, the clot of worms writhing together in the sun, to no conceivable purpose, sweating, giving off almost imperceptibly into the air their malevolent, wretched odors, roasted to the rigidity of objects. The inner side of the brick arcade, its paint faded, covered with graffiti, seemed to be falling, idly silently, to ruins, in the blue shadow. Then he looked at his straw hat on the counter and the face of Barrientos, who had come back and was standing there waiting, indifferent, ill-shaven, a swindler.

"You haven't touched your glass, chief," he said slowly. "I've got a little ice—forgot to ask you if you'd like some."

Without looking, Medina stretched out one hand and placed it around the precarious coolness of the glass. He scrutinized the bar-owner's dead-still eyes, dark and empty, free of any sort of expression, surrounded, in the semi-darkness, by the static gleam of the bottles and the bright-colored promises of the fly-specked posters. He found nothing and began to divert himself, to surrender to the fury of failure.

"There's no need for any," he said. "The soda's cold." He contained himself and sighed; he downed the glass in silence, not at all thirsty, in little swallows. The flies buzzed invisibly, the years-old smell of vegetables, blood and fish began to seep out from the market counters and the paving stones.

"Another one, chief?" Barrientos asked.

"No. Who's that man?"

Barrientos didn't turn around toward the back of the man with the pipe, who went on pouring himself cane brandy, muttering, twiddling his thumbs. He continued to look at Medina, or more exactly, he revealed to him without insolence his expressionless eyes.

"I don't know," he said. "I've never found out what his name is. When he asks me for credit he notes it down under the name 'the Englishman.' He always pays up, before the tenth. I think he gets a pension from the railroad company. He never picks fights with anybody."

"He's lucky. Not to have to."

"To each his own fate," Barrientos said quietly.

Medina smiled and sighed again. The sensation of everything

being a game, the certainty of the usual triumphant ending, that familiar territory, marked off by risks he could get out of, which he took pleasure in exaggerating.

"To each his own fate," he repeated.

From somewhere, from behind the shelf full of bottles, the optimistic advertisements and Barrientos's bald head, held motionless, awaiting something inevitable that couldn't really matter to him, an old woman appeared, walking along without a sound.

"Chief," she greeted him. Medina bared his teeth at her and stroked the stiff ends of his hair. She brought her mouth close to Barrientos's head as he leaned it backward but didn't move away.

She had gray braids, bright mocking eyes, dirty skin; it was not so much a matter of age as of slovenliness. She muttered something calmly, indifferent to the result of her long, intermittent, alms-begging phrase.

Barrientos said no, barely moving his head. Her eyes remained open, looking in the direction of Medina's hard profile, which had leaned backwards and was now aglow with a wicked, joyful grin. Barrientos shook his head again and the woman slowly went on her way, as though she were afraid of offending him. "Chief," she repeated, bidding him farewell.

When the woman had gone, Barrientos moved away from the shelf full of bottles and placed his hands on the counter.

"Will you have another one now? You haven't come to visit us on Saturday noon for quite some time, chief. The dog's not feeling well and she's scared. She's never had a baby and she can't have any."

"Yes," Medina said and turned his profile to give him a happy, furious look. "Such things are understandable. Bring two, please; some sort of wine, on me this time."

Barrientos stepped back, with a real expression in his eyes now, with a slight disillusionment that soon dissolved as his mind became occupied with other concerns. He brought the bottle and two tiny glasses.

"Cheers," he said, raising his little glass.

Medina turned around again toward the violet shadow of the brick arcade, toward the fragment of the frieze traced by miserable wretches that he could make out from the counter. Without looking, he took hold of the little glass of sweet wine with two fingers and drained it in one swallow.

"And what can you do," he said. "Get them all together once a year, for the distribution of food that isn't enough to appease their normal hunger of even one day, not counting the hunger pangs left over from the last three hundred sixty-five days. Get them together in the courtyard of the Detachment, or if there's not room enough for them there, in the square with the poor horseman cast in bronze who's always threatening to take off at a trot and never does. Once a year, on the day set aside to honor and be honored by the police. And tell them, with the aid of a priest, of an ugly woman, of a man representing the governor, that it's not right to steal, to cohabit with a common-law spouse, to drink alcohol. That the package, which not all of them manage to get, wrapped in tissue paper of the same colors as the nation's flag and which the young ladies of the Police Auxiliary Corps distribute with smiles and without getting sick to their stomachs, is going to have to do them to feed themselves all year long, till the next anniversary."

He had been toying with the little glass as they talked, slipping it onto his fingertip like a thimble. He put it down carefully on the counter and contemplated Barrientos with a sweet smile, almost that of a child. But Barrientos was searching his eyes and understood.

"Where is he?" Medina asked, in the same sad, ironic tone. "I've already wasted as much time as I care to." He picked his hat up off the wet, grimy counter and pulled it down to his eyes. "Let's go."

Barrientos gave him a quick look full of hatred, scorn, sadness. He put the bottle away and dried his hands on a cloth; he came out from behind the counter and suddenly halted, almost touching the Englishman's back.

"I gave him my word I'd never tell you."

"Yes, but he doesn't know what's good for him. So I have to do his thinking for him. Let's go," Medina said; erect, white, he began to follow along behind Barrientos.

They made their way through the almost deserted area full of tables piled atop one another, walked through a broad dirty zone where the darkness too was piling up, where their feet clacked like tongues. Barrientos led the way, swaying back and forth, his back a little hunched, his silent protest and his contempt showing only in his arrogant, motionless head, to a wall of wooden planks that seemed to loom up all of a sudden. From over Barrientos's shoulder, Medina grabbed the fist he'd raised to knock on the door.

"Wait," he muttered. "Do you figure he's drunk? I know how he gets."

Barrientos shrugged; Medina came around in front of him and stood feeling the gap in the doorframe, the wire that apparently was held the door shut. "It's okay. You'd best leave."

He silently opened the door onto darkness and a disgusting smell; the door gave a feminine moan, and threatened to collapse. Someone to the left sat up above a screeching of metal that went on vibrating, slowly dying away in the silence. Medina waited for a moment; then he gave the door a kick that made it knock feebly against a wooden partition, and searched in one pocket for matches.

"A friend, Medina," he informed the darkness in a cheerful voice. "An old and faithful friend who doesn't hold a grudge against you for despising me."

Now he heard, above the shaking of the bedsprings, an expectant panting, a heavy breathing whose violence the metal coils couldn't drown out. He scraped a match and once it was lighted held it up. He could barely make out the skinny body leaning on its fists, the gaunt face; he searched about for the switch to turn on the light bulb hanging down very low in the middle of the cubicle.

"Okay," Seoane said from the bed, in an even, high-pitched voice, as though it had just been given to him or returned to him and he were trying it out so as to learn how to express something. "Okay."

Medina found the switch halfway between himself and the man, who turned into a youngster with his mouth wide open, feeble, naked, once the light filled the room with silent fury.

Medina gave a crooked smile, let the match fall to the floor and came one step farther into the room, without looking toward the bed. The wall at the far end of the little room, if there was a wall, was covered up as far as the ceiling, close overhead, with crates for empty bottles and others full of empty bottles. On the floor, next to the head of the mattressless bed covered with a tattered blue cloth, were two bottles, a glass, a candle, cigarettes, a pair of socks, a pile of newspapers. Being careful not to dirty his suit, keeping with slow and noticeable repugnance from brushing up against the bed, forcing himself to keep his back to it, Medina placed a crate on the floor and covered it with newspapers so as to have a place to sit down.

His legs crossed, his long body hunched over, he took out a pack of cigarettes and put one between his lips; barely moving, he dropped the pack on top of the youngster's narrow chest, grabbed the pile of gray clothes lying at the foot of the bed and threw it toward the youngster's flat blond belly. The thin old summer suit didn't have the heft of a garment with a weapon concealed in it. Once he'd lighted his cigarette, he also tossed the box of matches toward him; after exhaling two clouds of smoke he smiled again and then, curious and expectant, looked frankly at the sick and anxious profile that swayed from side to side as the youngster struggled to put his trousers on.

"How long a time it's been since we last saw each other, years," Medina said, in a deep, indolent voice that made mock of itself in the final inflection of each phrase. "Only months, to tell the truth. But for two very good friends the absence grows longer, time flies by. Though I had news of you the whole time. Maybe I sought it without realizing it, maybe by chance, by luck. It's not possible for two real friends to separate for good. Real friends are rare."

"Okay," the boy repeated. He had put his trousers on and his head, glistening with perspiration, with drops of sweat again running resolutely down his forehead, was panting as it leaned against the wooden planks of the wall. He was sitting up on the bed, his bare feet shrinking back timidly alongside Medina's shiny shoes. The voice had learned to express, awkwardly, tedium, a pale cynicism.

"I found out you'd gone to the capital. It wasn't hard to guess as much. Two thousand fifty-one pesos," he recited, "won't take you much farther. What I mean to say is, I found out you'd rented a car to take you beyond Puerto Astillero, heading north, an amazingly cunning move. From there you took a fruit boat and kept going on north to El Rosario, to the railroad station. From there to the capital. I kept finding out things before they happened, maybe before you'd even made up your mind to do them. And I didn't want to arrest you, who knows why. It's puzzling. Maybe because friendship is sacred and there are few real friends. Or because I was paralyzed by my admiration for your intelligence, for your cleverness at throwing me off your track. It must be a gift, that."

He had spoken as his eyes contemplated his cigarette end, held between two fingers, which was burning him, the almost straight lines of smoke rising in the gloomy unbreathable air toward the heat of the light bulb. From somewhere in the market came the din from a poultry dealer's stall; reluctantly, slowly. Medina went over to the door to close it and protect the false night of the room. He came back and sat down again and looked at the youngster as he sat motionless smoking, his cigarette hanging from his half-open mouth.

"I'll finish my cigarette and we'll go," he proposed, stammering, his head learning against the wall.

Then, for the first time since they'd met in the room. Medina looked straight at him. Almost beardless, his face smooth and white, his golden hair mussed, but not that young after all. It wasn't possible to put a finger on any sign of age, touch a wrinkle, point to areas that had withered away; but time, and more than time the hanging about with life, brazenly contemplated Medina from the blue eyes turned cold, from the mouth gone soft.

"I'm no good at pity," Medina warned. He leaned toward the bed and lighted another cigarette.

"I'm not thinking about pity," the other stammered, with amazement, with dispassionate insolence. "That's of no concern to me, it's of no importance to me. None."

"Or almost none," Medina corrected. With a smile he looked at the black butt of a handgun peeking out from beneath the cloth wadded up into a ball that the other had used as a pillow; he scrutinized the trembling of his mouth, of the little hands crossed over his belly. "Friendship always mattered to you. That must have been why, out of an appreciation for what's sacred, you never sold the regulation pistol you stole from me. Not for any other reason, I'm certain. Anyone else in your place would have used it immediately or would have immediately sold it. And love also matters to you, maybe it still matters to you, love and wine, love or the need to turn into a dog or a bitch. Right?"

The boy leaped to his feet and stood swaying back and forth on his wide-splayed legs, the hollow of his stomach, his agitated ribs, threatened to brush against Medina's face. The boy's expressionless face slowly contracted and he spat the cigarette in the direction of Medina's head, without succeeding in hitting it. The boy stood there, moving his mouth, thinking without being able to say what it was that he was thinking, his impassive eyes open very wide.

"No," Medina advised. "Don't spit at me." He sat there for a moment watching him gasping for breath and then rose to his feet;. Almost without touching him he reached his open hand out toward him and made him sit down on the bed. He took a step to the right and handed him a bottle of wine. "Take a swallow. It always goes down well when a person first wakes up."

He watched him from above as he drank thirstily, immediately after his mistrust and vacillation; he looked at his half-closed eyes, his mouth sucking furiously on the neck of the bottle, the two streaks of wine running down the skin of his neck, the tense possession and surrender. He sat down again and examined his linen suit, the sides of his white socks. The boy rested his mouth on top of the bottle and sat breathing loudly as his face set in a wicked smile. He threw his head back and took another drink, more slowly now, growing drowsy.

"That's how it was," Medina's indolent voice said again jokingly. He had stopped looking at the other, he was turned toward the door which was miraculously still standing. "And after the capital, after she got bored with being there, or was a flop, despite the hopes the newspapers gave all of us who were interested in her career as a performing artist, and she didn't get her contract renewed, or wasn't able to establish long-term relationships with any of the admirers who took her out to dinner after the show. Right after all that she faced up to her failure or thought that if she stayed in the capital the moment would soon come when she'd have to face up to it. Right after that she returned, with no memory of her defeats, to Santa María, within a week, let's say, you came back to the city, into the wolf's mouth; crossing the river by ferry at Salto, wearing a mustache and dark glasses. You phoned me from there, but I couldn't do anything. I couldn't even go to the port to welcome you or look at you, from afar, as you came down the gangplank. Perhaps, once again, the astonishment, the envy, the admiration for your intelligence kept me from making a move. I knew all the time that you were in Santa María, hidden, impossible to find. It was enough to know that she, your false wife, Frieda or Margot, if I may mention her name, was going on singing at the Casanova or at the Central. I refused to look for you out of disgust."

The boy had finished dressing; as he sat on the bed, with an unlit cigarette in his mouth, his fingers were fumbling underneath his chin, trying to tie his necktie. With a quick glance, Medina examined his patient half-smile, his face slightly flushed and anxious; his dirty misshapen shoes holding up the not-yet-empty bottle.

"Out of disgust and out of pity; out of a strange sense of shame that I don't know whether you can understand. Moreover, I didn't have, nor do I have, a duty to look for you. Your debt to Santa María—your debt to me is another matter—amounted to no more than a regulation .45 Colt pistol, one hundred forty three thousand zero, zero, seven that I'd taken with me to Lavanda. As a souvenir, out of homage to friendship, without any ill intent. You stole it. Some day you were going to come back so as to return it. I promised myself that and had a clear conscience. I'm happy you've kept my word. And I had no duty to look for you because within forty-eight hours of your mysterious disappearance, I gave back the two thousand fifty-one pesos. Today it would be easy for me to do that; when you went away, ten months ago, it was very hard."

The boy bent down to get the bottle; sprawled out on the bed, he downed what was left in it in one swig. He carefully placed the bottle on the floor, lighted the damp cigarette that he had been holding between his lips and rose to his feet.

"Okay," he said. "It's all the same to me. Let's go. Nothing matters to me. Nothing."

Medina raised his head and blew the smoke from his cigarette, gently, toward the young smooth-skinned face. He smiled, baring his teeth.

"Or almost nothing. It's all the same to you except for your Señora Seoane. Everything. Except for that poor dirty whore, Frieda Margot, if my lips are worthy of uttering her name. I don't think she changed her luck; just her name. I'd like to know—I'm not asking any questions—if she still prefers women. If she still goes by the name of Frieda." He gave a feeble smile, exhausted all of a sudden, and spat on the floor, feeling nauseated. ("It must be my heart, or whatever the doctors say it is.")

He rose to his feet, slowly crushed his cigarette underfoot on the floor and walked over to the head of the bed, awkwardly brushing against the other in a deliberate attempt to provoke him. With two fingers he removed the pistol from the bulges formed by the pillow. He hid it in his pocket. "This is it. I don't need to look. A hundred forty three thousand, zero zero, seven," he muttered, smiling. "I knew you were going to give it back."

"Okay. Let's go," the boy said, a patient, bored expression on his face. He let the cigarette fall from his mouth to the floor, rigid, not moving his head, his arms dangling forgotten.

Medina slipped one hand underneath his suit jacket and laid a little pile of money on the bed.

"We're not going anywhere, nobody needs you. Today, thanks to you, even though you don't understand, it's easy for me to get money. Buy yourself some clothes, move to a decent place and come to see me. Or offer Frieda a bouquet of orchids, invite her out to dinner, pay her for a night, have her sing 'Prefiero que me lo digas,' just for you alone. Even though maybe you're not all that rotten yet, even though you'd rather I didn't tell you so."

The boy was as rigid and deaf as a soldier, his impassive, still-young face trained on the light bulb hanging from the planks of the ceiling. Medina brushed against him once more as he went past him and stopped.

"Julián Seoane," he murmured, mockingly. The other's face didn't move; he looked with his cold, dilated blue eyes at the row of crates full of empty bottles climbing up the wall. "Julián Seoane," Medina repeated pointlessly.

He waited a moment longer then, without moving his body, he hit the boy's raised jaw with his fist, heard the thud of the blow and saw him fall to the floor sprawled out and not moving. He gently placed on his left wrist that Gérard-Pérrigaux watch that had been a birthday present.

THE SIESTA

Medina looked at his shoes before taking them down off the desk, where they had rested between the pile of recent daily papers, unopened, and the empty bottle of beer.

"If it's not dust it's mud," he said in a low voice.

He opened a drawer, took out a yellow cloth for cleaning cars and hunched over to polish his shoes.

"Who knows what you get yourself into, chief?" Valle said, and laughed just once, with his usual laugh that never expressed happiness, that was only his way of underscoring the sentence he'd just spoken.

"Not everybody can live along the river, boss," Martín said gently, with a bit of a twang, giving an exploratory smile.

The three men were in their shirt sleeves, lolling in their chairs, finding a bit of relief when the air from the little fan hit their sweating faces. It was six p.m., the hour when they usually met in Medina's room to talk over the few mysteries of criminal life in Santa María, or chat about fishing, about well-planned murders that had happened a long way away—an acceptable classic, Medina would announce—about women who were strangers in town, the weather, the municipal events that each day marked the slight growth of the city.

"I don't choose what I get into and I assure you that from what I see it's going to be easier for years to come to live along the river rather than farther away," Medina answered, putting the cloth away.

He went over to the window and lifted the curtain without looking at the square. All he saw was what was in the window frame, the yellowing, motionless beginning of dusk, the anomalous light that foreshadowed a storm.

Without turning around, broad-shouldered and mild-mannered, eagerly offering to the fan his intellectual's forehead, his curly hair, his permanent expression of slight enjoyable suffering, Martín murmured:

"It's odd. What you were telling us, chief? That the guy let himself be caught while he was taking his afternoon nap? With the corpse of the woman out in the street?"

"Come off it," Valle said, impatiently.

In the window, looking at the other triangle of the raised curtain, Medina thought: "What's odd is something he doesn't imagine, doesn't suspect: himself. That he's a cross between a lap dog and a fat spinster, that he's the most capable man on the police force I've ever known, who doesn't stop following a trail or let his mind wander it till he's sent the dossier to the judge, that he's never needed to beat up a man who's been arrested, not even to make him confess or just for the pleasure of it or to take justice in his own hands or to calm his nerves." He lowered the curtain with one tug without looking at the tail of the horse in the statue and walked slowly over to the desk.

"Come off it," Valle said again. "The guy wasn't attempting to escape. A criminal, perverted mind. He threw her down from the balcony as though he were killing a bedbug that was keeping him from sleeping. Don't you think so, chief?"

Medina collapsed in the revolving chair and nodded his head toward Valle's half-open mouth.

"That's the story, Deputy Martín. It must have happened the way we were told by Officer Valle, that monopolizer of medals and hoarder of days off, an old customer for orders of the day and little celebrations in the courtyard for acts of bravery in the line of duty. That's how it must have been. The man was sick of hearing her gripe and confined himself to throwing her over the balcony. He got rid of her without consciously realizing he was committing a crime." He hesitated, glanced with one eye at the neck of the bottle; then he bared his teeth; an impersonal hatred. "How long have you been married, Deputy Martín?"

The three of them laughed and it seemed as though the heat was dying down a little. Medina noticed that Martín looked away and gathered up the remains of their laughter with a child's pout. He was determined to answer, without, as usual, the least trace of humor, of situations over and done with, of poking fun at them in turn.

"Less than a year," he said, calmly.

Medina lowered his head and rummaged through the pile of newspapers. He went on unfolding them noisily, paying no attention to the tired chit-chat of the other two. ("He's right, he'll always be righter than I am, not because he's more intelligent, but because he has his beliefs and sticks to them.")

"It's like I was telling you," Medina said. "I still haven't gotten permission to take a vacation, Martín. Just put up with things, the way I do. I've already told the two of you that there can come a time when a person gets fed up, all of a sudden, just like that, or else after knowing for weeks that he's fed up and refusing to accept the situation and exploding, fed up with opening up a filthy, badly put together, badly written, badly printed newspaper from the capital, and reading, almost exclusively, the way a student reads nothing but textbooks, the articles by reporters on the police beat. And a person, that person, does it out of curiosity and love of his work. For no other reason than that miserable thing, if you take a good look at it, love of his work. I'd like to turn into a vocation, though not one for me anymore. But this filth written under dictation can't help me in the least."

He lifted up the papers to throw them down at the foot of the desk, taking care to make the wild gesture as dramatic as he could since he'd just discovered that he didn't know who it was he was lying to. Above the soft, low-pitched rustle of the newspapers on the floor the muted ringing of the telephone was heard.

"Well," Valle said, "it seems that they don't leave you alone even on the eve of your vacation."

Medina leaned across the desk to reach for the phone. The voice of the *mestizo* switchboard operator said hello and began to speak, piercing and insidious.

"He says he wants to see you about a personal matter. It's Barrientos, the one from the market, though he didn't give me his name. A friend. As though any dog wouldn't recognize him. I didn't say whether you were in or not."

"All right," Medina said. "I was just about to leave, but it doesn't matter. Did he come by himself? Tell him to come on up."

He looked at his men as though they were enemies; he looked, as he piled papers on top of each other without sitting down again, at their different ways of putting on weight: Valle obese, with his bones tired from the weight of the flesh on them, a middle-aged man, bald, accustomed to anything and everything with no need to ask questions, recognizing each happening as he would a man whom he'd at least have heard of. Shorter and plumper, white and young, Martín, full of caution, self-assurance and ambition. ("And patience as well, convinced that he'll get everything he wants if life, death, gives him time, brick by brick, smile by smile, kindly by profession and out of calculation. The important thing is not how much he suspects his wife; the amazing thing is doubtless how much he agrees to suspect, the exact dose that allows him not to recognize how stupid and how big a cuckold he is and not compromise his career, his relationships with me and with her.")

The other two were talking now of smuggling; Valle was

telling an incredible story and Martín, kindly and in no danger, was nodding with a smile. Night was failing behind the curtain at the window, the light of a stormy night, yellow, violet, would be hard and hollow around the statue of the Founder, viciously eating away the horseman's back, the horse's greenish haunches. There were two knocks on the door, with an interval between, a resigned rage.

"Gentlemen," Medina said, "perhaps they're coming to tell us something about contraband goods." For a brief moment he beamed a mysterious smile at them. "It's best that you leave me by myself. And don't wait for me to come back. It's Héctor's turn to yawn tonight. As soon as I get rid of one I'm going to go down to the river."

He answered their goodnights and watched them go out, meeting in the doorway the man who was coming in, wearing a black mourning band on his arm and his Sunday best.

Barrientos walked toward the desk with a black hat, which he had never once worn, dangling from one hand. When he came within two or three meters of him, Medina saw his look of antipathy and obstinacy, and then heard, repeated in his voice, the furious resignation of the knuckles that had knocked on the door.

"Sit down," Medina said, "and put your hat down somewhere. All I could offer you is coffee; but not even that at this hour. I can come to the market one of these nights and stand you anything you like."

He sat down behind the desk, opposite the square torso of the other man, who had placed his hat on his thighs so as to concentrate his attention on his hands. Medina put his feet on top of the desk and sighed.

"The sky looks stormy," he said as if his statement were a question.

"Thanks, I don't want anything to drink," Barrientos answered. "You must know why I've come."

"I've no idea. There are friends who come just to visit me.

When Valle left, he said jokingly that you were coming to tell us something about contraband goods. In any event, I'm glad you've come."

"Contraband goods," Barrientos said slowly, pondering the words. "There are lots of people, I suppose, who could tell you more than I can. All I have is a few bottles that I bought or that were given to me as gifts. And they're out in plain sight of everyone."

He seemed to grow tired and old all of a sudden, as though by walking to the Detachment in the afternoon heat he had gained on his misfortune, and the latter had just now caught up with him, sitting there in the chair with his legs apart, with his brand-new hat on his knees, his crooked black bow tie getting in the way of his chin.

"It was a joke. How's the dog?"

Barrientos took a tired hand out of the hat and raised it up to remove something.

"Er . . . Old, he's a very old animal and he's been dying for years now. He's my wife's child. You know what I mean? Everybody asks and sympathizes and pokes fun. What I mean to say is, they don't understand and yet it's easy. It's always easy to understand when it's a person's own dog."

"I wasn't poking fun, Barrientos," Medina said gently. "What breed of dog is it? I've never seen it."

"I know that, I suppose. You weren't poking fun, chief; at least not in that way. He's a fox terrier. He could be anything now, he's fat, all swollen up, he doesn't move."

He gave a weary smile, accepting his misfortune as company, a habitual, bearable climate.

"You didn't summon me, chief. At least you didn't ask me verbally to come, or send me a note. You know what we're talking about. Your men have been there since that Saturday, two of them, standing guard and every so often they'd come over to me and ask for a drink and question me. I gave them drinks and told them that yes, that the boy was still in the little storeroom. After you came to visit him, two or three days afterward, he went out and then came back dressed in new clothes from head to foot. He was happy and ate dinner with us that night. Without getting drunk. A nice boy. I don't know if I'm the right age: I would have liked having him as a son instead of the dog. But in the morning he came and woke me up, brought several bottles from me that he paid cash for and stayed holed up all day long, drunk. Well, when I went to see him again, I don't know how many days had gone by, he was as dirty and in as bad shape again as he'd been before. Your men asked intelligent questions, with no sign that they really wanted to know the answers though, and I told them the truth: that he was there in the storeroom. Till yesterday, in the morning this time too, he came and woke me up again. It was four a.m., there weren't any police around. He wanted to kill himself, he promised my wife and me that that was what he'd do, after killing somebody else, I don't know who. He hasn't come back. Since four o'clock yesterday morning. This afternoon I thought it best to come and tell you so. There was some reason why your men were hovering about like flies ever since that Saturday when you came to see him and left him with me after you'd knocked him out cold." He raised one hand again to cough into it and said, thoroughly tired of the whole business: "Chief."

Medina relaxed his chest muscles and gave a calm, affable smile as he looked at the shiny tips of his shoes.

"Yes? So first he bought himself some clothes, then he came back and got drunk, and yesterday he announced he was committing suicide. That's no concern of mine. I thank you, as a friend, for having come to tell me. But what he may do is no concern of mine. It might be a good thing if he kills himself." He took his legs down off the desk and smiled once again with a shrug. "I did everything that could be done. I've known him since Lavanda. I thank you, Barrientos."

"That's the only reason why I came," Barrientos said as he

rose to his feet, his hat against his chest. "I wanted to tell you, just in case." All of a sudden his mouth grew tense and his eyes sought Medina's. "What's more, chief, I had to punch him yesterday. He was rude to my wife, though she didn't pay any attention to him. But later on he tried to heal the dog by putting him in a barrel of water. I too left him while he was asleep; I forgot about him and he disappeared. To tell the truth, if I came to tell you it's because this time I'm sure he won't be back. And he not only drank; he was out of his mind, a drug addict."

"Okay, thanks, it's not important. There's nothing to do, Barrientos. From now on my boys won't be coming around asking you questions."

He smiled and put one hand on the man's shoulder. He walked over to the window and saw that the storm was irresolutely spreading over the square, over the gesture of the horseman that the shadows blurred.

"If you came here on foot I'll drive you back to the market. Forget this whole story. Neither you nor I had good luck."

The drizzle began almost the moment that they got into the car. There was still a little blue light in the sky, behind cornices and tree branches in the distance.

"It's just a rain cloud," Barrientos said. "Maybe it'll be over in a matter of minutes."

"And maybe it'll rain all night long." He was expecting that the old, oft-repaired engine would overheat. "Every night or every morning, when I go back home, I have to think about the damned road they're letting fall to ruin."

"Politics," Barrientos murmured.

Medina drove the car straight into the rain and drove around the plaza. As they neared the market, they went through the part of the city that he liked best, illuminated now by the first street lamps and the neon shop signs and the bright gleam left by the rain.

"RED"

The car drove unhurriedly over the gray, slippery, badly paved street; in the sultry night, at the imperceptible beginning of the hot season. It turned smoothly at the deserted street corners where the slanting rain illuminated the still-pale zones around the street lamps. Barrientos was silent, stolid and resentful, with his big mustache tips turned toward the fog on the windowpanes, sitting as far away as possible from Medina, with each of his large, dirty, misshapen hands resting firmly on one knee. The windshield wipers barely cut through the time and the silence. The car drove cautiously through that section of the city where the remains of villas surrounded by trees, fallen down and covered with moss, with stubborn, solitary symbols of wealth and pride, were being besieged and invaded by underbrush or brand-new, white, business establishments, with smooth façades that were all alike or new and pretentious residences, with large and unnecessary iron doors painted black and unnecessary windows never opened, behind monotonous metal scrawls. Carriage gateways for nouveaux riches who kept their cars in the Shell garage and entered their houses by way of modest, unassuming entrances, protected by doors made of cheap wooden panels.

"Just look at that," Medina said. "This side of the city. In my young days in Santa María, when I had just arrived and until a year or more later, when I still hadn't resigned myself to having

178

come here to settle down for good and when it was still possible for me to go about completely on my own, I used to wander all over this neighborhood." But now the car had entered the city proper by way of the Avenida General Latorre and was effortlessly rolling along the wet asphalt, pierced by the colored neon lights of the shops. "It was like those feature articles from twenty-five years ago that *El Liberal* puts out today. Have you ever happened to read them? Well, the paper reprints what it published all those many years ago, inaugurations of this or that, public celebrations, anything. It was like looking at the history of the city; and one could even touch it, guess its past and its future and not be wrong. This part of town, halfway between the riverside and the railroad line; and nobody knows why the city began here. The Café Confederación, as you know, was located here; people say that it was once a grocery store and that a Latorre ball was given there in the months when Santa María was the capital. I used to go to the Confederación and watch from the windows the story, a much more interesting one to my mind, of rich people who were replaced by others. Do you know what I mean? That story is still going on. I'm speaking of the new things and the businesses that are being built on the land where the villas of this neighborhood once stood."

"I beg your pardon, but I wasn't listening to you when you first started talking," Barrientos said, uninterested and gloomy. "I've got things on my mind, chief. But I do understand that last part. The city's rich people, or those who were rich and went broke or those who came and still keep coming to push them out don't interest me. None of them really worked, or maybe, in certain cases, the fathers or the grandfathers did. Latorre's balls, or his mansion, on the island, or the portraits that you can't help seeing even in the soup don't interest me. Hereabouts even the gringos who've just arrived speak of Latorre as though he were God."

"True enough," Medina said and stopped the car. They had left the Avenida Latorre and were driving down a dimly lighted street that came out almost alongside the market. It was a street full of dirty houses and high old front walls, with little doors above two or three stone steps; of wretched shops that had almost no merchandise for sale, of general stores with bar counters, some of which still had the little twisted hook of a hitching post outside.

"Excuse me," he lied as he scrutinized the street intersection. "I want to light a cigarette."

He held the pack out to Barrientos who refused one, raising a hand and shaking his head. Medina pushed in the cigarette lighter on the dashboard and then raised the red and white spiral to his cigarette.

"Don't you think, Barrientos," he said slowly, pretending that all his attention was focused on puffing on the cigarette, "don't you think that Latorre was God, or very nearly so? Or perhaps Brausen, a more modern one."

"I'm of the same opinion as you, chief." Barrientos's indignation, not given completely free rein, made his voice sound younger and caused his mustache to tremble even more. "Latorre was a son of a bitch, a thief, a boorish, ignorant *gaucho*, as all of the rest of them were. Just look at the fortune he left behind, the leagues of land he kept buying for pennies or through influence as he was fighting for freedom and the fatherland. Look at the list of those sent before the firing squad by mere whim; and more than a hundred *gauchos*. They were all alike. All they were after was power." He sighed and relaxed for the first time during the trip back to town. "I don't say that's true of you, but I don't take it back either. I was saying that I understand that business about rich people who take off for somewhere else and about the ones who throw them out. I won't say anything about Brausen. If you've lighted up, chief, I'd like to ask you to keep going. My wife, the dog, the bar."

"Of course," Medina said. "I stopped so I could listen to you."

He put the car in reverse and drove on quickly toward the downtown section of the city. He had seen Julián Seoane's blond head leaning against the grimy windowpane of a general store, twenty meters behind the place where he had stopped the car. ("Nothing else, and only for a second, just the uncombed hair falling down into his eyes, the bearded profile, the unbuttoned shirt without a tie, an arm stretched out straight on the table, between two bottles. On the corner of Gerifaite and Cucha Cucha in the Turk's place; he must be drunk, dirty, an imbecile; he may even be living there, the Turk has a shed for coal, potatoes and wood; he hasn't moved very far away from the market, at least he didn't move any nearer the Casanova, where she sings every night except Mondays, between ten o'clock and one; he must not have a cent left of the money I gave him.")

"That business of those who go and those who come," Barrientos was saying; he angrily rubbed one hand across his mouth as if he'd just had a drink and were wiping it. "Some people throw others out. With their elbows sometimes, and sometimes with no need even to get close to them. That's how they threw me, or threw my father, out of the Colony. I understand this very well, as I told you. All of a sudden, or gradually, some of them come to occupy a place and the others have to leave. The difference between what you told me about the villas of the neighborhood is that we worked. My father and mother did, at least; maybe what I did couldn't be called work. But I was helping out and sharing the suffering as soon as I could. I understand that, chief. A cart, early one morning, loaded with the junk that nobody wanted to buy or that a person decides to sell because it helps to go on believing that there's such a thing as a family, that it'll continue to have a house to live in, that as individuals we really have a place in the world. There's no need for you to turn around, it's almost stopped raining by now. Today, as I told you, I have the same mistaken impression about other things that don't really matter; her, the dog that refuses to die, my worries about the business, chief.'

"No,' Medina said. "I'm taking you to your door."

("Maybe Frieda doesn't matter to him any more, maybe she's only an excuse to be drunk and high on drugs all the time. That would be less nasty and also, insofar as it matters, less serious.") He let Barrientos out at the black rain-soaked arcades of the old market; it was as if he had arrived at a depopulated expanse in the dark of night, at the edge of an abyss, a sea of a desert. The dampness heedlessly entered the car, fogged up the windowpanes and the chrome. "Thank you, chief." He was bent over, holding the car door open, his mustache gleaming in the rain, his eyes troubled and unforgiving.

"Wait," Medina said and smiled at him as he searched in his trousers pocket. "I'd come in and have a drink with you and your wife, but it's gotten late." ("What is he trying to absolve me of?") "You know, Barrientos, that I'd never think of giving you . . . You know that I've never given you a tip, the few times you've let me pay. Please take this for the dog. I don't know, a few sweets, some medicine." He reached out and opened his fist full of wadded-up bills.

Illuminated by the pale glow of the car's dashboard, Barrientos sought Medina's eyes and looked into them for a moment. Then he hopelessly shook his head and gave a tight-lipped smile.

"No amount of money can do anything for the dog now, chief. He's so bloated he's about to burst; he doesn't move, he pushes his food around with his muzzle and his teeth, but he won't eat. The only thing left for him to do is to die, and then it's going to be very hard on her and on me."

"I'm sorry. It's a shame. I understand," Medina said and put the money away.

"Thanks, chief. Believe me that I'd like to tell you with all my heart: 'Come whenever you like.' But it's Saturday; you're the chief of police and you can come in even though you've not been invited." He closed the car door almost without a sound and quickly disappeared into the shadow of the arcades.

Medina lighted another cigarette and absentmindedly repeated an insult. He started the car up. ("Chief of Police of Santa María. That is to say, I could gather together the little goodness and spirit of justice that I have left; the pity and unselfishness that I already have, and it keeps growing, and in the right circumstances, it would be infinite. And it would never be enough, it could never equal the conventional friendly gesture of one of them. The only tolerable authority is God's; and maybe not for everyone at that. I, Medina, Chief of Police of Santa María.")

He parked the car up close to the curb, in front of the Turk's general store and stood there looking with curiosity and reluctance, through the blurred car windows and the fine rain, at Julián's head, now held at an angle of longing and petulance, with a cigarette dangling out of his mouth. "Red" was also sitting across from him.

("And now I'm going to get out of the car, I'm going to close—paying no heed to the drizzle, my eyes searching the cloudy sky—the car door with an abrupt, precise, decisive slam; I'm going to take three steps, go up to the little stairway at the entrance, enter the Turk's cheap bear with a chummy, soothing smile, knowing that I'm broad-shouldered and heavy-set, twirling the car keys around my index finger, recognizing the sudden silence, the hurried obsequious greetings, the mistrust, the respect and the swear words swiftly coming to mind, in the air that smells of a cellar, of damp earth and filth. I'll walk over to the table like I owned the place and we'll smile at each other again. I'll spoil the moment for them, the night maybe; in any case, I'll interrupt them. And yet, if Seoane should happen to die some day and since he was born to be forgiven, it's not impossible that they've set aside for him as a paradise getting drunk at the Turk's place, with 'Red,' some twenty or thirty blocks away from the Casanova, where she'll be singing 'Prefiero que me lo digas,' leaning on the mahogany-colored piano or where, at least, there'll be a photograph of her on either side of the grimy curtain at the entrance, her gigantic head, badly tinted, fastened to oblique squares of cardboard, above her *nom de guerre*, the corners of her mouth forever about to break into a smile, her expert gaze, never wrong, prophesying the events of the night two or three hours before they happen, in a warm, eternal drizzle—some fifty or sixty blocks away from the little house she rented along the river, near mine, where she'll dance as dawn is breaking, innocently and intimately, with her girlfriends from the Casanova, as her men friends uncork bottles and unwrap packages of food; where she'll sleep with some man or other about whom all she can recall, if anything, is his preferences. Maybe this is her paradise and I'm going to yank her out of it.")

He got out of the car in the drizzle, closed the door with an abrupt slam, entered in the dim light, the smell of a grocery store and the toilet of Chamún's place, smiling and twirling the keys around one finger, indifferently measuring the sudden silence, the effusiveness of the distant greetings, the ensuing expectancy surrounding the billiard table.

"Hi there," Medina said. Seoane took from his mouth the cigarette, which had gone out, and examined it in surprise. "Red" greeted him several times with a nod of his head as though he were agreeing to something. Medina was almost certain that Seoane didn't have on the same suit that he'd seen him put on in the room in the market: this one was brown, tight-fitting and dirty, with a tear under the left armhole. Seoane slowly stretched out one hand till it reached the matches and lighted the cigarette, which he put back between his lips. He grimaced and gestured for him to sit down.

"Hi there," he said in turn and raised a hand to ask for silence as he frowned.

Then he raised his other hand and clapped one against the

other to ask for service. But Chamún was already standing behind Medina's back with a smile on his face.

"The same," Medina ordered.

"Hi," Seoane said again. "I was waiting for you. What I mean to say is, I'm always afraid you're going to turn up. No matter where I am, even when I'm sleeping, like the last time. It was the last time, right? It's not getting punched out that I'm afraid of." He shrugged and thrust his skinny stubbled face forward above the table.

"I see," Medina drawled. He took the glass that Chamún had brought and poured himself a drink out of the two bottles.

"Red" emptied his glass and his head teetered.

"Good night," he said; "see you around."

"Ciao," Seoane answered.

"Anything else, chief?"

"Nothing, just let me be." Chamún went off. "Well, it was only one punch. And maybe I gave it to you without really wanting to, simply to fulfill a promise."

"It doesn't matter." Seoane gave a very slow, distracted, and cowardly smile and stroked his wet chin. "It's marvelous. There's nothing in the world, now that I really think about it, that can be compared to it. Wait a minute." He raised his hand, his face furious, and then he smiled patiently and mysteriously. "I don't know what time it is. And I don't care. Do you realize? Just a minute, don't say anything."

He put a few drops of vermouth in his glass and then filled it up to the top with gin from the square bottle. He held the glass up with a trembling hand to the level of his eyes as he looked at the scene reflected in the damp, greasy window, still smiling. Then he unexpectedly pushed his body away from the edge of the table and drained the glass in one gulp. He sat there for a little while with his eyes closed, waiting; without making a sound, he gently put the glass down next to the bottles, closer to Medina than to himself, and sighed in a fury.

"Better?" Medina asked in a low voice. He looked at the white face, which was thinner now, where only little reddish areas below his temples left space for youthfulness and nobility. His unshaved cheeks lent freshness and color to his mouth; his long copper-colored sideburns formed curls alongside the lobes of his ears; his innocent blue eyes regained their brightness, their complicated happiness, and sized up Medina's expression.

"Chief," Seoane said slowly, "in the market, that time, I wasn't drunk, but asleep. I said it was of no importance. I'm not afraid of getting punched. Some time ago, months ago, every night, more or less, I'd come across guys who felt insulted and socked me. No. What I'm afraid of is sermons. I'm afraid of the rosary of well-meant stupidities that a friend can force me to listen to, for example, one who doesn't have a care in the world and stupidly speaks up from outside. I don't want to offend you, chief. I myself sometimes talk to myself from outside; I give myself advice, I make plans for my life and promise myself to follow them, I make fun of the truth. But it doesn't last long; it generally lasts till I go to sleep. And when I wake up I remember with regret what I'd been telling myself; I stop being split in two, there is nothing of me left outside of me and I feel hopeless, there's just me, Julián Seoane, having to put up with things again. Never happy, naturally, and that will always be true. But in any case it's better than when I split in two, judge myself and give myself advice. I think it was marvellous and incomparable, I said. That certainly that I've reached the end, that I have nothing, neither now nor tomorrow. Absolutely nothing," he said with an amazed smile, pouring himself another drink out of the bottle. "Naked. They can't take anything away from me except my life. And life is no longer anything more than this; such a trivial thing, nothing."

"Yes," Medina said, looking toward the counter. "You may be right; you may not go outside yourself, not even one minute a day or minutes that don't count. A man like that will always be right. However, I won't give up and now even less than before.

When we were friends you had lots of things about you that one could like or admire. There were also things deserving of respect. The most important thing, essentially, because in the last analysis it's the most important thing, was your intelligence. The mother of all virtues, if you look at things in the right way." He fell silent, apologizing in an affectionate way; the three men standing in the background, separated from the Turk by the bar counter, were half turned away, pretending not to be paying any attention to them, maneuvering with their billiard cues.

"That's all right, chief. I haven't entirely lost my memory. I'm not making fun of you, it doesn't interest me to make fun of you. I'm going to go on drinking. The only thing that matters to me is to be left alone. But I can go listening."

"Thanks. I was saying that the most important thing was your intelligence. And the only thing that makes a person persist is having evidence that your intelligence hasn't disappeared or been ruined. That's why I'm determined to persist as long as I have to."

"It's no use, Medina. We're different; everybody is different, I mean. And nobody understands anybody. And maybe people who don't try to understand are the ones who understand more. But nobody is better than anybody else, chief. Everybody different, but nobody better. And there's no need to persist in saving somebody else. Only God, out of caprice, could do that. And you . . ." He smiled and went on drinking, slowly and carefully.

"God," Medina said. He drained his glass and lighted a cigarette. Now the sound of the rain could be heard again; a train whistled twice and again there came the unhurried sound of summer rain falling on the roofs and in the streets.

"And you," Seoane went on, "as far as I know you never got beyond being chief of police."

Medina turned round toward him in surprise and for a moment they looked at each other with the smile, the amused eyes and defiant eyes of years before.

"Well," Medina said then. "May I ask you a question?"

"Yes. It's a good time, I don't have anything to defend, I don't have any reason to lie."

"Are you in Santa María because of her?"

"Yes."

"Do you see her?"

"Never. It's been months. The last time I tried was . . . a failure. What I mean is that before she used to throw me out herself. That night she had somebody else throw me out. I was watching her sing at the Casanova. The whole bit, everything you can imagine. They hadn't let me come in there for quite a while. But that night I had money and I was able to sit down at a half-hidden table, against the wall, a long way away from the piano, from her. I got drunk, naturally."

"What was she singing?" Medina asked with a big smile, raising one finger. " 'Prefiero que me lo digas'?"

"Go to the head of the class. That was exactly what it was. She always told me everything. And I sat there there at the table in a dark corner thinking that she was singing for me. That she knew I was watching her and listening to her. And at the same time she was sure it was impossible for me to have gotten into the Casanova. Maybe she also thought I'd gone off to the end of the world or had shot myself. I promised her very often to do both of those things. But at any rate, I convinced myself she was singing for me and I paid I don't know how much to hire a taxi to take me to the house at the beach that she'd rented. I don't know whether she's still living there. Sometimes I work, believe it or not, for a few days at the port. And there's a lawsuit over a plot of land in the country that might or might not have belonged to my mother, a lawyer who's hoping that it did and gives me money when I can make him feel sorry for me. What I mean to say is that that night I had money and went to wait for her there with bottles and a bunch of flowers that I stole with the driver's help. A long time ago. She came home with some guy just as it was getting light and had him throw me out. An old story. I'm here because I don't care if I live somewhere else and I like it better being close to her. What else?"

"Where is it you're living?"

"Nowhere since you made me leave the market. Or convinced me that it was best for me to leave. Barrientos doesn't like you and invited me to stay on. What's more, nobody likes you. You may possibly have noticed. I sleep anywhere I can, right here some nights, upstairs above the billiard parlor, after they close. Sometimes I go to 'Red's' shack. Why? Anything else?"

Medina raised the ringer with the car keys and the Turk came out from behind the counter.

"How much?" Medina asked. "This round and the one before."

"Nothing," Chamún said in surprise, picking up the napkin.

"No," Medina said. He put a bill on the table and looked for a second at Seoane's mocking smile. "Here, take it." He pocketed the change with a yawn and tapped the label of a bottle with one finger. "No other questions. Like you, it's all the same to me to be here or somewhere else; let's go to my place, or to Campisciano's. He still has an empty room left. You're not obliged to live there. It'd be for when you want to sleep or eat. What's more, my vacation will be beginning in a couple of weeks. We can go fishing and get bored together. I've got enough bottles for a year. Yes, let's go down to my place on the river."

"And all this in honor or my intelligence," Seoane murmured.

"Yes, for the most part."

"And there won't be any sermons? Or not many?"

"No. One a week, maybe. When I get plastered too. Shall we go?"

"Wait a minute. I'm of a mind to tell you yes, I'm coming, that it's all the same to me. And I don't mean to be rude. I'm now going to drink the last glass in the poor part of Santa María. But I want to tell you that I don't know how long I'll stay. I'm not making any promises. I don't know whether getting drunk there will make me feel as happy—well, that's one word for it—as it would if I got soused in one of the gloomy bars around here. If it stops raining some day, I'm going to get some sun on the beach. I don't know, you never can tell. I also need to tell you two things. Two. One at a time. Number one: nobody likes you. I liked you when you were my father, when I needed one. Three things and we'll be on our way. The second, now that I remember, is that you're dead. Frieda said you were always playing at doing things. Never doing them for real."

"Margot?"

"To the head of the class again. Margot. Names still **mean less** than words. That you played, she said, at eating, at amusing yourself, at having arguments. I agreed. We said that the same thing happened with elderly people when they wanted to be nice to young people. We said that it was the fear of failure. But she, Margot, went further and discovered something else. She discovered that that was the only way you could be, that you were more than old, you were dead. Now—we're still in the second thing—if the envy and rancor of an old man toward young people is always awesome, even though it's contemptible and sad to see, how frightening the rancor and the envy of a dead man must be. That was what Frieda Margot said, and I agreed. She's very intelligent and you might try to save her too. I don't know from what; but I think it won't be too hard for you to imagine. And now I've said what I had to say, chief."

"Yes," Medina said. "But there were three things."

"Three? The third is precisely that. Salvation. The chief of police who wanted to be God."

"God," Medina repeated, rising to his feet. "It seems impossible, but it's easy. The difficulty lies in the fact that if a person begins he has to go on. Shall we go?"

"Yes. It's all the same to me."

THE RECONCILIATION

It was in the car, on the way to the riverside, in the gentle night rain, that Seoane coughed as he smoked and spoke of the pistol.

"The Colt. A hundred and forty three thousand and a little bit more. Did you give it back?"

Medina grunted. He may have said yes; but he had it under his armpit.

"It's odd," Seoane went on. "Maybe you understand it or maybe you can't. In order to understand it a person needs to have a past. And you don't have one, despite your age, despite many things having happened to you or your having been mixed up in them." He laughed, leaning forward toward the gleam of the twisting road. "I've brought along a little flask of cognac, it's in the same pocket where I used to pointlessly carry the pistol around. Can I take a swig? Or two? Can I offer you some?"

"No," Medina said. "I've got better stuff at home."

"I expect so. That's why I'm coming." Seoane drank from the flat flask and laughed again. "Two marvelous things, if a person can get used to them, if he can go on living. As I was telling you though; nothing matters to me any more."

"Ah, yes. Or almost nothing."

"And the fact that a person reaches the point of accepting that it's impossible to understand. That he has to get along with what he understands without believing in it."

'Yes," Medina said. "Now comes the bad part of the road. None of the councilmen lives or has a house in Villa Petrus. Nothing matters and nothing is understandable. And a person goes on living or does something like it. And what then? Because it's a good thing to learn that early on. And living is also a good thing; the one possibility, moreover."

"I don't know." Seoane put the flask away. "I was speaking about the pistol. It's odd to think that at this moment it may well be in the holster of some cop in the provinces. That pistol now . . . That meant something to me."

"The same thing happens though, with people with and things. Didn't it mean you were sorry you'd stolen it from me in Lavanda? In Frieda's apartment, no less."

"Never. It was like a life insurance policy, a death insurance policy. All I needed was to see it and touch it; nothing could go completely wrong for me."

"No, nothing," Medina said. "But I can get you another one. A toy one."

He turned to the right and the car entered a narrow mud road, brushing against the drooping branches of weeping willows. They went downhill in the train, Medina following the trail, guided by the odor of the soil and the scent of orange blossoms. They climbed up the five wooden stairs and Medina pushed with his shoulder against the stubbornly resistant door, which creaked as it opened.

"The dampness," he said. He turned on the overhead light and the lamp on the corner of the table. He went to the kitchen and came back with a bottle and two glasses.

Seoane was standing in the middle of the room, looking around, protecting himself with a crooked smile.

"There aren't many things that have changed," he said. "That's a consolation. And the bottle of cane brandy, like a fatted calf . . . Is it the same stuff Barrientos buys as contraband and sells in the market?"

"The very same," Medina said from the armchair next to the dirty fireplace with the stains and smells of the winter. "But I don't pay for it. What else about the pistol?"

Seoane looked at him from the table, with his glass in the air. He gave a quick shrug and raised a mocking, flushed face to take a swallow.

"Nothing else," he said. "If you could understand, what I've told you would suffice. If you could imagine and remember."

"I can and I refuse to. It's useless. Everything pleases me, I like being happy despite everything. That happens when a person catches on in time, and really understands, that nothing matters and that possible understandings are infinite and uncertain. I enjoy living. When a person catches on in adolescence and ceases, right there and then, to be an adolescent, to fool himself and seek refuges and safeguards. It's also a good thing to catch on before you die. A question of luck, of course; and what's more a question of instinct. You were thinking about the .45. I thought the inventory of property belonging to the Detachment indicated that it was worth five hundred pesos, the price paid for it, for this particular one and another hundred and twenty or two hundred and twenty exactly like it, on the day they bought it. And it's funny that five hundred pesos are still five hundred pesos. A theft amounting to five hundred pesos. I thought about what five hundred pesos meant when you stole the pistol. And I thought about what five hundred pesos mean nowadays. Maybe it'd take that much just to invite Frieda to a table at the Casanova and have a meal at daybreak. I think the absurd disproportion, nowadays, between a theft and what can be had for the money from it makes a farce of crime. We're talking now of the man who committed a theft for nothing, the one who pulled a dirty trick just so he could invite a woman he was fond of out for a night. Not to make himself feel happy; not for any future longer than ten or twelve hours. So there's no crime involved; a friendly joke, innocence, almost. I think if the five hundred pesos had been worth what they used to be, everything would have been different. Maybe you wouldn't have escaped with the pistol, or you wouldn't have escaped at all. Because five hundred pesos in those days would have been enough for the trip, the ferry and the train, in first class, two lunches and two dinners in the dining car and with what you had left, five pesos or a hundred, you wouldn't have been able to pay for a hotel room in the capital, not even for just ninety minutes. She of course would have been able to. She didn't give a thought to five hundred pesos in those days, nor would she today. She has millions now. And then, perhaps, that tenth or twentieth version of the idyll wouldn't have lasted as long or maybe it couldn't even have begun. The dirty trick, in any case, would have fouled things up before that and probably today you wouldn't be this curious, extraordinary piece of trash in love with an ambisextrous whore."

Seoane went on drinking, sitting at the table, drowsy and all by himself; his head with the cigarette dangling out of his mouth tilted toward the muffled, listless sound of the rain on the windowpane; at equal intervals one of his hands scratched his dirty, copper-colored, tangled hair.

"Inflation as an element that distorts tragedy," Medina said with a yawn. "Or reveals it. It turns your theft into a mere childish prank. It makes your unquestionable, long-standing sense of pride and bravery, the one you had when you escaped with the woman and the Colt, unbelievable. It makes it impossible to take Julián Seoane seriously; to really believe in that reddish-blond, unshaven, hollow-cheeked, cowardly, miserable wretch who plays at being drunk and in the depths of despair."

"No more sermons, you promised, chief," he finally said. "I'm going to sack out, I'm only going to listen to one last sermon. It'd be a good thing, then, if you thought it through carefully, whether it's worth my listening to and then going back, to the Turk's storeroom. I haven't seen her for a long time—Frieda, I mean. I haven't been trying to find her either. It'd be possible, if you kept your mouth shut, to stay here and begin again or start over in some other way."

"Yes." Medina leaned toward the fireplace and examined the thick soot stains on the bricks. "A person can always try and try again. There are very few people who matter to me or have mattered to me; and so I have a mania for telling them the truth."

A Son

("What is the falsehood between him and me," Medina thought, "that obliged me to go on loving him and trying to impose on him a happiness different from the one that he's enjoying now and that I stubbornly persist in calling a misfortune, and why do I persist in doing so? There's a falseness involved, a fake feeling; it's not a question of friendship, it's not only that I want to save him from going on binges and getting addicted to the drugs that Frieda gives him or sells him, I'm sure. To save him from humiliation and suffering. In all truth, I've never really loved anybody. It's not possible, there's no way to go beyond the need to act like a human being among other human beings. There's something more, something stronger and purer than affection, than friendship and any sort of love; I don't know what it is, but it must be something like dignity and pride.")

And perhaps the boy had thought about the same thing. Moreover, he had a great deal of time to think and get bored, to choose or accept an idea and mull it over as he sat on the wooden planks of the pier with the primitive fishing pole that he had chosen, held idly between his knees, taking no interest in whether the fish bit or not, indifferent to Medina's advice and his scornful remarks. He would come up, naked to the waist, deeply suntanned, from the pier to the house to eat and sleep. He drank only a glass of wine at lunchtime and Medina noticed, to his surprise, without being reassured, how much the boy kept imitating, with increasing perfection, the Seoane that he had first seen, years before. The same placid, amiably cynical good humor, the same serene self-assurance, the same spirited swiftness of his movements and his ideas.

He never left the house, or the grounds around the house or the fringe of sand and underbrush along the riverside. He didn't want to visit the city, he didn't seem to recall that Frieda's beach house was only some two hundred meters from the pier of faded wooden planks where he sat down to fish or stretch out in the sun or where he obeyed a languid impulse to take a dip in the river, which at that time was carrying very little mud along with it which grew deep and translucent in the midday sun. He didn't talk about future plans and greeted with neither rejection nor enthusiasm the ones that Medina invented to sound him out. He smiled in apology showing his teeth that were whiter now, asked about anecdotes, about the personnel of the Detachment.

"She's still at the Casanova," Medina said one night. "I feel like going to see her, maybe talking to her. But I'm tired, the city is becoming more important by the day, making me work harder; as soon as I can get away from it I'll be off. Maybe I'll start my vacation next week. We could go away, take a freighter and go up north. But it's been a month now that my vacation keeps being put off till the following week. She's still singing there and since they just sold a harvest in the colony, it never fails, every month the gringos keep selling a harvest of one thing or another, the cabaret is always full. She still sings 'Prefiero que me lo digas.' What I mean to say is that the world that matters to you hasn't changed. The big hit, the show-stopper is still 'Prefiero que me lo digas.' She wears three dresses a night now and as far as anybody knows she doesn't have a serious lover or a live-in girlfriend. What else? They've now put up a neon sign. I'd like it if the two of us went there some night. This very one, it's still early, if the idea appeals to you. And they say that she's bought or else is about to buy the Casanova. Which means that she'll be around Santa María for a long time. Yes, it's true."

Seoane had listened to him with a smile, leaning back in the easy chair smoking, with an attentive gleam in his eye, as though he were waiting to hear something that never got said.

"I haven't been to the Casanova," Medina concluded. ("Maybe he thinks this whole test is a prologue; that I went and spoke to her, that I have a message for him from her, a sign of regret, an apology, a never in the world, a never again.")

"She says she doesn't have the money to buy it. But I know her," Seoane said after a little while. His face was young and calm, at present bent over the disorder of the dinner on the table. The hair at the nape of his neck was very long, stained by summer. He slowly took out a cigarette and sat loosening the tobacco between his fingers. Turning toward Medina, he suddenly smiled. "Even though there aren't any limits for a woman. If she's really a woman, I mean. But it's true she has millions now."

"I agree with you," Medina said from the armchair next to the fireplace; he looked at him with bored eyes, with a kindly and stupid expression. "I understand; they never manage to be this or that for good. But it seems that she's really going to buy the Casanova. And the neon sign in the doorway alternately shows the name of the cabaret and her name. In letters the same height. We can get in the car and visit Santa María. I brought a dozen bottles of Barrientos's cane brandy home."

"None for me, I don't drink," Seoane said. "I don't feel like going to the city. It bores me. Out here I get bored in a way I like. I don't think she'll buy the Casanova even though she's got the money to. It's not her way of doing things. What's odd is that you know so many things without having been anywhere around there."

"I haven't gone there, but maybe I will tonight." With his legs over the arm of the chair, Medina looked, closing his eyes halfway, at the boy's bare brown shoulder. He wanted to be nothing but a voice, a challenge, a cautious provocation. "But the police have been by there. The boys, Martín, Valle and Ruiz, were there, on several nights. The throat-slitter of Enduro had held up the gas station for boats at the port after killing his wife. He'd bought himself a suit, shoes, a silk shirt, a tie. He'd been asking for the works at the barbershop in Ainsa. A guy like that, if he couldn't escape from Santa María—and we were almost certain that he hadn't—and had money burning a hole in his pocket, was bound to end up drunk in one of the cabarets. He turned up at the Casanova. A fat man less than thirty, with a mustache, acting out the fear of reaching the point of not believing in himself. And so he'd slit a woman's throat. She wasn't even that: he slit the throat of what he'd had and used for years for a wife. Then the boys went to the Casanova several nights in a row, waiting for him. They took him away drunk and begging them to recognize I don't know what secret pact between men that went back thousands of years. They told him they would. And the next morning he was still drunk and he cried as he explained to me, all upset and almost bursting out of the new clothes that he'd already had time to soil and wrinkle, that by now must be stained with the yellowish sweat of fat men who are scared. I didn't have any need to go to the Casanova; but maybe I'll go there tonight, without any need to this time either."

"I'm going to bed," Seoane said. "I'd like it if you could find out whether she bought it or is thinking of buying it. I'd bet not."

Medina didn't go to the Casanova that night. And he also thought it was another test to bring home with him the following Saturday a record with Dinah Shore singing "Prefiero que me lo digas" in English and get drunk after dinner and play the record over and over with the persistence of a drunk, till dawn, till Seoane got tired of listening to it and making jokes, and rose to his feet, shaking off his drowsiness, to go to bed.

"I don't remember anymore," he said. "But I'm sure she sings it better. Or in a different way, with something in mind that I like better. It'd be curious if you were to fall in love with her, if you were to turn into a miserable wretch and a drunk, if I had to invent plans to save you."

But Medina hadn't gone back to the Casanova, he hadn't seen Frieda. ("Why?" he thought. "I don't love him and haven't been able to love anybody for years. The more I see that he's freed himself of the need for that whore, the less he interests me, the more I feel him to be ordinary and replaceable. Saving him from that wretched state he was in was a whim, an obsession that has nothing to do with what I know about myself. And after all, he cured himself because he wanted to, without my help, because the illusion of love and need mysteriously wore itself out. Next week we'll go upriver and when I can convince him to leave Santa María forever I'll have lost all interest in him. He wasn't what mattered to me; it was his unhappiness, his enslavement.")

And perhaps Seoane had thought about the same things during the days he lived at the beach, during the lonely hours when he sat on his heels drowsing after throwing the hook with the little piece of bloodless bait into the water. Because there was the night he accepted a glass of contraband brandy, just one, and broke off an inconsequential conversation to say in a loud voice and with a vehemence that seemed to have been rehearsed for some time, that he knew more about Medina than Medina knew about him; that Medina didn't know anything and he, Seoane, knew everything.

"We've already spoken of this, and more than once, I don't recall how many years ago. You've always wanted to have a child, probably since the first time you slept with a woman. You said so, I remember. What you felt when you were on top of a woman was so important, so unrelated to any other sort of possible experience, that you needed to make it eternal, or enduring, or palpable, with a child. I never understood that; I still can't, at least in the case of a man. I never wanted to have a child. With Frieda less than with anyone else. And this is true, even though it's also true that Frieda was the only woman I'd had aside from prostitutes in ports. She didn't want to have one either. We loved each other too much to need or even accept that something be added to it. But you always needed a child. Maybe not only for everything I mentioned: eternity, enduring through time, the act of love made concrete and occupying a place in space. Growing, moreover. Maybe you also needed a child so as to justify your staying on top of a woman, to apologize and be forgiven. By whom? That's another problem. I'm better, after all is said and done and before, because I realize I don't understand anything and admit all the possibilities that I don't understand. Maybe that virtue—basically, the indifference you think you're capable of having—that virtue has developed in my case in the afternoons on the pier, where it's impossible for me to avoid the visits and the prattle of that pig of a neighbor of yours named Mr. Rey. He comes here by walking across bridges, or in his motor boat, always fat and seemingly asleep, always dressed in white and freshly showered and shaved after his siesta. At any hour. And from the confused prattle, from the terrifying stench of the barely stinking terror that reaches me from the defunct intelligence of Mr. Rey, I could extract two jewels of wisdom. First: it takes many different sorts to create a world, my friend. Second: God has strange boarders, my friend. I'm sorry not to be able to say it with his accent, with his shortness of breath. But, in any event, I believe in those two pillars of Mr. Rey's philosophy; and I cling to my faith. We didn't talk about that. We talked about your old, perhaps congenital need for a child and of the bad luck that kept you from having one. Then, ever since you've known me, or since long before that, you wanted to play at my being your son. No love involved, really: the pleasure of dominating, the petty, vainglorious satisfaction of dictating fates and contacts. No deductions involved, really: you led me to understand that many times, you unintentionally confessed it."

And all this pile of sentences spoken without alcohol, without vehemence, without the shadow of a desire for revenge. It was a Saturday at the end of January and Medina had been promised that he could begin his vacation the following Saturday.

"It may be true," he said with a smile as he walked over to the bottle of cane brandy on the table. "It never interested me to analyze Medina, to know about Medina; I let him live and help him. I try to treat others in the same way. With no need of Mr. Rey, I've learned not to look at myself. I simply am; I'm in the world and I do things. In this case, in the last chapter of this case, it occurred to me that you were too intelligent for the price of self-destruction that you were paying to be a fair one." He drained his glass, set it down gently on the table and moved closer to Seoane who was looking at him from the moon in the open window, with an expression of tamed rebellion, with an incredulous smile. He came close enough to be able to slap him gently on the cheek. "What you've said tonight, whether or not it's true, at least goes to show that it was worth the effort. Everything we know, you and I, shows that that bitch isn't worth a cent of anybody's money. That whore, I said." He waited a moment, breathing the slow-moving air rising off the river and the lemon trees, without shifting his gaze from the bright blue eyes, which remained vacant, only slightly curious, slightly insolent.

"And whenever you want to leave . . ."

"I don't want to leave," Seoane said slowly, shaking his head in the attenuated blue glow. "At least, when I leave it's not going to be on account of her. But it's not fear of insulting her and what's more it's of no use. I know her. I'm the only one who does."

"I'm glad. Yes, it always happens that way. Thinking about it carefully, it's only right that I beg your pardon. I thought that . . ."

Seoane raised his shoulders and one hand. His rejuvenated face seemed to grow thinner, ironic and knowing.

"I've talked a lot. There's nothing more to say. I'm going down to the river to have a look at the hooks and then sack out. Goodnight."

And the next morning, with the sun already high in the sky, when Medina went to get the car in the arbor, he could see the boy sitting on the edge of the pier, almost naked, broad-shouldered and fine-boned, holding above the water the useless curved fishing pole.

A black barge was clumsily making its way upriver; at the beginning of the invisible suffocating heat, to the right, the motor of Mr. Rey's boat purred.

THE FIGHT

That morning, Medina got up late in the little house on the beach where Gurisa, who had come back from Colón, sat yawning over her breakfast. The day was warm and peaceful; Medina walked unhurriedly along the usual path, cursing under his breath the Detachment, Santa María, returns and their uselessness.

Standing outside Mr. Wright's house, with its front door only partially closed, he heard groans and long, stammered complaints, a waste of breath since they were uttered in the Englishman's native tongue. He listened for a moment and then slowly opened the door and entered the yellow light. He waited for a short while, listening to the sounds: in the geometrical dark shadows, in the odor of a wine vault and dead air, in the curve of cement stairs. There was a cot; crates and bottles against the walls, a desk surrounded by chairs with bowed legs, with padded seats. He went on looking at the white shoes and trousers, the fat seated body, the infantile and repentant expression on the big round face.

"Chief," Mr. Wright murmured, his head swaying, letting out a laugh like the protest of a chicken.

Alone, his legs spread apart, and sweating in his chair as though this were a conscientiously fulfilled task, with one eyelid drooping down and turned a deep purple, his stubby nose swollen, his pink lips parted in a smile, Mr. Wright welcomed him, rocking back and forth above the creaking chair. Alongside several books lying in a pile on the table were his panama hat, a bouquet of jasmine, a bottle and a glass.

"How to escape the eye and the arm of the law? Not even in the stinking depths of this catacomb. I'm prepared to confess, without being pressured into it." He half closed his good eye to look toward the stairway over Medina's shoulder and then between his legs. He gave another laugh, slowly making once again his sound of a henhouse as dawn broke; he took a swallow from the glass and spread his tiny white hands. "I don't have another chalice to offer you, chief. Neither syphilis nor tooth cavities, for many years now. This cane brandy is the real thing; I don't know whether he paid import duties on it." The high-pitched voice seemed to laugh from underneath the impassivity of the little blue eyes, between sighs and stifled coughs. Medina lighted a cigarette and went over and sat down on the desk.

"Good morning. I was passing by and I heard. What kind of a fight were you in?"

Mr. Wright took his handkerchief wadded into a ball out of his trousers fly and kept shifting it from one hand to the other to wipe away his perspiration.

"Did she send you, chief?" Preceding the question, the growl resembling a laugh, the stupid, frightened, confidential expression on his face.

"Nobody said anything to me. I heard swear words and came in."

"Fulfilling your duty," the fat man said in a trembling voice. "But there's nothing going on here. And my asthma has been getting worse and worse for hours now in this filthy hovel. Do have a drink. I didn't even get up to greet you. But there are a hundred and twenty kilos, chief, sitting here in this dressing-table chair." The round pink face turned serious, slightly infuriated, the cheeks puffed out so as to breathe. He filled the glass and took a little sip, passed the glass to Medina and with furious attention watched him drink. "Real cane brandy, chief." He began to laugh and to cough, kneaded the handkerchief between the palms of his hands. Then he suddenly turned serious and looked straight ahead, frowning. "What do you want me to tell you, kind sir?"

"Tell me what kind of a fight you were in?" Medina put the glass down on the table, near the left arm of the man dressed in white, huge and drunk as a lord. Medina raised to his nose and mouth the bouquet of jasmine with a stem tied around it and slowly waved it back and forth. ("I can choose, any memory, and direct this white perfume toward him like a blinding light that will make his last wrinkle show.")

"Oh," Mr. Wright said. "I'm not complaining because I don't have anything to complain about. That's the only reason; I like to complain and I admit it. I admit everything." He laughed once again and touched his little round injured mouth with the handkerchief, holding it up with both hands. "Chief. Do you know who punched me?"

"No," Medina said. "In any case, it must have been a brave man." ("But what do I remember that matters to me? The last real scent of flowers is the one in the room where Teresa lay dead and invisible and the flowers had been offered her by persons unknown.") He let the branches of jasmine fall on the table and with a smile filled the glass and put it on top of the handkerchief that the panting fat man was holding in his hands.

"They like me and they hate me," Mr. Wright said, swiftly shaking his head back and forth to counter any objections. "I don't do anything, I live on a pension and a few dividend coupons. They love me because I'm a good-natured fat man. I'm nobody's rival. I am not personally acquainted with anyone who hates me, but they necessarily hate me. That's the way people are, chief."

("It's summer," Medina thought, separated from the heat by

the cool air smelling of years cooped up in the room, "summer. The renewed exhibition of faded hopes, the ingenuous and astute impulse to choose to believe for three months. And the way one says no out of habit and clear-sightedness without thereby being any saner than the person who accepts and gets involved.")

"A fat bachelor gringo who could have had grandchildren, who has a pension from the railroad company, who feels happy without being ashamed of it. Chief," Mr. Wright said, looking at him with brief desperation, cackling once again, "the only reason they have to hate me is that they realize I'm happy; what's more I tell everybody so. As I was telling you, the heat woke me up early this morning and I went down to the pier for a while playing with the doors and laughing because the morning had been made for me. I shaved and took a bath, I got into the boat and went to see him, but everything was all closed up. I was bringing him dozens of branches of jasmine for his wife and beating my hands on his pier and along the path till he came, all smiles, with a fishing pole over his shoulder, dressed in bathing trunks, half asleep and unwashed. Then he went to get a bottle and we sat on the pier under the willow trees, with our hooks in the water just for the fun of it, because I explained to him that with last night's strong current we weren't going to catch even a catfish. And we talked about the river, about Europe and about Santa María, and got to talking about places to get drunk in and be with women till we got around to the Casanova, which he said, indifferently, he'd never set foot inside of. And as we were talking we got around to her, the boss, Frieda. And lazily, jiggling the pole above the water out of habit, certain I wasn't going to catch anything, I told him what Frieda was like and how much she cost in cold cash. Even though sometimes she hasn't cost me anything, or not anything that could be paid at the moment anyway. And when it seemed to me that they'd taken off with the bait I started to pull the line in and he shouted at me as though he were laughing: 'Stand up, Fatty; do me the favor of standing up.' I got to my feet and saw that he was waiting for me with a smiling but determined expression on his face, standing there half naked, his arms hanging down, shifting about so as to get a firm footing. I asked him something, raising my hands, and he started punching me. I think I fell on the pier and there was nobody there when I was finally able to get to my feet to ask him to explain. I stood there rinsing my face off—he'd shut himself up in Frieda's house—and when I got tired of waiting I climbed into the boat. They're lovers, everybody knows about it. But that's no justification. That's all there is to it, chief."

"I see," Medina said. Before walking away from the table he stood there smelling the jasmine. "It's of no importance."

He felt that something had reached its maturity and rot had set in as he walked toward the stairway; that for years he had been swallowing the same thing over and over again, something that made him sick to his stomach and now he had to vomit it up.

"Good day, Mr. Rey. As usual, on the pier, any morning you like."

He remembered Mr. Wright at his feet, with his laugh trembling like the respectful coo of a dove.

SANTA MARÍA

Campisciano thought he ought to bring the news in person. But it was a night when there was lots to do in the restaurant; he decided that one of the waiters should run down to police headquarters with it.

He was a short skinny lad, an emigrant from the Swiss Colony who trotted through the streets repeating almost audibly the message that he was to pass on, which he didn't fully understand.

He had just put on his white waiter's jacket, which seemed to prolong the brightness of daytime in the calm dusk of Santa María, with no lights turned on as yet.

The police officer on guard at the door—wearing dress shoes, with his two hands leaning on the muzzle of his Mauser—impatiently nodded his head and ordered: "Go on in."

Timidly, the boy entered the patio and finally came to what was called the office of the chief of police. Vast and dirty, with its damp walls and its tattered wallpaper, it revealed its history as the former reception room of a wealthy family. The days when they were "at home," bejeweled women whose perfumes sold by Barthé mingled, the tea table in the center of the room, with the always brand-new set of chinaware and the big cake made by the mistress of the house. And the incessant prattle: abortions and adulteries, true or not, malicious predictions, the cost of food, the newest styles and knitting.

He saw Medina seated at the table that he used as a desk, with his uniform jacket unbuttoned and a swinging lamp hanging from the ceiling. Invisible to the waiter, some men were talking together on his right. He waited a moment and softly clapped his hands together.

"Come on in," Medina said without looking at the door.

He entered slowly and cautiously, with a respectful bow. Then he saw the men who had been talking together and two hens lying on the floor, with their feet tied together. One of the men was a policeman dressed in long pants, a jacket that had once been part of an army uniform and a revolver tucked in his belt. The other was skinny and dirty, dressed in clothes that were too big for him, and shoes each a different shape and color; their gaping tips were either yawning or asking to be fed. He wore a black neckerchief to show that he was in mourning.

"You again," Medina said with feigned despair.

"People have to live, sir," the man with the neckerchief said in too high-pitched a voice for his body.

"To live. And why do you have to live?"

The man looked at him in surprise, opening his dark eyes which he had managed to protect from filth, from misfortune, from his own life. His hunched-over body straightened up. "I don't mean me, sir. My family, I mean."

"I know the whole story. In exchange for two hens Barrientos or the Italian gives you a demijohn of that wine that they call a local vintage and that sets your insides on fire. It also helps a person to forget that his family's hungry."

The waiter stood there quietly, disconcerted, calculating the time that was going by, increasingly aware that he risked not being back at the restaurant before it opened for dinner.

Medina waved a pencil as though it were a scepter and asked: "Which of them is the fattest?"

With his right shoe, the yellow one, the man pushed the gray hen forward.

"Okay. Take the other one with you. And don't come bothering me for a month; I don't like seeing your face or getting a whiff of the smell of you. And kindly be quick about it."

The man leaped forward, squatted down agilely and stood up again with the scrawny hen flapping its wings, its feet tied together.

"Thanks, chief. If you'll open the outside door for me . . ."

Medina pressed a button, a harsh bell rang and the man disappeared. With the pencil Medina pointed at the policeman in the long pants and then at the fat hen.

"It's yours, Héctor," he said.

The corporal—he was still wearing sergeant's epaulets—smiled in mock protest. "But, chief . . ."

"That's an order. You're all dressed up in a carnival costume; I owe you two paychecks. Next time you're the one who'll get the skinny chicken."

Once he was alone with Medina, the waiter felt the message slipping away inside his head.

"Speak up. What other sort of con game has your boss thought up?"

"He says to tell you that there's a banquet tonight. Lady friend of yours. The German one got drunk with one of her friends. The banquet is in your honor. But you don't have to come."

Once the waiter had left, on the run again, Medina summed up or translated "Frieda had ordered a midnight supper. Five or six women who knew him from Lavanda. He, Medina, was the honored guest; but they didn't want to set eyes on him. There would, of course, be a chair at the head of the table that nobody would occupy. Something bad, since it was a practical joke Frieda had invented when she was drunk and stoned. And Don Aldo Campisciano would charge for six people, as in the meantime he sent him a word of warning of what the sextet of females was up to, just in case.")

Shortly before midnight Medina passed through the last

211

remaining traces of the Plaza, now permeated by the full-bodied odor of Italian cooking. He made his way into the dampness of passageways twisted out of shape by recent masonry work, traversed easy and pointless labyrinths.

These were not the remains of a city razed by the troops of an invader. It was decay, poverty, the ironic heritage of a generation lost in cars that no one remembered, in nothingness.

A few traces remained: dust atop a leather easy chair, abandoned and missing a leg; mirrors stained with spots of whitewash, framed in cream-colored wood; little plaster roses, scattered in disorder on the walls. Guided by the oregano and the garlic, he reached the restaurant.

At nine o'clock that night, he'd telephone Díaz Grey.

"Evening, doctor. It's Medina, of course, the man with the golden voice. Nobody dead for the moment. To ask you a favor. I've worked up my nerve to call you because I know you don't go to sleep till the sparrows start bothering you. A favor. A witness who can testify. Be at Campisciano's place around midnight. It's true, when I think of that place downstairs I still call it the Plaza. It must be old age. Thanks, doctor."

Medina went past one side of the three women's noisy table. There were only the three of them. Almost without looking he greeted them with a polite bow and went to the end of the room, where he curled up, with his back to the wall, at an empty table. He asked for a bottle of Paraguayan cane brandy and two glasses. He was sitting in profile to the tableful of women, and as he slowly drank and smoked he began waiting for Díaz Grey. ("Only three of them and I thought, I believed I remembered that I'd made it with many more there in the south.")

Díaz Grey came in talking with Seoane; they halted for a moment and then the youngster stayed to join the women. Even though it was a warm night, the doctor was wearing a hat (a Stetson, I'm sure, Medina thought) and removed it to greet the women at the table presided over by Frieda. Medina greeted him with a big smile as he looked at the doctor's thin face, the circles under his eyes, his sparse reddish blond hair with traces of white.

("Of course," he thought, "Petrus's daughter, more than twenty years difference; thought she's stupid, so skinny, she looks as though she's anemic, as thin as a rail; but when it comes to women, nobody ever knows beforehand. If somebody were to give me a hundred dollars for every time I was wrong.")

They spoke of the heat, of the ferry, of the way the Plaza had gone downhill.

"Everything in this city," the doctor said, in a dull, muted voice. "We're suffering from dermatitis, every day we lose a bit of skin, or a memory. Or a cornice as well. Every day we feel more lonely, as though we were in exile. And every day the gringos of the Colony buy yet another section of the city. There's hardly a business establishment that doesn't belong to them. Even Campisciano, despite his name, is just a front of theirs. Sometimes I think they gave him or lent him the money to buy the Plaza. So he'd go on destroying it and making it uglier and uglier by putting up wooden partitions. It's a boarding house today. This very dining room, if you recall the way it was."

"I know. I live here. I have one room with a bath and a window. When I'm not at the little house on the beach."

"Yes, it's all very sad. I don't go play poker at the club anymore. There's nobody left from my day, from our day, I mean. I wait at home for sleep to come. Games of solitaire and chess."

(And a drug injection every so often, Medina thought, ironically and impassively.)

"I've already made up my mind to die here. Even though it's not out of duty." Díaz Grey smiled. "But you. You who managed to escape the clutches of God or the devil. Quite frankly, I don't understand why you came back. Unless you were attracted by the famous nostalgia for filth."

Medina moved back from the table, still looking the doctor in the eye.

"Yes," he said cautiously. "I escaped in one boat and came back in another. Police chief of Santa María. I came on a visit, an inspection tour. Or so I believed. Later I discovered I had some things to do. Without much conviction, naturally. Nothing ever happens here."

He brought his body back to the edge of the table and as he filled their glasses again he heard the sound of the talk and the laughter of the three women at the next table; Seoane was also talking. A fit of rage came over him and he downed his brandy in one swallow. Then he smiled and his manner became cordial once again. ("No, I won't ask him yet; with all his faults, he's the most decent sort in Santa María. I don't want him to think my invitation wasn't a disinterested one.")

"We haven't seen each other for quite a while. I forgot to congratulate you on your marriage."

"Thank you." A mocking smile lingered on Díaz Grey's face. "Excuse me. It's been almost a year. All the people who congratulated me thought that I was marrying the hypothetical millions of old Petrus and the not at all hypothetical mansion on pilasters, without a mortgage. But I'd been in love with Angélica Inés since she was a little girl. And because she's not an adult and never will be, I'm still in love. Then later on, through the mysterious help of Braunsen, who moreover doesn't exist, we won the case against the railroad. We now have millions in money that's almost worthless. And we don't need it. I could say, though I'd be lying, that I'm telling you things in confidence. But the truth is that I never hide from anyone either my love, mildly perverse, or the millions that came afterwards."

Medina nodded his head and sat stirring, slowly and with a thoughtful look, the liquid in the glass.

"Thanks for your trust in me, doctor," he murmured in a tone befitting a wake. "I'm a friend. And what's more a friend who's understanding and respectful. That's why I tell you, as a friend, that I'm going to talk to you some day about money and a project. But don't get the idea that it's anything commercial, I'm not going to set up a shop to give the gringos competition. It's not a matter of buying and selling. It's not a matter of making a profit. Quite the opposite. That's why you'll help perhaps, only one person like you. And I swear to you, by whatever you hold most dear, that I'm not flattering you."

He raised his head to look at Frieda's face; she had come over so close to the table that she was almost pushing against it with her thighs. The Presidente brandy danced in the glasses for a second and then settled back down.

"Excuse me, doctor," she said, smiling. "I didn't want to bother you. But since the chief of police, my friend, decided to make himself comfortable in the dining room without anyone having invited him . . . Police headquarters must have a good intelligence service."

"Will you join us?' Díaz Grey asked her politely. "We were talking about Santa María. We were saying that nothing ever happens here."

"That's true,' Medina said. "We were having a quiet talk together. But I wouldn't mind if you—or let's drop the formal you and use the familiar *tú*—if you took part in the conversation."

Frieda, who hadn't quite finished her smile, now directed it toward Medina.

"Oh," she said; the smile gradually spread to the corners of her mouth, which a moment before had already started drooping with sarcasm and scorn. She drew up a chair and sat down; she was wearing a black dress that fell in shiny folds. Medina noted that she wasn't wearing pearls; just a brooch, on her bosom, with a black design, difficult to make out, which was repeated on her bracelet and her ring.

("Lesbians used to wear ankle bracelets to show that they belonged to a sisterhood and scare men away. Today that's gone out of fashion, this must be what they wear now. A goddess of Gomorrah, the shield of Bilitis.")

"Oh," she said. "Just for a moment, I'm very well-mannered; especially since my relatives, tutors, executors, accountants were called to the great beyond. There's been an end to niggardly money orders that always come late. Everything's mine today. Moreover, thanks to Brausen, they got over their shame at knowing that I was alive and breathing in Santa María and was sleeping with anyone I cared to. I include you among them, chief, even though our illegal marriage took place in Lavanda."

"And where you go on loving," Medina said, in a vulgar, superior tone of voice.

"Am I de trop?" Díaz Grey asked politely, in a grandfather's affectionate tone of voice.

"No, she's the one," Medina said, and handed Frieda his full glass.

She drank and then threw her lips away in disgust.

"This is ordinary stuff and it burns. I've always been told that policemen lived like rich people on the bribes they took. And that they extended invitations like rich people."

"Absolutely true. In Lavanda I lived for some time as the husband of a very pretty woman who sometimes said she loved me. That was a bribe. She even put up with poor Juanina who, as I'm coming to see now, might have been interested in you. But I don't like the game you're playing with Gurisa. Gurisa to me. Olga to everyone else. Here, unfortunately, I could bribe only Campisciano. And with no hope of anything but credit and a lower price."

"Do stay, doctor," Frieda said.

"Perfect. I had called on him to be a witness to so much predictable stupidity. Grown women and Seoane, who's just a kid."

All of a sudden Díaz Grey stopped being a grandfather. He sat up straight in the chair and said in the voice of a diagnostician:

"Here everyone apologizes for being a bother. I'm going to be one who doesn't apologize. That boy has already been to the bathroom three times and come back feeling happy, or so he believes or feels, with shining eyes. I can see by the way he moves that he's an addict. He's drunk, and stoned besides. You, Medina must know where cocaine is available in Santa María."

Medina spoke in a parody of a chief of police. "You have some in your office."

"The amount that's necessary and perhaps even less."

"Thanks. I have to know how it gets in. I'd at least like to save the kid."

He leaned back in his chair and in a moment he shook his head. He looked in the air as he said, as though reciting: "Two places. That's one of them. Maybe you shouldn't have asked me. doctor." Without looking at Frieda he said happily: "And now, with your permission, I'm going to take Gurisa away with me."

"Several books back I could have told you some interesting things about alkaloids," the doctor said, raising one hand. "But not any longer."

"Yes, I've learned a little," Medina commented, standing up. ("As a matter of fact," he thought, "they can all die dripping drugs out of their ears. Who matters to me?")

Gurisa saw his signal and came over to the table.

"Doctor," Medina asked, as they said goodbye to each other, "do you know a fellow they call 'Red'? I've seen him prowling about around here. And people have told me something."

"Oh, it's an old story. We were together for a while at a house on the beach. A strange sort. The whole thing takes up any number of pages. Hundreds."

THE WAY II

And they kept on, knowing it, through the wine of the first Mass, the struggle for their daily bread, ignorance, stupidity.

They went on, content, distracted, almost without hesitating; so innocent, relaxed or tense, to the final hole in the ground and the last word. So certain, ordinary, silent, reciters, imbeciles.

The hole had been awaiting them without real hope or interest. They happily went on their way, some leaning on others; some of them went on alone, smiling, talking softly to themselves. In general, they discussed plans and spoke of the future and of the future of their offspring and of revolutions great and small recorded in books clutched beneath their armpits. One of them gesticulated with his hands as others rambled on about memories and their lovers and faded flowers that bore the same name.

MARUJA

And there was the night, another Saturday, when Medina stopped the little asthmatic car two blocks from the Casanova and slowly walked up the steep sloping street, smelling the air restively and in surprise, as though he had just discovered the scent of summer.

He had been gone on a trip to Enduro and El Rosario during the week; that afternoon he had brought the throat-slitter of Enduro to the jail in El Rosario in his car. Without handcuffing him, visibly storing away his pistol in the pocket of the car door, wrought up by the unbearable heat of the dry January afternoon, by contempt, by a puzzling hatred that the murdered woman played no part in.

The fat man sitting slumped down in the car seat to his right was sweating and stank. ("This is the phosphoric smell of anxiety grown cold, like that of fear, yet different because of its lack of cunning and aggressiveness. There is another sort of perfect crime, also impossible. A victim who would give rise only to respect and a touch of pity. A corpse without blood spots or with the spots so well distributed that they would barely underscore the death and the violence. The woman hung over the edge of the bed and her short stiff hair might have scratched the floor if there had been any more room on it for more scratches. Fat, although not as fat as he was, infected by the obesity of this poor devil as though it were a venereal disease. Her legs spread apart and doubled up so as to kick out with the worn, dirty stockings that she would call champagne-colored, one folded over below her knee and fallen, all out of shape, down over her ankle; the other stretched till it almost tore apart, tied with a knotted band of elastic. Without a face, since it had been obliterated by the crusts of blood that surrounded the only beauty that perhaps she never had, the blue eyes of a lamb, opened furiously so as to absorb the life of the wretched room, of the daily traces of existence, of the heat stored for weeks or months under the tin roof, of the light that overran the defenses of the bits of cloth in the two windows. He killed her at eight o'clock in the morning and despite all the confessions that he's made and will make neither he nor anybody else will ever know why.")

Medina drove along the rises and falls of the highway, narrow, gray, intense in all the landscapes it traversed, with only light traffic made up of enormous shaky trucks, carts swaying back and forth, sulkies drawn by trotting ponies. The car left the coolness of the river behind and went on between taut barbed-wire fences, amid dry fields, and distant cows, skinny and motionless. The fat man's body complacently offered no resistance to the car's jolting as he sat stroking his wet mustache with his index finger. Every so often he gave a sigh and summed up, with the surprise of a bridegroom, his thirty years of experience: "That's just the way it goes."

Every half-hour, Medina lighted a cigarette and handed him another one and the dashboard lighter. He tried not to brush his hand against the man's fingertips. He drove with one arm, leaning back in his seat, his furious eyes narrowed to slits riveted on the shaky edge of the road. When they reached the mountains of the countryside around Gradin, where the highway goes steeply downhill in hairpin turns, the man asked permission to get out.

"The beer the boys gave me," he explained; his little, barely visible mouth tried to frame a sentence and an apologetic smile.

From the car, scratching with itchy fingers at the lid of the side pocket in the door where he had put the pistol away, Medina watched him totter off, numbed, squatter and shorter with each step he took, his shadow closely resembling that of the trees that were beginning to grow long and tinged a dark blue.

When at nightfall they reached the edges of the stench of tanneries that envelops El Rosario, the fat man coughed and said: "That's just the way it goes. Some ten years without getting either a yes or a no. She never gave me a reason. And I brought the reasons from outside or invented then, unjustly. The cane brandy, maybe. No: I don't drink it any more. I got the idea that she'd slept with Tabárez, and she gave a laugh, but from the look in her eyes I thought I had proof."

"Bullshit," Medina said idly. "I've heard that lots of times."

("He killed her at eight o'clock in the morning and stood there looking at her or walking around the room, stopping up her throat with little bits of wood wrapped in rags. And he must have paced around drunk and bare naked, his buttocks slapping against each other, a man so fat he made a person laugh.")

He handed him over, they fawned over Medina for having brought him in all by himself and without handcuffing him, they invited him to get soused and go out to eat together, and for dessert they gave him, like a reward they hadn't wanted to waste or cut down on by giving it to him before then, the right to go on vacation beginning on whatever day he chose.

"Thanks," he said, certain that they were doing him a favor. "Beginning this minute. Nothing's happening in Santa María. Not one robbery, not one horse that's gotten out of a barbed-wire fence, not one kid who's drowned one Sunday, there are drunken binges and scandal, but there are few topers who kill anybody. I'm glad because they say the fishing's good. I'm glad because Martín is going to be able to play at being chief of police for two whole weeks."

He made his escape from the restaurant by lying, saying he still had a few matters to settle in Santa María, thinking he'd begin his vacation immediately, with some woman or other he could get right there, in El Rosario. He went into a couple of cheap bars and in the second one he chose a skinny woman who smiled at him from the counter, with a reddish hairdo that made her smile look a little like Teresa's.

"Hi, there, dearie. How're you doing?" she said, and drank down half of her syrupy drink.

She showed her young teeth again and Medina examined the outline of her half-open mouth, the colors of the glints in the coppery hair that fell over her ears.

("A resemblance, almost but not quite beyond recall, though growing fainter by the minute. A resemblance like the ones that I invent for the masks she wears to look at me in dreams from the other side of death.")

"What's your name?"

"Maruja."

"Okay then, Maruja," Medina said. "I have to be in Santa María before midnight. You can have another drink and charge it to me without drinking it."

She gave a quick, cheerful smile, nodding her head and once again there was a resemblance for the space of a second, perhaps not to her, perhaps only to a mood of hers, to the times when Teresa raised the tip of her chin, to the tone of her voice when she said: "Now that we've gotten this far . . ."

"I'll have another drink," the woman murmured, bringing her face closer to his across the table, with no possibility of repentance and confession.

"Not me," Medina said. "Maruja." Now the woman with the indifferent face was nothing but a skinny red-headed whore, putting a slow, lewd, assiduous tongue into the thick green drink.

"Maruja." He called the waiter over and paid and sat there laughing so as to be forgiven for seeing the ghost of Teresa. ("The color of Frieda's hair is closer and a truer likeness, as I remember. But because of its difference the hair of half a dozen women who are waiting for me at the Casanova tonight is an even closer likeness. And that's exactly where I'm headed.")

Still naked, she tucked the two bills into her handbag, took out a round mirror and busied herself putting make-up on. Then she smiled as she carefully straightened the folds of her blouse.

"A little piece of trash," he said timidly, with a smile.

THE CASANOVA

Without dreaming and without remembering, Medina traveled back to Santa María through the warm, dusty night, repeated in the dark the easy curves of the road, the ups and the downs. It was twelve-fifteen when he got out of the car two blocks away from the Casanova and walked down the Calle América with his nostrils flaring, with a kindly and sustained fury, looking at the summer with half-closed eyes and entering it.

The sign "Casanova," with the last two letters gone out, in that blue that was almost violet, at once resigned and exasperating, of the signs for funeral hearses, twinkled, sick and sibilant as a firefly trapped vertically, on the narrow wet sidewalk. They had improvised a tiny window, they had dug a hole in the wall with a protective pane of glass over it in which to keep and display two bottles of expensive liquor, empty ones perhaps, and the large photo of Frieda. Loosening his tie, forcefully and irritatedly, Medina contemplated for a moment the oblique face in the gold frame, the white hair held tightly in place above the nape of her neck and the eyelids that threatened to cover the desperation of the look in her eyes, the slightly tragic, slightly mocking mouth. ("She's the same. There are women like that, if one had the patience to remain curious; but they inevitably go on being the same person. They can change their eyes, their mouth, their

224

nose; what never changes is the way, the manner in which those things combine to form a face.")

He pushed aside the new greenish plush curtain and did not look at the fat black dwarf, dressed in red, who smiled at him lowering his shoulders and murmuring a welcome that ended with the word "chief." He walked on in the semi-darkness toward the brightly lighted circular area where a man was playing the piano and another was apathetically accompanying him on a set of drums. He stopped on the edge, suddenly aware that he was still wearing his hat, with his hands in his pockets and the long strides of a man who owned the place. He removed his hat and walked on toward the right, to the edge of the brightly lighted circle, without stepping into it. He chose a table against the wall and waited for the set to end so as to have a look at the people in the room. He lighted a cigarette and tilted his chair back over the face of the woman, turned toward him.

Then, out of the white, circular silence that now encompassed voices and soft laughter, there came the white tuxedo of the waiter and his gradually lowered, servile voice: "The usual, right?"

"Yes," Medina said. "It's been so long since I've been here that the usual is going to be a surprise. But I don't want to be alone."

"I'll see, chief. It's a bit late."

"It's the Casanova, it's Saturday night, it's summer."

The pianist began to play with just one finger, slowly, searching for the keys with a crystalline sound. There was a woman standing next to the piano and the man was propping up her enormous mulatta's head with one hand. Beyond the circle of light a woman was singing, deeply moved, making mistakes, a marching song from the Spanish Civil War. Despite the hour, the smells of dawn were beginning to be perceptible in the thin, defenceless air.

"The usual," the waiter said. He put the glass on the table and opened the bottle and served Medina his drink with a friendly and triumphant air. "There's nobody here. But I sent word to the Seville, asking Trini to come over."

"The name doesn't matter. Gin and ginger ale. Isn't Frieda going to sing any more?"

"I don't think so, chief. She stopped singing a minute before you got here."

" 'Prefiero que me lo digas'?"

"She had to sing it again. Everybody still likes it."

"Trini, then, if it's possible."

"Right away."

Now the mulatto was playing a bolero and the placid fat man of about fifty who had been playing the snare drum with one or two little metal brushes, was scraping the bass strings of an enormous guitar and keeping time with his head and one foot. The woman in the background was singing drowsily; the clearness of the sounds, the echoes repeatedly bouncing back and forth foreshadowed the dawn. Medina drank and toyed with the box of matches. ("I can get along without a woman tonight, or else tonight a woman isn't worth the price of putting up with her chatter, her perfumes, her mere presence before and afterward.")

He saw her coming, walking toward him, moving, leaning on the other semi-darkness, that of the counter, which was separated from his by the white circle of light that contained the pair of musicians and half of each privileged table. He saw her silver hair and the tight-fitting black dress, he recognized—in another distance, one of years—the calm movements of her head, that slow raising of her hands, the prolonged motionlessness in supplication and expectation. He saw her, with her back to him, throwing her head back dramatically, laughing with the bartender, her laughter now including the dishwasher who appeared behind the counter. Leaning against a column, fat and faintly white, the waiter seemed to have given up trying to get hold of Trini.

Frieda turned around; there was only one other thing to do, she was incapable of imagining new pretexts or procrastinations. She turned toward the circle of light that the probability of dawn had shrunk, toward the corpulent pianist and the phlegmatic, plump, elderly drummer. She turned around with what remained of the forced laugh that she had addressed to the bartender and his helper; she was leaning her elbows on the counter and her black breasts stuck out underneath the glints of the gold chain around her neck and the smile that refused to die. She said something and the waiter lazily slid his back down the column to take an interested and apologetic look in the direction of Medina's shadow. He pretended to shake off his drowsiness as he repeated the order to the musicians. The mulatto squeezed his ribs with his elbows and began softly playing; the fat, elderly one, overcoming his reluctance, began to dust off "Prefiero que me lo digas" on the drum.

Medina went on leaning, slowly, carefully against the wall and smiled at the woman for a second, as an equal. Then he put out his cigarette and let her come ahead, saw her move her body away from the counter, cross through the semi-darkness, distant and innocent, step with false torpor through the disk of light and tired music, glide into this half-protective shadow. He watched her stoop and loom larger, he was certain that he had sensed her smile before he saw it.

"Good evening, Medina," she said; she barely leaned her hands on the sky-blue tablecloth, so as to show them, so as to offer to make peace.

"Yes," Medina said. "Do sit down, won't you?"

She leaned over as she raised her long skirt, as she made her face assume an expression of patience and disappointment.

The waiter filled Medina's glass. The musicians let the last notes of "Prefiero que me lo digas" die away, awaited for the space of a yawn and began to play the same thing again, discreetly and respectfully, knowing that they might well be obliged to go on doing so till noon.

"What about you?" Medina said.

"No. I've already sung and I've already had a bit to drink. That's enough for today."

"Best that way." He shook the glass to mix the gin and the tonic and desire and contempt slowly mounted inside him until they touched his diaphragm.

She glanced toward a movement at the front door and then turned imperiously toward the piano; the mulatto was now playing "Prefiero que me lo digas" very softly.

"Me," she said. "What made me come over to sit at this table? And what's going on with Seoane? And why, and above all how, did I buy the Casanova or am I about to buy it? And why is Seoane a poor kid? And why didn't I ever have a son? And why did you walk in tonight as though you owned the world, and why should I waste my time answering any questions? Tell me that, chief."

Medina drank calmly and slowly, taking dozens of seconds, as though he were alone at the table and alone in the Casanova; he lighted a cigarette and began to smoke it. He twisted around toward the woman, toward the place where, through the smoke, there was no denying that the woman was, an exhausted smile and sigh.

"Something's up," he said gently, envying the full-bodied, hoarse voice of the mulatto pianist who was now speaking in English to the piano keys. "Something's up to make you come sit down with me and talk so much without saying anything; to propose things to talk about, to spread them out in front of me for me to choose from. Something you're in need of to come visit me instead of wrinkling up your nose from a distance. You can ask and we'll see. Some difficulty about buying the place, or a little hysteria that lay hidden and growing until this summer night, or some scheme involving friendship and reconciliation?

Out with it. I didn't invite you over to my table. Why did you come?"

He spoke without looking at her and without hatred, for his amusement, idly thinking of Seoane, of the ride in the car with the fat throat-slitter, of how good it would be to be really alone in the dead summer midnight, to be listening to the low scattered notes, resonant, hollow, interminable without seeing or remembering the musicians. All of a sudden, he saw her shrug and not bother to smile to express disdain or fortitude. He saw the gentle, noble curve of her nose, the unquestionable intelligence of her eyes, the courteous movement, patient and mocking, with which she thrust her lips out for a moment.

"What is it?' he persisted, leaning over his glass; it was now rage that was being mixed with his desire.

"Nothing, chief," she said. "At least none of all that. It's true that we agreed, foolishly and without having said as much, that it was better not to speak to each other. It's true that I came over to your table without your having invited me. But don't worry; it's on the house. I don't want to ask you anything that resembles a favor. Simply . . ."

Medina looked at her, and as he tilted his body so as to lean on the wall of reeds and photographs and cross his legs, he frankly accepted his desire. She didn't invite it; her cold, beautiful face, almost masculine when she chose to cast challenging looks, scarcely moved, austere and sad. But he preferred to be unjust, he preferred loyalty not to himself but to resolves of long ago. ("It would please her, of course, to force me to go to bed with her, and especially to see me determined to seduce her, to see me refuse to listen to my own objections and the ones that she would cast my way, one after the other, each one feebler than the last and expressed with increasing vehemence. She'd like that, and she's out to get it, and that's why she came over to my table, she'd like to feel my fury and my surrender on top of her body, to feel me apart from Seoane, her ally or at least neutral."

"I don't think you've come over to my table out of fondness for me. There was a time when I was Seoane's friend, I was his friend, his only one, and more or less his father. He was the one who was responsible, you understand. Then, when things began to go badly, when I had to convince him that you were all the things you are and his downfall besides, I hated you and I would have liked knowing that you were dead. The thing is that . . ."

Frieda smiled as though she had heard words of praise, signaled to the waiter, and whispered something alongside the flabby cheek that the man bent down toward her.

("It could be, why not? Go swimming tomorrow with Seoane and as we're drying off on the thick planks of the pier tell him that I slept with her and with just one sentence cancel out his friendship and his love, and be free of this stupid submissiveness that's gone on for years now. It's possible.")

"What's happening, what you don't know is happening," she said as the waiter put the two bottles on the table. "is that a person doesn't have the courage to see friendship through to the very end. With love it can be done, a person is capable of doing it, perhaps because all of us know that love can have an end but not friendship. If it were possible to be friends till the very end, I would have crushed you long ago. Or at least it would have been up to me to do so."

She stopped aiming the invincible maternal smile his way and mixed the gin and the tonic. A group of five came in timidly, stopped to talk something over in low voices and then resolutely walked over to a table near the piano, beyond the circle of white light. The music went from a whisper to passion; anyone could see, behind the backs of the five of them, the pianist's white teeth, the drummer's zealous patience.

"Look after the customers," Medina said. "And tell me why you wanted to talk to me. I'm sleepy. And since you forbade the waiter to go hunt me up some female or other from the Seville . . ."

"Yes," Frieda agreed, with enthusiasm and sadness, as though she were listening to a more nostalgic and distant music than that of the piano and the drumbeats. "I told the waiter not to go because I wanted to talk to you. Moreover, the Seville has permission not to close till three. You can go look for what you want there, chief. We're decent here, the police only let us stay open till one."

"I couldn't say," Medina murmured. "The corruption in Santa María is no business of mine, the only thing that interests me is my own. You wanted to talk to me, I asked and we'll see. I know you're at this table to ask me something. I know women as well as though I'd given birth to them. If I no longer have the body of a twenty-year-old, that's the reason, because of having given birth to all of them. Out with it."

"Yes, chief," she said humbly; and it could be said that her sarcasm was confined to the metallic whiteness of the glints of her hair, to the surprisingly stubby fingers that held the glass to her mouth till she'd emptied it. "Did you know that we're neighbors? We're quite a way apart, but the mud street we both live on has the same name."

"Out with it," Medina repeated. "I can take you home; even though I'm falling asleep. I suppose that Seoane knows we're neighbors, that each one of his drunken binges knows the way to your house by heart and in the dark. The poor guy."

"No, it's not that either. I didn't come over to ask you for anything and Seoane never comes to my house. You"—the two women and three men who had gone over to sit down at the table next to the piano after stopping near the front door to hold a whispered conference once they'd traveled too boldly and swiftly through a vast area of linoleum and empty tables, had thrown their heads back and were laughing, playing at the game of who could raise the longest peal of blind laughter to the ceiling on which there had been painted in poor perspective a cupola of leaves, indefinable fruits, and taut, curved reeds from the Indies;

and had brought in with them in their hair and their garments the heat and the mild dampness of a summer day dawning, memories and promises of summer that spread all through the deserted and somnolent place along with the exaggerated vulgarity of their laughter; the pair of musicians emphasized the low notes to raise a swaying wall against the trembling air filtering in from the street that indifferently announced the end of Saturday night, the vulnerability of forgotten things and impulses—"you, who have given birth to all of us women, will die without knowing for sure if a woman had an orgasm with you or just made you think she did, without knowing whether your son is yours, without even knowing why they lie to you or whether the woman who lies to you even knows why she's doing it."

She made her face an impenetrable blank, turned around to mumble something toward the piano and the musicians who began to play "Bolero de la jungla"; she looked toward the table of five and bringing her face closer to Medina she gave him a deliberate, mysterious smile.

"I didn't want to ask a favor of you, chief. Just ask you a question. I'm thinking of buying the Casanova. You hate me now; if you're against me, I can't get very far. I wanted to ask you: shall I buy the place or shall I go away?"

("It's curious, but it's okay. The same face, the same way of not making up her mind to smile and of not looking at me, the same burdensome and bearable weight of fate in her swollen eyelids, and an identical way of spreading to the corners of her mouth memories of childhood and puberty that she presumes are moving ones. That was how she used to look at me when we were alone in Lavanda. Then maybe she went to bed with me to strengthen her bonds with Seoane, with Seoane's world. She'd do it tonight—if not as an old, almost unconscious whim—so as to separate me from Seoane, to convince me that she's the one who's right, so that it becomes impossible for me to admit she's right.")

"Go away," Medina said and made his cigarette moan inside his glass. "It would be better if you go away provided you can manage things so that Seoane won't follow your trail. But if you decide to buy this modest brothel and stay, you won't have any more fines than the ones you deserve. Moreover, there's a man who has an even more sordid joint than this in the old market. His name is Barrientos. He's got an old wife, he's got an old dog; or it's the wife who's got a dog. Both you and I, it occurs to me, and you especially, would have to thank him for having a drink with him and for the privilege of shaking hands with him. And yet, I don't even let him give me the usual drink offered gratis to police officers by bar owners. So what I drink isn't on the house. So if you really don't have anything to ask me, go check the cash register receipts and send me the waiter."

She shrugged again and smiled patiently, as though she were more mature than he was, calmly sensing each one of the experiences that Medina had suffered through.

"Go ahead and pay," she said as she got up, "since you seem to enjoy it. I asked you a question and you didn't answer. I already knew that I can either go or stay. We're still neighbors; maybe you'll feel sorry and come visit me to tell me if I should go or stay. You know what?" She seemed to lean down to get a better look at him and bring her smile closer; without turning her eyes away, unlike Teresa, but comparable in the distracted way in which she made herself necessary, tall with small firm breasts, she scratched at the package of cigarettes with her long fingernails. Pretending to lean on the green curtain, the black dwarf was trying not to fall asleep, with his back to the gentle, cool wind blowing steadily off the river, finally ashamed of the provincial night.

"You know what?"—she was smoking with the already damp, stained cigarette dangling from her mouth, and accompanying the music with her hand and the gold lighter—"I'm going to do whatever you tell me to. Go or stay. Whatever it occurs to you to tell me; like tossing a coin. But, in any case, I swear to you,

Seoane hasn't seen me for months; and if I went away he wouldn't know where."

"I'm glad," Medina said. "Tell the waiter to come over, please."

("And she's living with him, if it can be called living, with him drunk and stoned every day. Though maybe Frieda wakes him up when she comes home from work.")

She bent over the table just a little way, leaving behind a slightly different smile, with the mystery diluted in sarcasm and patience.

"Goodnight, chief," she said aloud and the two musicians suddenly fell silent.

"I can take you home. I'm sleeping at the beach tonight because I have to settle certain things. I'm leaving Gurisa at the Plaza because I'm going away early tomorrow morning. Two weeks in the capital."

"I've got my car," Frieda answered. "Making the trip together can make you forget or remember. Till, one of these days, we become friends again. And since there's a moon I'm going to wash my hair in the river. Fresh water. Some other time."

Medina, almost without moving, looked at the nape of her neck, her buttocks and her ankles. ("But since I can't understand my joy, others can't kill it and can't even see it. Perhaps I'll go by the Detachment right now and say goodbye (listen to Martín's oily voice, I can just hear him clapping me on the back with the comical solemnity that sets the style for our relationship, flatteringly call me 'chief') and pretend to be interested in some new clue about smuggling, in some drunk who's sleeping his binge off, in some miserable wretch. Or maybe I'll leave it till tomorrow and go sit on the pier now with a bottle, with my legs hanging over the ends of the summer night that we'll believe is endless, above the black and almost deserted river. Maybe I'll sit myself down relaxed and lazy and silently ask for explanations of things that were promised, that are of no importance because it doesn't matter whether they're in the past or in the future.")

The waiter picked up the bill and counted out the change. The notes coming from the drum and the piano were low-pitched, with long silences between them.

"Is that it?" Medina said.

The waiter had put away his bill fold and was waving his arms toward the ceiling and the green curtain where the dwarf was keeping watch, hopelessly, over the damp night. Then he bowed, still shaking his head, prolonging his admiration for the joke that Medina hadn't made.

"He's not a regular doorkeeper here," he explained. "They, the musicians, hire themselves out along with the dwarf. If there's no work for the dwarf, they're not for hire either."

"But why is it obligatory to hire the dwarf too?" Medina asked. "Is he the son of the drummer or the pianist?"

"Nobody knows," the waiter said sadly. "I think the dwarf is the drummer's brother, but I couldn't tell you for sure. They're very fond of him, but they hardly speak to him. They take care of him, the best food is for the dwarf and every Saturday night, when they're through work, they let him get drunk. They go to the Bavaria, which doesn't ever close now. Many thanks, chief."

The waiter tottered off to lean against a pillar near the table occupied by the three men and the two women. One of the women began singing again, paying no attention to the music: she had a pure voice, which didn't go at all with her cold, rancorous face. The song, a very old one, alluded to things that she had had only a presentiment of in the year that she learned to sing it and that she had never experienced. ("It wasn't love, it was an approximation, it was myself," Medina thought, killing time. "And sometimes Teresa thought it was lack of love, she couldn't understand the foreplay, she couldn't understand that because I wanted her I made her strip naked and kept dragging the whole thing out, drinking and smoking, looking at her on the sly, talking to her of serious things and foolish ones because when I opened my mouth I breathed better. She didn't understand it and mistrusted the whole thing, she felt uncomfortable and immodest. But it wasn't love; it was, the way it is now, the pleasure of prolonging the waiting for the rare important certainties that life gives me.")

The woman stopped singing and the other woman shouted "bravísimo" as the men laughed and applauded. Medina turned around, looking at the smiles of the two musicians, the colorful table at the edge of the white circle of light on the floor, the group of three at the counter going over the accounts together alongside the cash register.

("I haven't seen him for months. And she keeps him hidden, drunk, close at hand, under her thumb, next to the toilet at her place, snoring face up on a cot, swallowing with his mouth wide open the shut-up, ammoniacal smell.")

He got up and put on his hat; he walked to the door, the greenish felt, the dwarf who had trouble turning his smiling round head. He stopped and walked back to the table, passed by the musicians, who had calmed down now, waving his arms, his hat on the back of his head, containing the enthusiasm in his eyes, skirted the table for five full of bottles, and headed toward Frieda, who had climbed up on a stool and was sitting, her face drowsy, smoking through a long transparent holder.

A CHILDHOOD FOR SEOANE

Medina didn't know when Seoane had been born. But some time before, on a lonely night, horizontal and all by himself in his bedroom in the former Plaza, bored, hearing the rain beat down persistently in the distance, with a bottle of Presidente cane brandy and a carton of lung-scraping, dark-tobacco cigarettes, he remembered the unfailing recipe and had the boy born in the cold dawn of a day in the Colony: July sixteenth. He had seen that he had such reddish blond hair that he managed to convince himself that he was not his son. The boy continued to call himself Julián, María Seoane was his mother's name, but his father was a Swiss gringo. It was a good idea to give Seoane a childhood for his birthday.

He had been born, then, in July, in the Colony, twenty years before, on a (mysterious) night surrounded by a (mysterious) landscape peopled by (mysterious) beings. That was all he was able, really, to find out. Later on, they passed on to him—his mother, with the gentle, superior air of someone who's making up stories—toned-down versions of emergencies and terrors, words that alluded to prayers, first aid, resignation and a calm, a manly and yet asexual acceptance. They were—they and the beings who inhabited the environs—immigrants, pioneers, colonizers, greedy and rapacious; the women, moreover, could give birth and suckle their babies; but almost nothing else of any

237

importance differentiated them. Alien days, apart, not really lived, like bricks that kept piling up. Legend placed above the fear and the learned patience, above the whip-cracking racing of a tilbury driven by an already elderly doctor, a bright moonlight easy to imagine clearly, and close at hand but already dead, almost invisible. Another sort of moon, fantastic people impossible to understand moving mechanically and awkwardly in that variable landscape of twenty years before, freezing cold and forever destroyed by time and blind, comical human activity.

So that, at times, he made do with the enormous blood-soaked bed, the light of the kerosene lamp, the candles in front of the religious prints on the shelf that ran along three walls of the room; and himself being born of his mother with dizzying gentleness. Sometimes the old doctor lent a trembling hand; at other times he kept on trotting beneath the waning moon without ever arriving in time.

Then, the father pounding with his whip handle on the desk of the Registrar's Office in Santa María, so stubbornly certain that he was protecting himself from violence, so certain he was fighting for the truth, or, at least, for an isolated and invincible truth, that he didn't show how moved he was when he folded in four the paper which confirmed his right to name the son he had come to declare as his Julius and not Julián.

Then, another nothing, a happy supposition, warm and believable, several years that ended in the discovery of rites and laws, of an elderly and taciturn father, skinny, standing tall and straight, never wrong, with a meager handful of beard that was turning gray, and of an ample, disillusioned mother, not placid and smelling of cheap perfume.

Then, the instinctive and eternal alliance with the woman; and not for aggression but simply for defense; and against or in the face of the world, persons or animals, the heat and the wind, sadness, the indefinable threat of certain hours; not against the very tall and self-restrained, bearded man, and the world of obligations that he silently imposed each afternoon when he returned from the fields; long-legged but moving with ridiculously short steps that befitted the small boots, the legs of them almost hidden by the white balloon trousers that would again be immaculate in the morning. The foreign embroidered jacket, the neckerchief worn in mourning.

Then, the complicity, more frivolous, in acts of disobedience that the smiling woman had suggested: sweets, siestas, hours whiled away in the hen-house and the rabbit hutch, the suits made of velvet and lace sewed in secret, worn fleetingly when all alone. The laughter and the suffocating kisses, the woman's oppressive and protective beauty: his ally, his bliss.

Then—although perhaps he never knew it—the battle begun when seven of the twenty years were almost over. The traps and the overt fight to keep the silent man with the gray beard from loading the boy into the two-wheeled carriage or into the newly purchased truck—with the indispensable details that would fill in the terror of separation: a brand-new valise, a basket full of fruit, a couple of hens with their feet tied together—to climb unhurriedly the road to Santa María, going without stopping on the way and without curiosity through the city which at the time was giving birth to a house a day, and at the end of the afternoon, after a journey of four or six hours, finally handing over everything to the superior of the Jesuit school in Colón. The pretexts, the calculated fits of weeping, the dramatic, genteel attacks of shortness of breath during which the thick dark braids, younger now than the woman, ceased, by their own will, to wind round her head, fell and came undone. And the mornings when the boy baffled and healthy, was sent to bed and the woman shut herself up in the bedroom, worried, with a brave smile, ready to weep as long as necessary.

Until the man with the little white beard said one night after supper: "tomorrow"; and the woman bribed a farmhand to bring her the old doctor and made arrangements to meet him in the alley of twisted young trees that had just been planted from the door of the house to the road, of mud or clods of earth. And she also bribed the old doctor, the same one who had or had not been present when she gave birth, depending on the whims of her false memory. Until she, that same night, went up to the attic and calmly rummaged in silence through the pitiful objects, the little stories, that filled the trunks, and was able to find a yellow European document, a diploma vaguely authorizing her to teach children.

"But not in Spanish," the tall skinny man, the man who had called the child Julius and therefore believed that he had rights over him, said shortly after dawn, at breakfast.

She smiled. The man with the white beard hadn't thrown the paper in the fire on the hearth. She brought coffee to the table and crossed her arms over her still-firm breasts.

"Children, things, everything's always the same everywhere."

She saw the man who could have been her father to the door, smiled at him maternally when he turned his head before he put spurs to his horse.

Then, the prompt farce of every day and here the memories limited to dusk falling late in the afternoon in winter: the translucent porcelain lamp on the red velours table cover with thick S's and gold trefoils. María's slow, cheerful voice—sometimes she spoke with her eyes shut and it was as if she were recounting a dream, hardly believing it herself—the smell of lavender warmed in the neckline of her dress. The farce quickly invented and staged, more swiftly, calmly and believable as they became inured to transgression. The voice of the sparrows pretending to go mad in the sky and the garden, as afraid of the dark as though it were the first night, searching for a tree. The games, the disguises and the stories were coming to an end. She was maturing without suffering, she was playing the role of the only woman on earth as she withdrew her ample hips, her ankles of a girl to the window. She placed her forehead against the glass, the tip of her short nose perhaps, and forgot the little boy for a moment, immersed herself in the purity of being without memory or presentiments.

Then, she lowered the curtains over the last orange of another short day mistakable for any other; lighted the lamp, spread out notebooks, books, her hands wearing rings on top of the now-appeased blood of the table cover. The man with the little white beard was announced by voices saying goodbye and the horse's hoofs. He passed by them without caring to look, he saw the woman's smile, and went into the bedroom to change his clothes.

Then, the afternoon that ended differently without anyone's having announced it, the afternoon ten years after the old doctor's unlikely trip in the carriage beneath the light of the moon that had perhaps existed, the afternoon when the very tall, lanky, numb man arrived at the usual hour, this time in the two-wheeled carriage, accompanied by a not very fat, not very convincing priest.

The supper which the priest shared after the hasty blessing and which he enlivened with stories and jokes, to an excessive degree for the other three, accustomed to silent yet not dreary meals. And when the tablecloth was removed and coffee was brought, the priest wanted to know what the boy had learned since the day on which she had dusted off the absurd teaching certificate with a heading in Gothic letters. The man with the short beard smoked his rustic pipe, patiently, resolved not to voice his prejudices. The woman listened, in tears and with her cheeks flaming, as though it were the little boy who had been humiliated. Furious, unearthing old reasons to take revenge, for the sudden betrayal, for the years in which the old man had allowed her, had induced her by indifference and silence, to perform the comedy of giving lessons, of passing on knowledge that was not hers to give, that perhaps she had once had and had forgotten, carefree and smiling in the face of the things that count in life. Not out of tact, but because partial victories did not matter to him, the man older than she made no comment after taking the priest back to the seminary and returning around midnight. He lay down next to her without listening to her crafty justifications and dropped off to sleep with the same heavy, personal snore as usual after kissing her on the forehead.

"On Monday I'm going to take him to the seminary," the old man said at another breakfast. In the window, in the door standing ajar that the restless dogs keeps going through, perhaps in the same dark living room smelling of smoke and threadbare plush, it was already autumn, deft and serene. "His clothes must be gotten ready."

He finished eating the thin slice of lean meat and sucked up the maté in silence, showing her that he wasn't listening even though she kept going back and forth without a word. From the door, where he stood, tall and white-haired, surrounded by the yapping dogs, he turned his head halfway round; he had already kissed her, he had already finished with her till noon or nightfall, because he was now going to put up wire fences.

"The seminary so as to please you. Because I for my part would take him out into the fields tomorrow. It's enough if he knows how to write and keep accounts."

He, the boy, although he didn't say so, preferred the seminary, friends, surprises and mistakes. But she didn't speak of a choice. She only asserted, hiding her tears and showing them to him, holding him on her knees that afternoon, that he, wasn't she right?, never wanted to leave his mother. She took him to the attic then, to the confusion of mingled dust and spider webs, of valises and trunks that had turned, years before, once and for all, into pieces of furniture that would never travel anywhere again.

From the door that reached nearly to the sloping ceiling, halted in his tracks by the dampness and the probable odor of rat filth, he saw the woman crouch down, looking radiant and young, alongside the trunks with heavy convex lids, protected by moldy brown leather straps. He saw her open them and turn toward him for a moment, impetuously and indifferently, her face, which had taken on the gleam of tears and of a smile that neither the boy or the old man had ever seen. The soft golden sunlight came through the one dirty windowpane, to spread out with precision over the bound braids, the whiteness of her back, the patent leather shoes arching up from the floor.

"Like me," she said in an aloof, cautious, calculating voice as though she were approaching a bird. But she was standing motionless above the echo of the squeaking trunk opened with difficulty and lifting out a girl's pink dress, with bows and lace edgings. "Like me, when I was this big and there was going to be a party."

He allowed her to put the dress on him, feeling embarrassed but without protesting and even pretended to dance about in a semicircle in a pair of worn-out high-heeled shoes in front of the woman, who had sat down on the trunk and now without crying was singing incomprehensible words and clapping her hands in time, half asleep.

Then, there came the dawn when he was dragged out of bed and became all excited at having a man's boots and farmer's clothes to wear. In the big room where they ate he added his silence to the father's stillness without promises and both were served impartially by the woman who moved back and forth accepting old age, the shock of running into the wall, the lack of love in the future.

A Childhood for Seoane II

There then began the work on the farm, the discovery of a world of which he had been deprived, of which up until then he had known only echoes, reflections, empty forms—or ones stuffed absurdly full—despite having had it right next to him, surrounding him. In the beginning he hated the transplanting and the failures and exaggerated his need for consolation. He did not address a single cultured word to the old man; he sought his mother's eye and nothing was easier to find or harder to escape; they looked at each other and the look was a tacit agreement to meet later. She would escape from the enormous, grumbling, perhaps already eternal bed; steal away from the invariably uninterrupted snores, it seemed, all through the precise eight hours of sleep, and leave the door of the boy's bedroom open so as to continue to hear them and be able to mingle her tears with her son's in peace. She, at least, didn't hate the old man, she did not make him responsible for the little boy's sufferings, for the early risings in winter, for the falls from the horse, for the sleeve caught and torn by a threshing machine. She would kiss and care for his bruises; she learned little by little to look the future in the face, to accept that there was nothing to do but hate life, the passing of the years, the differences in people's fates.

So that the change in the boy was incapable of taking her by surprise. She realized that something was happening long before he himself was aware of it, shortly before she was able to discern the signs of the change appearing in the boy's body and movements. It must have been the end of the second year; his father had already been paying him half the wages of a farmhand for a year; with an obscure rancor that kept returning on seeing the dirty bills counted out on the table after dinner on the last day of each month, the boy took the money and didn't keep it, he simply slipped it into the earthenware piggy bank, he eliminated it.

And it wasn't that he'd stopped pleading with his eyes for nightly visits from her. Things seemed to go on as they always had and she didn't want to think any farther, she refused to imagine the possibility of events being different from the usual everyday ones. Something was happening, she wasn't able to discover what it was and she put herself on guard. The lad must have been twelve years old or so and he had grown a lot but he was still weak, languid and handsome. And there must have been a short period, an instant, a flash of lightning between the moment when she suspected the change and the moment long after when she began to see it. An instant, a flash of lightning when she understood everything, as though she had smelled it with whatever womanliness she had left in her, with the feminine side of herself so slowly come to an end in her thirty-two years; like a pain.

She was prepared for that and for everything; in order to put up with it, because the only thing she could plan now was solutions, consolations, passive remedies. So when she saw the change, later on, she recognized at once something animal and age-old and one of her cautious foresights.

She saw that during the nearly silent meals something was being added to the boy's respect for and fear of the old man. It was a hot night and she was walking from the kitchen toward the table, preceding the mulatta maidservant, when she heard the old man, as he was holding up a big loaf of bread and skilfully slicing it, say to him, amiably, absently, as though to himself: "The bay mare's a really wild one. But we're going to tame her."

And she saw that the boy, overwhelmed and hesitant, was allowing himself to be trapped by the magic of that plural and smiling at his father, who wasn't looking at him. She saw him smile without parting his lips, merely puffing them out, in a knowing and cocksure gesture, learned from some farmhand. She understood: it's all right to show your teeth to women when you grin at them; but among men, among comrades, that kind of smile is sufficient.

She didn't want to risk seeing his eyes until the pot of camomile tea that ended their meals had been brought. Their eyes didn't meet then; she saw what she had sensed and smelled: the boy's dirty, strawberry-blond head grown serious through meditation and keeping secrets safe; his eyebrows, much darker than his hair, almost meeting, his mouth with a strange firmness and above it the gleam of sweat and the timid shadows of his first mustache.

Her eyes finally met, as they were sitting at the table after dinner, the deliberate pleading in his, fulfilling the duty or the pious act of asking her to come to him. She didn't come to see him that night. She stayed in her bed, face up alongside the snores, weeping without desperation, imagining the look on her own face in the distant light of the summer moon, trying to resist without grimaces the tickling of her tears, determined not to think, lying awake until morning listening to the irregular beats of the windmill turning.

Then she realized that she was incapable of feeling rancor and remembered what she had always known, since the impressive and tacit first family council when she reached puberty and the reticences, the curious eyes, the rigid gestures of affection allowed her to sense that she had become impure and sacred, as an uncle, or a great-uncle, gigantic and austere, read the Bible aloud, with long pauses, and her mother and her mother's sisters-in-law added flounces to her child's dresses. She remembered that she had been born for a blind and stupid waiting period, for a short summer, for a series of unfailing disappointments from which it was necessary to construct a life.

She was incapable, therefore, because of the early warning, of prolonging her rancor and, above all, put up with it. But on the day following this memory she included both the boy and the old man in her active and respectful aloofness. She no longer sought the boy's eyes, she observed them with prolonged curiosity each time she unavoidably met them gazing at her with outworn childish pleading.

Drunk, Medina heard the sound of hail falling that gradually pushed him toward the torpor of sleep and, just before that, the sound of the bottle rolling along the floor.

THE AMBUSH

Leaning the growing weariness of his legs on the window sill, Medina kept the binoculars trained on Frieda's house and on the narrow winding muddy street turned white by the moon that had just appeared. The moon climbed like a balloon leaking gas and quickly lost its orange color.

He relaxed when the quadrangular light of the woman's door leaped out onto the street for a moment and he then saw her silhouette, in a swimsuit, cross the warm darkness before dawn and lazily amble toward the water's edge. He watched her lean against the trunk of a willow and a little while afterwards the sound of her dive into the river reached him. Medina left the binoculars on the table, sat down on the bed and decided to wait but not knowing for how long, fearful of being in too great a hurry or arriving too late. He could count, thinking about an ascending staircase of numbers, a thousand numbers, two thousand.

("I'm waiting out of sheer stupid superstition. And no matter what moment I make up my mind to go I'll be greeted with a feigned cheery welcome. A little cry and a laugh and a nickname dragged out of the past, of a bedroom and a bed. But here I am, not budging, waiting for everything to fit together, for the moment of my arrival to coincide exactly with the one I've imagined, with the one I'm playing with and repeating as though it had already been, as though it were a question of playing tricks with a memory not all that old, a little faded but still clear, made out of light already seen and retaining its angles and curves.")

Medina got up from the bed, smiling because he was trembling; another wait and he went out into the white brightness without being bothered that his footsteps were crushing clods of earth and moribund leaves. He strolled along calmly in the heat, not hurrying, not dallying. And he discovered that everything was a perfect reproduction of the memory he'd invented.

Frieda: he recognized the body and her favorite position, she was lying stretched out on the ground, face downward, her head not visible, perpendicular to the edge of the brook, murmuring as it slowly ran down to swell the river. Medina gave a whistle to lessen the surprise, wished her good evening even though dawn would soon be arriving and plopped down beside her, he too contemplating the water and its broken moon.

"Nervous," Medina confessed. He began to take out the bottles of toiletries, the bathing cap, the towel.

"I wouldn't be nervous. The capital doesn't interest me anymore." Her voice seemed to be coming from the water; the woman was rinsing her short hair, again and again.

"I suppose so," Medina said. "You probably don't remember Margot's stay there very well. I'm not saying that to get your goat. It's just that I still don't understand why you went there, why you took it into your head that you knew how to sing. What I mean is, without at least giving a thought to the competition there. And why you took Seoane with you, since he doesn't wear skirts. Except that you're changing. It might not be bad on a night like this."

"Ever the boor, never understanding anything. If I took the kid with me, it was out of sheer pity."

"Yeah. You couldn't sleep thinking that he wasn't living in a drunken stupor and without drugs. Hard or soft ones?"

"You utter idiot," Frieda murmured raising her head out of

the water and shaking it as though she were furiously denying something. The water splashed the man's mocking face.

"No," he said. "It doesn't matter to me anymore. There was a time when I thought the whole business of drugs had something to do with your nightclub or cabaret, or whatever it is. I also have my suspicions about poor Barreiro. But now I'm going away and the whole thing's behind me and I may possibly discover a way not to come back. Maybe I'll come across an opportunity or two in the capital. Medina, private detective. How does that sound?"

"How does it sound? Like one of those jobs that Quinteros and I invented to keep you from starving to death. And also, to a very minor degree, to humiliate you. It was all your fault: you didn't like being my gigolo."

"Yes, the whole business was very complicated. But there's one thing I ought to thank you for. In Lavanda I was always able to paint, either badly or well, pure academic stuff. Here, in Santa María, it's impossible to imagine a chief of police with an easel."

She was drying her head with the towel. Then she leaned down to look at the moon. And with her hair plastered down by the dampness, for a moment she looked like an ephebe, like a homosexual adolescent that Medina had known years before. ("The combination of defiant gentleness and toughness born of pride. The mouth so thin and straight, the nose, almost without curves, giving the finishing touch to the expression of arrogant hauteur, of false aloofness, as typical of him as a habit, a mania.")

"As nervous as though you'd never been in the capital. Besides, what's the point in sleeping if the ferry leaves at five?"

He placed his hand on the arched vertebrae and slipped it underneath the little patch of cloth that was the bottom of her bikini.

"Hey there, chief, take it easy, pal," she drawled, her contralto voice lilting and laughing girlishly.

"RED"

Medina's relations with "Red" had been like those spring days, a hazy sky, a sun overcast by clouds only to shine furiously for a few moments.

"I don't know why the devil you insist on these meetings in your office," "Red" said. "It's dangerous and you compromise yourself."

"Red's" shoulders were drooping, as though stubbornly determined to give him a premature hunchback's hump; when he spoke he bared a row of tiny teeth, like a child's.

"It's better this way. People think that I'm arresting you for vagrancy."

"What about the money?" "Red" said. "We need lots of it."

"I know, it'll be coming along. So you can go on living for the time being." Medina left on the desk a couple of bills, two brausens, echoes of a fake laugh, and moved away till his back was leaning against the wall.

At other times Medina detached himself from the wall where he appeared to have been embedded for some time and moved forward toward "Red" 's insolence as he sat at the relic of a desk, mutilated and dirty, to order: "'Ten-shun!"

"Red" slowly rose to his feet with a tired smile and did as he was ordered. Medina took over his usual seat and the other took a few ambling steps so as to face him.

"Like how much?" the chief of police asked offhandedly. He was thinking of the packets of foreign banknotes hidden in his room at what had once been the Plaza and in his little house on the beach. He was thinking of what had happened in Rome, London, San Francisco.

"Red" answered by asking another question: "How long has it been since I brought you a budget?" And he added: "Even the luxuries are noted down."

"That's the hangup. I've got the budget in my briefcase, there's no problem there. The Meteorological Institute, the electric tower, the telephones. I think it's excessive. But it's okay, I don't have anything to say against it, on paper it looks perfect. But I'm thinking of a budget for the poor, for us. If sometimes all it takes is a cigarette or a radio that hardly plays. How much?"

"But what I want," "Red" argued, compensating for a smile with two fanatical points gleaming in his eyes, "what I want is to ensure my innocence. You're the one who puts up the money, there's no doubt of it, but I'm the one who risks his neck."

Medina bargained so as to protect himself, to ensure his innocence too, that particular innocence—or fear—among so many others, of a different sort that he had probably lost indifferently or joyously in all the many days he'd lived through, in all the many contacts with people now forgotten or present once again in moments of recall and melancholy.

Moreover—and there were interviews at secret hours in the little house at the beach, so close to Frieda's—"Red," half-drunk on the transparent Paraguayan cane brandy, could assume the pose of a knowing interviewee.

He would then strip the petals from the compass rose, speak of suitable and helpful materials, of other rebels and traitors. All this colored with memories of triumphal feats carried off perfectly, of others that had not been so completely successful. He spoke of surprises, of imponderable negatives, of almost unbelievable escapades, of blows given and received, with an abundance of the former. And he kept repeating: "I'm not saying this to blow my own horn." And he repeated names of places (because he'd traveled all through Spanish America) as though they were names of battles already forever recorded in history.

At a certain level of the bottle he stopped saying "I" and began to tell his tales in the third person: "Then 'Red' realized that the whole business wasn't going to be as easy as he'd thought." Or, " 'Red' hid out for three hours, not moving a muscle."

"I don't want the whole business to begin in slums, in shacks built out of tin and cardboard," Medina always relentlessly insisted.

"I've already explained to you, it seems as though I'm talking to walls. It has to be that way for a hundred reasons that I've already told you. Either we begin that way or it's no go. Maybe 'Red' is wasting his time in Santa María. He'd do better, I think, to try his luck in the Colony. Or go much farther away. There's already been too much talk about the subject."

"Those unfortunates aren't guilty of anything."

"Like you and 'Red,' chief. The whole lot, rich and poor alike, are the same filthy trash. And just think: maybe they'll turn out to be winners. Maybe Brausen will have them build palaces."

FRIEDA IN THE GRASS,
IN THE ASYLUM AND
IN THE SCHOOL

From the window opened onto the sunlight and the midday heat, Díaz Grey threw a handful of birdseed against the battle of doves and sparrows on the terrace.

Motionless in the big armchair, Medina was making an inventory of objects: a life preserver with illegible letters on the wood-paneled wall, an enormous compass underneath, a shiny, freshly painted helm. Two thin, crossed oars were fastened together above the fireplace still black from the fires of the winter before. ("Some of what old Petrus saved from the shipwreck.")

Díaz Grey came back rubbing his hands together and sat down in front of the desk again.

"There was very little I could do, chief. This has to be an official interview. In the slums, for so many long years, I saw many disemboweled drunks, women beaten to death, children like skeletons with big swollen bellies, dead too. Sometimes the neighbors called me, barefoot kids came to my door and clapped their hands together to summon me. When I was the doctor whose specialty was forensic medicine, eighty rupees a month, the jeep from the Detachment came to get me or gave me orders by telephone. You surely remember."

"Of course," Medina said. "As for the jeep, it had to be sold."

Díaz Grey, with the light at his back, looked older and wearier, a sick man with a slow, angry voice. He did not look into

Medina's eyes, he appeared to be searching in vain on the surface of the desk for something that didn't exist.

"You know the whole story better than I do. You were in the capital but you had to come back immediately and the people you still have no doubt told you all the details about all the horrors. You know that the hospital closed down. Dr. Rius fought desperately to keep it open, a part of it at least. He didn't succeed and went off, no one knows where to. Today it's an asylum for elderly Swiss from the Colony. They take care of each other. I think there's still a male nurse, or something like that. I went to visit it a while ago and now I have to go back. Interrupt me and ask me questions whenever you like. But I want to unburden my conscience by confessing everything, as though it were my fault. Everything I had to go through, everything there was no way for me to keep from seeing."

"Of course. I'm here to listen. Perhaps, unwittingly, you'll tell me something new, something that might be useful to me."

"It's possible," the doctor said. "At the beginning of this abomination Martín came to wake me up. Between seven and eight in the morning. He came in the car you left behind. Don't forget this business about the car because I'm going to remember it for a long time. Martín rang the bell, or rather, he leaned on it till the maid decided to get out of bed and open the door. We were all asleep. I rinsed my face, drank two cups of coffee and went out and got into the car. As we were driving along, Martín told me that that young girlfriend of yours, Olga, had found Frieda lying dead alongside the brook."

"Yes. She's in custody. I call her Gurisa."

"And Frieda was Frieda von Kliestein. Your girlfriend said that she'd gone to the little house on the beach to tidy it up. And on her way back she saw Frieda's body. The body was now lying face up—it was face downward when Olga discovered it—and one of your blockheads, Valle, had sat on top of it to help her vomit up the water. That's what the stupid ass told me."

"Yes, they're dumb the way dumb animals are. But basically good men. And I don't have many left. They prefer to go off harvesting."

"Some of them are still around. But that's of no importance. There's an animal in them, in their belly or their chest. And with a serious, self-important expression on his face, certain that I, as the doctor, was going to congratulate him."

He stretched out his left arm, rescued a paper knife from the confusion of the desk top; shortly thereafter he smiled faintly and nodded his head without conviction, dubious himself about the story that Medina already knew.

"The rest; unbelievable, like something invented by a sadist gone mad. There are sadists, you know, whom people take to be normal. We went into the little house to call the judge and there the boy was, stretched out on a bed, with all his clothes on, almost dead, an overdose of some drug. I'd naturally brought along the classic little black bag and I gave him an injection of Coramine. A slight risk, because I didn't know what drug it was he'd taken."

"Yes," Medina said. "I have him in custody too. For the moment he says he has no memory of that night."

"Well, it doesn't matter. For the time being anyway. The judge. And people are obliged to call that son of a bitch 'Your Honor.' He's living in a stately house in the Colony now. And he didn't even answer the telephone. It must have been nine o'clock or thereabout; but he was still in bed and couldn't be bothered to answer us. Martín tried to talk to him; I tried. Nothing doing. He sent word authorizing the body to be taken away but not to the new hospital that the gringos have there. The message said that the thing had to stay in Santa María. The thing was Frieda. The nightmare begins at this point; I prefer to believe it wouldn't have happened if it hadn't coincided with your vacation." He went on, avoiding Medina's eyes; at times he directed his gaze at the bright-colored tie that Medina had bought for himself in the capital, at other times it was directed upward as far as the police chief's recently combed hair. "Because Martín says that before taking Frieda away with us she has to be photographed. From at least three angles, and that unfortunately his camera's broken. I have three of them at home, or rather, they belong to my wife. But I don't want to have any part of this whole stupid affair and just keep my mouth shut. Thereby compounding the confusion, doubtless, because Martín has a confidential talk with one of the blockheads and he leaps up, salutes and takes off like a shot for the city in the car you left at the ferry terminal. So there we were, the rest of us, surrounding Frieda von Kliestein's body and staring at it, at the towel, at the soap dish, at the bottles of women's toiletries. And the sun was already climbing through and above the gigantic willow tree, it was beginning to climb up her wet legs, soaked by the dew on the grass that, even at that late hour, hadn't yet evaporated. And the boy there inside, a motionless heap on the bed. I for my part, listening to so many stupid remarks that they made me wonder why Brausen handed out the use of speech so indiscriminately; also looking at the cyanosis of the lips and the dried blood in the woman's nose. And so we come to the comical beginnings of madness. We heard the tires of the car that was arriving at top speed burning rubber on the sand. The blockhead had brought that poor old cripple who wanders around the square offering to take pictures of couples with his camera set up on a tripod. The camera decorated, practically covered with gray and yellow postcards. And the old man, trembling, almost whiter than death, hobbled around sweating and finally managed to take the pictures from the three angles that Martín had spoken of. This was the beginning of the end on the beach. I forgot to tell you that His Honor also ordered, listen carefully, an immediate autopsy. And I was the only one who could do it and I had no duty to, nor any certainty whether or not what I, a mere private individual in this case, might report would be added to

the dossier. Nor whether it would be of any legal value whatsoever. But I agreed because there was no other doctor in what
was known as the jurisdiction of Santa María. And, besides that,
because I was very curious. Now then, the only suitable place
was our asylum-hospital."

"Excuse me," Medina said in a clear voice. "Had you already
calculated the time of death, doctor? I caught a plane almost the
minute I received the telegram."

"Just by looking at her? No, I calculated it later on. But
that fact isn't mentioned in the report. Because of unexpected
developments that I shall permit myself to go on telling you
about. I can say with certainty that her stomach was full of water,
as were her lungs, and nobody could say at what time she'd
eaten that night. I'll go on with the story; I've a feeling it's
necessary for you to hear what you weren't able to see. Imagine
the trip. Martín and I in the car with the woman and her still
semi-rigid, with one leg sticking out of one of the windows of
the car like a branch of a tree. Finally, sick from the heat, we
arrive at the asylum. The majority, I suppose, of the oldsters and
the madmen, because there was some of them too, were in the
garden, a patch of yellow lawn. One of them had opened an
enormous useless book on a chair. Wearing thick glasses and
leaning over so far as to cause a person to conclude that he was
reading by means of his sense of smell he shakily beat time and
all of them began singing, out of tune and at the top of their
lungs, songs in German that must have been hymns. Almost in
rags, in heavy cotton uniforms, barefoot or wearing espadrilles,
undernourished or bloated. Old people, very old people, joined
to life by some invisible cord. They were or must have been the
day laborers of the Colony, the poor no longer able to do
anything except beg. I think Mersault's mother died there
though that's impossible. And that's how it is: those wretches
must have arrived in the first wave of immigration; as poor
relations or general servants.

"Martín, as I think I told you, was in uniform; he must wear it for pajamas; I've never seen him going about the city in an ordinary suit. He got out of the car, they saw the uniform, Martín walking toward them and the singing stopped. All of them stood there rigid, looking at the fence, some with their mouth hanging open, frozen in that position. Martín was talking, I don't know in what language, with the choir director. A very tall blond who had once been athletic and who kept moving his head, to affirm, to deny, whose eyes then swept in a semicircle around the motionless old gaffers and finally he decided to follow the officer of the law and come closer to the fence, to the car, which had one wheel on the sidewalk. I don't know if Martín's words had prepared him or not. What I remember is that the man looked at Frieda, then to either side of her, as though he were trying to keep himself from being locked up, shouted 'She's dead!' and tried to hide his eyes with his long arms. Behind him, in the background, next to the front steps, an incomprehensible murmur that grew louder and louder as the man who'd seen the horror began to run, raising dust, stumbling against nothingness, against the terror that he was driving before him with his long strides. When Martín tried to go back into the house the shouting stunned me and the poor devils climbed the stairs, pushing and shoving each other, entered the asylum and shut the door with such a hard slam that for a few seconds it continued to echo in the heat. Martín leaning against the door, all by himself, banging with his knuckles and elbow, ordering, threatening, cursing the silence inside that the oldsters and the cretins were using as a weapon against him. Finally he decided to give up, requisitioned the big black book, which was a Bible in German with hymns and pentagrams on the last pages, and went back to the car."

"Yes; I have the book at the Detachment."

"The two of us asked each other aloud 'Where do we go from here?' and then sat in silence for a while, looking at the radiator and the sun's reverberation. I always believed that that charnel house was for both sexes, a short-wait way station for men and women. But we didn't see even one woman, not a single down-and-out old hag. They must be inside, I thought, fixing lunch or moving the cots or bunks around. Or perhaps that ritual with the songs was limited to men. The gringos have customs like that."

"Yes," Medina said; he swung around in the chair until he finally took out his package of cigarettes and lighted one. "The matter in hand took place in the school," he said as he waved away the smoke.

"In the school," Díaz Grey agreed; he stood up to take a bottle of whisky and two glasses down from the bookshelf. "I'm sorry, but I don't have any water here."

"There's no need for any, doctor."

They drank in silence, in little sips, attentively, as though they were distracted by the confused and defiant songs of the birds in the garden.

"In the school," Díaz Grey went on. "Martín suggested it and I thought that the heat had driven him mad. But he insisted. Apart from the church it's the only place where we're going to be able to find a big table. The one in the dining room; there are really only a few little tables in there, but they can be pushed together. I explain to the directress.

"When we got to the school I drove around it and parked the car, with a great deal of effort, amid trees and bushes. The thought occurred to me later that that was the clumsiest way of hiding the car. I waited, peeking at Frieda's corpse every so often, and then I made up my mind to move it and was able to leave it, not sitting up but at least entirely inside the car. Meanwhile Martín was talking, interminably and invisibly, to the head-mistress and the teachers. Finally he left the building and went looking all round without summoning me. He had managed to persuade the women and they gave the children a day off from school. We waited for them to leave, dozens and dozens of them, little ones and bigger ones, with the half-dozen women behind talking to each other, moving their arms and their mouths in unison, stopping every so often in the little path of brick dust the better to converse with each other.

"When the three of us were finally alone, Martín went in to put the autopsy table together. This time he didn't stay long and between the two of us we carried Frieda in and laid her down on the big table we made by putting four little ones together. I opened the satchel to get out my scalpel, cotton, compresses. I hadn't been forewarned so I hadn't brought along either a saw or shears or clamps.

" 'We need a saw,' I said to Martín, feeling like giving up, abandoning the whole business. Let the devil take over.

" 'There must be one in the storeroom'. And he left the room.

"I raised the scalpel so as to plunge it into the suprasternal hollow just where the knot in your tie is, a little above the top edge of the clavicle. Then I saw the little boy who had silently entered the room and was standing alongside the feet of the dead woman. He was as motionless as I was, as she was, with his white gown and the big blue ribbon of his school tie with a bow knot running all the way around his neck. Under his left armpit, books and notebooks. He wasn't looking at Frieda's hard breasts, he wasn't interested in her flattened, wine-colored nipples. He must have been six or seven years old, blond and very pale, with his mouth hanging open. Fascinated, sick. He slowly stretched out his free arm till he touched the surprise of her pubic down. And there his hand rested, gentle and protective, as though he were stroking a bird and was afraid of harming it or frightening it.

" 'Get out of here,' Martín shouted from the door, making the blade of a big rusty saw meant for felling trees vibrate.

"And that's all, chief. She died by drowning, I think they hit her and held her head under water for a long time. There are no signs of the blow. A hematoma on the nape of her neck, the hand that held her down, and two on her back. In my opinion the marks of two knees. And she may have died somewhere between five and seven a.m. If my calculation suits you . . . Your girlfriend discovered her around eight." He was now staring into the eyes of the chief of police.

"Olga Aramburu."

"The dampness from the stream, the shadow of the tree, the dew, the sun. There's no way of being certain. But at seven it's already bright daylight. Oh, no trace of rape. Although I'm sure it was a man. And perhaps an acquaintance or a friend if she allowed him to get that close to her at that hour."

Medina rose to his feet and went to get his hat, murmuring, "Thanks."

"Wait a minute, chief," Díaz Grey said. "For that work of charity that you wanted to do. Over there, in that dark wardrobe chest, in the first drawer are some bills. Take what you need."

Medina opened the drawer, nearly full of brausens in denominations of ten, twenty and a hundred.

A Faithful Son

What they went on calling the Detachment ever since the time of the real one, so white at the beginning of the story. With Brausen's red and black colors on the flag defying and humiliating any tone of blue or gray that the semi-sphere of the sky of Santa María showed. And that now was a big house abandoned because of the danger of its falling into ruin and that one of these days that we're living through with the permission of the highest authorities will be bought by one or another of the nouveaux riches of the Colony so as to tear it down and build another exotic little palace for our pink and white architecture, inherited from the Hispanic founders.

The church will be saved and the statue in the middle of the square, where the horse threatens to go off toward the south as the horseman tirelessly points the way with his naked sword.

In the new and very old building of the Detachment they still raise and lower the flag, faded now from sun and rains, from weather that certain people believed to be changeless, though still not transformed into a rag, yet admittedly torn by furious and very isolated storms that were battles without gunpowder. The black is now navy blue, the red is a bright pink. And there is no bugle to salute and revere it when the sun comes up, when the sun goes down.

Sitting in his shirtsleeves and wiping away the sweat with his wadded-up handkerchief, in the room that was once a special reception room set aside for tea with visitors, Medina finished listening to Martín's report.

"All right. Nothing of any use to us."

"All he says is no, that he was sleeping, drunk and stoned, Díaz Grey states, and that he knew nothing about any of it till the boys waked him up with buckets of water."

"Buckets of water and blows. They might well have killed him. So here we are with no deposition or anything else. We can't hand him over to the captain accused of the crime of sleeping. Let him rest for half an hour and then go on. After that it's my turn."

"Whatever you order," Martín said uneasily. "I wish you luck."

"It's not a question of luck. What's more, you have to get some rest too. You haven't been to bed for hours now. Please tell Héctor to bring the cane brandy and glasses. A good stiff drink won't hurt you. Oh, by the way, where's the woman?"

"In the big kitchen. There's no other place to put her. We put the chair with the straw seat in there for her. You know, chief, we still don't have any furniture, even though we've put in a thousand requests for some."

"I know I'm going to have a drink and then I'll interrogate her right away. Even though I know her. She doesn't have the courage or the strength or the intelligence to kill that way. Or any motive either. But take her out of there, let her sit on the bench in that pasture we call a garden. There's no need to be afraid she'll escape."

Héctor brought the bottle and two glasses.

"By your leave," he said and put the glasses down on the rolltop desk that never rolled.

"Three," Medina ordered. "Or have you been transferred?"

Héctor smiled at his much-mended uniform, the pounding of his boots full of cracks retreated into the distance.

As they waited, Medina said to Martín: "Get some rest, man," and turned his head to look at three o'clock in the afternoon in the window without curtains or blinds, the distant tops of the eucalyptuses, their leaves singed and motionless.

Martín had sat down, his face thinner now and framed by a beard darker than his neatly combed blond hair, glistening with brilliantine; he wiped the sweat from his forehead by dragging two fingers across it again and again.

Héctor returned and then the three men raised their glasses and said, "Cheers."

"And to think that the refrigerator still doesn't work," Medina commented, as though he were thinking aloud.

"I did everything I could," Martín said. "I've got a cousin who's an electrician, but he's not in Santa María, I don't know where he is."

"He's most likely working in some civilized place," Medina reassured him.

The girl, Olga, Gurisa, was putting together little wild flowers with hard petals as stiff as cardboard.

"Those aren't flowers," Medina said in a low voice. "I can't kiss you, or even look into your eyes—those are flowers for a cemetery and we already have enough of that sort."

"Was he the one?"

"Nobody knows, he refuses to talk. But I'm the one who has to interrogate you. And I can't think of anything to ask you."

"But what am I accused of if all I did was have the accursed bad luck of coming across Frieda by accident?"

"First of all," Medina said as he pushed her down onto the bench and sat down alongside the woman who'd turned into a child out of fear, "first of all, why did you have to pass by that way at eight o'clock in the morning?"

"But if you'd told me, before you left . . ."

"It doesn't matter, I don't remember. We have to do a lot of talking, to repeat that we love each other without ever saying so. Even though everybody knows it. Don't forget that this is an official police interrogation. Very serious, very long. I have to find out what I know by heart. But as told by you. Why at eight o'clock in the morning? That's how it all begins. What time do you usually wake up?"

"I don't have any set hour. It all depends on the night before. If we've been playing around till it gets very late, you and I . . ."

"No," Medina interrupted. "You're not to say *tú* when you address the chief of police."

She raised her hands and gave a little laugh; then, slowly, she lowered them and turned her eyes away from Medina's glowering face. She sat there looking at the flat expanse of land in the distance with little islands of very dry grass, beyond the loose wire fence that marked off one of the boundaries of the Detachment.

With twinkling eyes she recited: "Yes, sir. I must have been playing around in the apartment in the Plaza until around midnight with his honor, the chief of police," she lied. "And the chief of police told me he was going to the capital on the five a.m. ferry. The chief of police asked me, it's always a good thing when he asks me for something or needs something, he asked me to drop by the little house on the beach to tidy it up a bit and sweep it out if necessary. If I, as a woman, thought it was necessary. And I was also to see if the canvases painted by his honor the chief of police in secret, and always in the dead of night, before dawn, under artificial light, were all inside the locked closet. I gave him back the key to the little house and also the key to the closet. And I could see that there was a big painting, on pasteboard, representing a giant wave, all done in patches of different kinds of whiteness. The whiteness of paper, of milk, of skin. Such a thing never existed in this river, nobody can ever have seen a wave like that one. So I thought that the chief of police had imagined it or that it was a memory of another country, of another river or a sea that I've never seen."

She swallowed her saliva and leaned a slightly saddened face toward Medina.

"Shall I go on?"

Medina looked at his wristwatch. "A bit more and that'll be the end of this farce. When you saw Frieda, how did you know she was dead? In your first deposition you don't state that you have any knowledge of medicine."

"Oh," she said and trembled against Medina's shoulder. "I've already told why and it makes me sick every time I remember it. I see her again, lying perfectly still, as though she'd never moved. Her head sunk down in the water, her neck looking as though it were broken and no bubbles rising."

"I'm convinced. Very intelligent." He smiled as though he were speaking with a child who had hit the right answer; his face continued to smile, he lighted a cigarette and asked nonchalantly: "If she was lying face down and nearly naked, how could you tell it was Frieda?"

"I knew it was," she murmured. "That woman was always stronger than I was. And even when she's dead she's stronger than I am. I never found out who you were really jealous of. But I'm not your Juanina, the one who told you that all she had to do was to get a whiff of the smell of a woman to almost die of nausea. And you believed her."

"No," Medina said in a dull voice. "It's true I often felt a great desire, almost a need to believe her. At that time, anyway."

"I never told you and I'm not going to tell you now unless you swear that this won't appear in the report or anywhere else. That you won't tell anybody. It doesn't have anything to do with Frieda's death."

Medina lowered his head.

"I swear," he said; "but whatever it may be, I don't understand why you didn't tell me. When all is said and done there were many times when we thought we were only one person. That was what I believed, at least, and you told me it was true."

"It is true and now I'll explain. What happened was that for months Juanina and Seoane lived together at Frieda's place. And every so often I used to see them by the little stream or in the Casanova, and I'm not completely stupid and I realized what was going on."

"And what could have been going on that was all that amazing? Why didn't you ever tell me about it?"

"Because there are lots of Medinas. Because I didn't know how you were going to take it. You might have done something crazy. And that whole business didn't have anything to do with us and each night I prayed that the three of them would gradually disappear from your memory, would be of no interest to you."

"Yes, and at least one of them . . ." Medina started to say and immediately regretted this stupidity.

"Bah, as far as that's concerned it doesn't matter whether she's dead or alive. As far as your memory, your hatred and maybe your contempt are concerned, Juanina went back to Lavanda more than a month ago. She gave me a message for you. She told me laughingly that she was going away to visit an aunt."

"I get the message."

"And she told me, as cynical as always, that everything that could possibly happen had happened at Frieda's house. And she added that this time there was no danger of getting pregnant. Naturally: she went to visit your friend Díaz Grey any number of times. None of this matters at all. I want to know what they did with Frieda after the butchery. With what was left of Frieda."

"She's in the capital."

"In this heat."

Martín appeared on the edge of shadow at the corner of the building. He was in worse shape than before, more worn-out, skinnier.

"Chief," he shouted.

Medina got to his feet, slowly at first, then all at once. He understood something indefinable and unpostponable.

"Take this woman back to her cell. To the kitchen, that is, it's the same thing. I got something very important out of her during the interrogation."

Martín whistled and Héctor appeared.

"Take the prisoner back to her cell," Martín ordered.

When the two of them had disappeared, Martín stood at attention, saluted; with his eyes he sized up the chief of police.

"At ease, and tell me all," the latter barked.

"The young man under arrest, the number one suspect. Dead in my opinion, when I went back to the cell."

The cell was a room whose only furniture was a bed with a thin bare mattress and a tall straight-backed chair; pieces of paper with sketches of hustlers in pink and gold were coming, certain of their eventual triumph, unhurriedly unstuck from the four walls. A small window still bordered with decals of Disney cartoon characters suggested the shadow of a memory of a nursery, of children playing with dolls, lead soldiers, balls and colored blocks with capital letters; children now dead perhaps, perhaps still breathing but all the same dead now with their pot bellies and graying mustaches, their self-esteem and their pale, recurrent belief in a future life or in the eternity of the one that they were going through.

Influenced perhaps by all this improbability, Medina blasphemed Brausen in four words and did not want to crouch down but rather to look from on high at the body on the filthy floor, so serene in its fetal position, its knees almost touching the filth of a bird's wing feather that had once been white, its head lowered searching for the breast, its fists feebly clenched, the hint of a smile of expectation at the prospect of birth and life about to begin.

"Dead, no doubt about it," Martín said, piercing the silence and the thoughts that were so contradictory, so fleeting and divergent. "Dead when I came back to interrogate him again, following the verbal orders I'd received. I immediately telephoned Dr. Díaz Grey's house, but nobody answered. Even though five or six people live there, counting the servants."

"As if we weren't servants," Medina thought. Then he said, without meaning to: "Why the devil should dead people die?" He corrected himself. "Did they take everything out of his clothes, did they take his belt, his shoelaces away from him?"

"Everything," Martín said. "I can bring you the whole bundle right away. But none of those things was the cause of his death. You need only to take a look at his face, he didn't hang himself or slash himself to death."

"Yes, he's at peace. I've never seen him like that before. But how did heroin, cocaine, whatever drug it was, get in here?"

"He didn't shoot up with anything, chief. You can see the little bits of paper he left behind. There are seven of them, not counting the ones he may have hidden underneath his body."

They stood there listlessly, each one absorbed in his own dissembling.

"And how could a drug get in here? Nobody came to visit him and I'm not about to start mistrusting all of you."

"If you want my opinion, chief, the victim brought it in himself."

"You told me that you'd searched him, that there was nothing hidden in his clothes."

They were surprised to hear a big, heavy car braking to a stop. They slowly made their way to the room they called an office or a study. They waited, Medina seated facing the desk, Martín standing, both of them looking at the doorway still flooded with sunlight.

Slight and tough, the resolve to live forever showing in his eyes and in the bones of his face, the fleeting shadow of a body loomed up in the entrance of the Detachment. It came forward almost smiling and said, peremptorily: "Medina, Martín. I'm whatever you like, but for the moment I'm the judge, the one whom the gullible are obliged to call 'Your Honor'. And the Y and the H in capital letters."

The stranger took a few steps forward as the others nodded their heads in mistrustful respect, till he reached a chair in a corner and sat down on it, facing Medina.

"Say something, chief," Martín said.

And Medina spoke slowly, searching for words: "Your Honor, a few days ago, we called you, Sergeant Martín called your house in the Colony. We called you in desperation because it concerned a desperate case."

"Yes. And someone answered that Santa María was not within my jurisdiction. But it doesn't matter; it is now, through a decree of mine. Santa María is now your territory again, although no one has any way of knowing for how long. And to begin with, who was desperate?"

He looked only at Medina and the latter understood and remembered that he had hated that man, without ever having seen him, since the very first day of his life, perhaps since even before he was born. But it wasn't the hatred of one person for another; it was like the hatred of an inescapable thing. It was the hatred of all the sufferings—mingled like one wave with another, whether the sufferings were great or small—that had been inflicted on him by childhood, his first woman, the obligatory beginning of adulthood. As though that man had made his old hopes vulnerable and almost unbelievable, as though he had insisted on curbing his impulses, his rebellions, as though he had worked tirelessly to limiting him to being a policeman in a forgotten town, as though he, the almost imperceptibly mocking man dressed in black, despite the torrid summer heat, had guided him, persistently and patiently, to his encounter with two dead people which he, the man dressed in black, had foreseen and ordered long before.

Now they were face to face and Medina remembered the fleeting image of something he had seen or read, a man who was perhaps a fellow office clerk who didn't smile; a man with a bored face whose greetings were mere monosyllables which he endowed with a vague vibration of affection, an impersonal irony.

"I spoke with the guard at the door," the judge said, smiling thoughtfully in the silence. "The fact is, there's nobody whose case is desperate. Or, at least, it no longer is. And the guard at the door told me that there was someone else who was dead, although now, it would appear, another murder victim. In any event, an unbelievable statistic for Santa María. May I, may we, see the second body?"

Rising to his feet, Medina hoped that the judge would hold his hand out to him. But the man merely walked alongside Martín, without really waiting for the latter to lead the way, as though he knew the place very well, until the reached the room with the bed, the chair, and the dead body.

Medina remained standing near the door; a little sunlight was now coming in through the overheated window and moving along the stained floor, trying to touch Seoane, Julián, whose police dossier had a number that read the same backwards and forwards, a good luck sign, and indicated that he had been born in the Colony, twenty years before.

"Turn him over," the judge said to Martín. The body wavered for a moment face up, the knees of the pants faded from many washings, with twin darns, and then fell over onto its other side. Nothing interrupted the peaceful dream of the tanned face. A little scrap of white paper now appeared on the floor. It had been hidden underneath the left arm. The judge stooped down to pick it up; he appeared to have done so without bending his knees. He read it, handed it to Medina, and the latter stood there looking at it for a long time, as though it were an enigma, before passing it on to Martín.

"With that," the judge said and pointed to a pencil stub alongside the corpse's shoe.

"I don't understand," Martín almost protested, as though this might be a trick on the judge's part. "We took away everything he had on him before we locked him up."

"Yes," the judge said, with a tolerant smile. "Everything except that and this."

He slowly pointed to the little pieces of white paper whose wrinkles showed that they'd been used as an envelope. "Don't you see? Cowboy pants with enormous cuffs. They would have been able to hold everything he owned if he moved from one place where he lived to another."

Medina thought of the shaky letters of the message, of the hand that had lied before it fell, of the ambiguous and terrible purpose that had brought about the confession.

You bastard don't worry your head about it any more I killed Frieda. Julián Seoane.

"I was right," Martín said. "I suspected as much from the beginning. But there was no way to get a word out of him."

The judge gently took the paper away from him and handed it to Medina.

"Put it in his dossier, chief. It's a fine gold paper clip. Then send it to me. And a report of everything that's happened. From the discovery of the woman in the stream up until now." He pointed to the paper and the boy's body lazily licked by the sun now. "Have the body sent to the Colón hospital. I can almost read the autopsy report now: overdose of some filthy drug. With an occasional exception, perhaps, all those whom people call drug addicts will necessarily end up that way and the sooner the better. Doctor Díaz Grey doesn't want to know one more thing about such matters. I was with him all morning, with the telephone disconnected so that nobody would bother us. We talked about so many things; it was like a history of the city. I don't remember how old he is. But I go on loving him as though he were my son. A faithful son."

An Evening Before

In the little house on the beach, flanked a long way away by Mr. Wright's and the biggest one, Frieda's, Medina lighted the place with a heavy pot-bellied kerosene lantern:

He was seated on the bed and "Red" was pacing about with his head down, his hands in his trousers pockets. He seemed to bounce gently from wall to wall.

"And so?" Medina asked. "Is it enough money or not?"

"Red" halted and brought his face closer to the lamplight. His face was suddenly dotted with freckles.

"That's not the reason," he said after a little while. "It's hard to understand."

"Hard to explain," the chief of police corrected him. "We've got all night. I'm listening."

"Red" looked at the small piles of brausens laid out on the table. The bills were also reddish.

"Tell me what's going on," Medina persisted. "Isn't that enough money? It's all I could get. There isn't any more. And I got it by telling the truth."

"You told the truth? You're out of your mind. Who did you tell it to? I was sure I could trust you." He walked aimlessly, over to the bed; Medina smiled at him with a touch of pity.

"I told the truth. All I said was that it concerned a clean-up operation. Of benefit to everybody. Now it's your turn. Tell me what's happening, tell me if that's enough money."

"Red" lighted a cigarette and sat down on the table top, pushing the piles of bills aside with his backside.

"Listen to me as though you were hearing my confession. And try to understand. There's more than enough money for what we're going to do. Or want to do. Or what I'm going to do. I don't intend to be left without a cent. The ticket for the ferry or the bus or the train. What's happening to me is that I've thought about this and been wanting it for such a long time that now that it can really come off, now that it's a sure thing, I feel sick and on my last legs; what they call a depression."

"Have a couple of swigs of cane brandy and you'll feel better. Something of the sort also happens to me. But that's at the beginning, later on it goes away."

"And what's more, I'm thinking of the wind now. As we're being exhausted by the heat Santa Rosa is approaching, bringing the usual storm with it. It won't be long now. But who can guess which way the wind will blow?"

AT LAST, THE WIND

For three nights, like a virgin shepherdess awaiting the Holy Vision or the never-heard sound of Voices, Medina awaited from behind his window at the Plaza the resounding arrival of the Santa Rosa storm. He waited for it in the dark because during the afternoon he'd seen only flashes of lightning dissolved in the light of day, heard only distant claps of thunder, and because it's at night that great dreams come true.

Before Gurisa fell asleep happily with the double dose of Seconal given to her by Medina which she had taken unwittingly. They had made love, she with her natural mixture of innocence and perversion; he with a surprising virility that seemed to him, each time, strange and pathological.

She breathing in the shadow of the bed, he glued to the unchanging landscape of the window.

On the third night the distant compensations finally arrived. The flashes of lightning and the earsplitting, sarcastic claps of thunder, the brief and abundant rain, an unfettered wind that pushed trees from left to right and danced for an instant, hurriedly and disrespectfully, around the statue in the square, pedestal, horse and rider.

Fearful of entertaining false hopes, fearful of almost certain disappointment, Medina went into the bathroom to put on a prickly warm bathrobe. In the closet his seldom-worn uniform and his holster were hanging. He put the weapon, heavy and cumbersome, in the pocket of the bathrobe and managed not to break the silence as he walked through the room and took his place once again alongside the blackness of the window. The only thing he could make out was the gleam of a few puddles on the street that reflected the dim light of the hotel sign.

He tried, in vain, to see what time it was, to measure the passage of the minutes on his wristwatch. Time was going by—and he could feel it in his shoulders, in the sweat on his chest—without leaving any traces, without allowing anyone to capture it and measure it. All of a sudden a new ache of weariness at the back of his knees and a premonition of a clear light, very slight and a long way away at the far end of the city, to the left.

"The west," Medina thought, "can't be where an expected dawn comes from. And I told him not from that direction."

Gurisa stirred in the big bed and muttered incomprehensibly and irritatedly; the feeble sound of her childlike breathing then returned immediately.

The light, still to the left, began to move and increase. Already, very high, it slowly moved on above the city, violently parting the dark of night, bending down a little only to rise again, that same moment, now, with a sound of great canvases being shaken by the wind.

Medina felt the light fall on his face and the increasing, almost intolerable heat of the windowpane. He trembled without resisting, victim of a strange fear, of the always disappointing end of the adventure. ("I've wanted this for years, this was the reason why I came back.")

He heard a window blow in, in the place in the apartment that they called the kitchen. Pistol in hand, he went over to the bed. He felt the almost irresistible need to kiss Gurisa, but he was afraid he would wake her up before she was awakened by the din that was beginning to come from the street, from the hotel, the roof and the sky.

Madrid, February 23, 1979